PRAISE FOR *AFT*

"George Weinstein's *Aftermath* snagged me with the first sentence. Fast pacing kept me turning pages. Great writing kept me clenched in the fist of this small town. Its long-kept secrets, stuffed inside old boarding houses and concealed in modern mansions, remain just out of reach as Janet Wright struggles to find answers of her own. Weinstein's characters are vivid and developed. They support and betray—reveal and hide. They are both innocent and guilty, but always and foremost they are human. Weaving past with present, light with shadow, *Aftermath* maintains a perfect and engaging balance. This is one you don't want to miss!"
—Susan Crawford, international best-selling author of
The Pocket Wife and *The Other Widow*

"There should be a writer's genre called Keep Turning, for there are books that simply make such a demand of readers. George Weinstein's *Aftermath* is one of them. A full-force story of a small-town murder and that town's ugly, uncomfortable secret has a cast of characters that thrive on suspicion and conflict. You know early on that in the end all the right dots will be connected, but you don't know how the lines will be drawn—until you Keep Turning. That's the pleasure of it."
—Terry Kay, author of *To Dance with the White Dog*,
The Book of Marie, and *The King Who Made Paper Flowers*

"George Weinstein has a powerful contemporary Southern voice. His new novel, *Aftermath*, is fast-paced and grabs the reader in the first sentence. This novel tells the story of coming home, proving Thomas Wolfe wrong with a strong-willed protagonist, Janet Wright, the new owner of Graylee, a tiny Georgia town. And only in the Deep South can one inherit a town. Kept me on the edge of my seat until I finished the last page."
—Ann Hite, award-winning author of *Sleeping Above Chaos*,
a Black Mountain novel

"Another winner for George Weinstein. Luring you in with atmospheric elements—a small town hiding dark secrets and a woman determined to uncover her questionable legacy—*Aftermath*'s final, disturbing twist will jolt you and good. A gripping, suspenseful read."
—Emily Carpenter, author of *Burying the Honeysuckle Girls*

"*Aftermath* has everything I crave in a novel: the perfect blend of mystery and romance, flawlessly crafted dialog, and an unsinkable heroine with equal parts grit and heart. George Weinstein makes his characters flesh and bone—bringing them to vibrant life as he peels away the secrets of a small town with more than just murder to hide—and an estranged daughter determined to bring the truth to light in the wake of her father's death. Go to bed early, or prepare to stay up all night: *Aftermath* is unputdownable."
—Erika Marks, author of *The Last Treasure*

"Weinstein works miracles getting us to suspect everybody in *Aftermath*. This thoroughly satisfying tale of deceit and emotional devastation in a small town rings true."
—Fran Stewart, national best-selling author of the *ScotShop* mystery series and the *Biscuit McKee* mysteries

"A truly satisfying mystery is one that keeps the reader guessing until the very last page, and George Weinstein does just that in his latest novel, *Aftermath*. With skill and finesse, he moves the story forward at a measured pace as he introduces believable and sympathetic characters, and each of these brings depth and sometimes gentle humor to this finely crafted story. The dialog is realistic, the situations ring true, and the settings dovetail seamlessly with the plot and, ultimately, the resolution. If you only read one mystery this year, read *Aftermath* by George Weinstein."
—Raymond L. Atkins, author of *Sweetwater Blues* and *South of the Etowah*

"*Aftermath* artfully combines a story of shattered hopes with a dark mystery that will keep you turning the pages as you follow a trail of clues, hidden in plain sight, into the corrupt and disturbing heart of a small Georgia town. This is a masterful study of the unfortunate truth that sometimes, in order to fix things, you first have to break them again."
—Roger Johns, author of *Dark River Rising*

"To unravel the mystery shrouding the gruesome murder of her estranged father, heiress Janet Wright will do whatever it takes, no holds barred. Set in a sleepy Southern company town, George Weinstein's twisty gothic who-done-it will keep you guessing right to the very end."
—Ronald Aiken, author of *Death Has Its Benefits*

AFTERMATH

AFTERMATH

A NOVEL

GEORGE WEINSTEIN

Deeds Publishing | Atlanta

Published by Deeds Publishing in Athens, GA
www.deedspublishing.com

Cover by Matt King

Printed in The United States of America

Library of Congress Cataloging-in-Publications data is available upon request.

ISBN 978-1-944193-44-7
EISBN 978-1-944193-45-4

Books are available in quantity for promotional or premium use. For information, email info@deedspublishing.com.

First Edition, 2016

10 9 8 7 6 5 4 3 2 1

For Kate, whose love has enabled me to confront the mysteries of life without fear, for twenty-five years and counting.

1

ONLY ONE STOP, I PROMISED MYSELF, AND THEN I'D GO TO MY FATHER'S HOUSE — WHERE HE
had been murdered in July. I wasn't exactly looking forward to
that. On Main Street in tiny Graylee, Georgia, I parked the rental car I'd picked up after landing in Atlanta that morning. Seventy-degree weather in late December and BBQ smoke on the
breeze through my open windows reminded me I had returned
to the Deep South, way below the Gnat Line.

Though I'd been born in Graylee, I only lived there until I was
five and had no memory of it. I assumed the place would be just
another backwater burg, decorated as countless others were a few
days before Christmas. However, instead of check-cashing par-
lors and pawnshops, the town somehow supported quaint bistros,
boutiques selling luxury goods, and salons for hair, nails, and full-
body spa treatments, with upscale cars parked in front of each
one. Manhattan it wasn't, but it wasn't the sticks either.

How had they maintained such prosperity in the middle of
nowhere? Between that and the weather, the place was a modern
Shangri-La. If I were back home in the center of the universe, I
would've still needed the heavy coat I'd worn while catching a cab
to LaGuardia, and which now covered my purse in the front seat.
I pushed it aside so I could retrieve my hairbrush and lipstick. As
I touched up, I surveyed Main Street again.

The variety of dining and shopping options surprised me, but the best part was a silence I never experienced except when I got out of New York City. No radios blasting, jackhammers machine-gunning concrete, or car horns blaring. The hush and the temperature put me in the mood for a nap but that meant going to Dad's house. I just didn't want to deal with it yet. Too many conflicting emotions, including a helping of dread as big as the deli counter at Zabar's.

At least the remarkable surroundings made me stop wondering for a moment whether I'd been foolish to quit a good job on Wall Street, leave my friends and everything I loved, and return to a home I no longer remembered. From the looks of it, Graylee seemed like a fine place to start over. To give my life a little meaning. To finally do something that mattered.

After exiting my rental and locking it with the remote, I noted a few elderly shoppers jaywalking across the road to their Beamer. They didn't look like the type to hotwire a car and go joyriding. If I planned to live here, I needed to start blending in. Feeling ridiculous but determined to establish new habits, I unlocked the car. After all, probably the only crime committed in Graylee in the past six months had been my father's murder, and the police shot the guy who'd done that.

The phone in my back pocket had been vibrating periodically with texts from friends who demanded updates on my adventure "down South." A new one buzzed my butt. With nothing significant to report yet, I let the messages accumulate unanswered.

I pushed open the door of a gift shop, and sleigh bells jangled. The Christmas murals on the windows had been painted with skill, drawing me inside, but who could I buy a present for? With my father's death, I had no family left. My New York friends were much too sophisticated to appreciate anything from small-town Georgia. Andy Jessup had broken off our engagement six months ago, and—unheard of for me—I hadn't rebounded with another guy yet. I'd always feared I would be all alone at forty, and here I was.

A housewarming gift, I decided, glancing at the displays of yuletide cheer. For my new home, which I'd never seen. Perfect. I took a breath and settled into browse mode, letting my gaze drift over the aisles of goods as my boots led me up a random row.

"Can I help you find something, honey?" A middle-aged woman, wearing a snowflake sweater despite the warm weather, approached me from the back of the shop.

"Just looking," I said, picking up a plush reindeer and putting it back on the shelf. Did that sound too abrupt? "Thank you," I added, drawing out the vowels to sound less like a damn Yankee than a Southern girl who had gone to live among them when I was young.

The woman asked, "You passing through?" Obviously my twang hadn't fooled her. She wove her way among the displays of reds and greens, putting on half-moon glasses that had dangled from a beaded cord around her neck. "Oh, Ms. Wright," she said, taking me in from across a display of holly boughs and fluffy snowmen, "Um, welcome to Graylee."

Small town living, where everybody knew everybody else's business. Maybe someone had spotted me dawdling in my rental car and sent a warning to all of Graylee that Brady Stapleton's daughter had arrived in town.

"Thanks," I said. "Please call me Janet."

"I'm Paulina Lollybelle O'Shea." Her snowflake-clad arm reached over the shelf, and she shook my hand in a perfunctory way. "I'm sorry for your loss." Her delivery was robotic, chilly.

"I appreciate that," I said, hoping I didn't sound as puzzled by her tone as I felt.

"You take after your mama—right pretty, the spittin' image of Mary Grace."

The folksy compliment surprised me. I patted down the cowlick on the back of my head, a gift handed down from Mom. "You knew her?"

"Yes, ma'am, went through school with her. She was a peach. Never understood what she saw in your daddy, though." Her look suggested I had some explaining to do on my mother's behalf. "They made the strangest couple, with her such a petite beauty and him a big ol' bear of a man, bless his heart."

From photographs I'd found on the Internet, that described him well. I said, "I don't remember my father. In fact, I hadn't seen him, or even talked to him, in thirty-five years."

"I reckoned, what with you having your mama's last name." Her voice dropped then, as if the plastic Santa Clauses could overhear us. "Did she tell you about him?"

"No, she never talked about my dad."

"Well, he just about owned Graylee. We heard you were coming down all the way from New York City to be the new owner." She didn't look pleased by this latest Northern incursion.

I own a town, I reminded myself. It was impossible to wrap my mind around that. Paulina's sour expression and the possibility that the people here were already gossiping about my arrival got the better of me. Although I had inherited my mother's looks

4

and I carried her name, the one thing she would say about Dad was that I'd gotten his smart mouth. I snapped, "I promise to be a benevolent dictator."

Paulina's eyebrows rose over the tops of her glasses. Then her look of shock turned to delight, and I realized the depth of my mistake. Soon all of Graylee would hear about my snotty declaration.

Damn. I needed to make friends and allies, not score points. Wincing, I shook my head. "Sorry, bad joke. What I meant to say is I'm not planning on running anything—my father seemed to have put really good people in charge. It's not broken, and I don't want to risk breaking it."

The apology seemed to mollify her, or at least she realized what poor manners she was displaying, too. She re-spaced some holiday tchotchkes on her side of the shelf and changed the subject. "All of us sure are glad about what happened to that Wallace Landry."

I nodded at the name of the drifter who had murdered my father. "I guess everyone was spared a pointless trial."

"And fifty years of that horrible man on Death Row," Paulina added, "filing endless appeals. I know it's not the Christian thing to say, but he got what he deserved." She looked at me hopefully, as if seeking something we had in common, a means of building a bond. Either that, or she was setting a trap to get some more juicy quotes she could broadcast.

I said, "You're right, I guess. Although I would've liked to ask him why he did it."

"Because he was evil, you hear? Came into the shop one time, and I knew the moment I laid eyes on him that he had the devil inside. What he did shook up Graylee something awful. We hadn't had a murder in years."

"He probably made everyone here feel nervous about strangers…but, uh, I hope I fit in and won't be considered an outsider much longer."

"Plan on staying, do you?"

It seemed more like a threat than a question, but I soldiered on. "I thought I'd volunteer, maybe start a charity. And work on a book I've always wanted to write."

"Why, honey, we already have an author: David Stark. Maybe you've heard of him?"

Who hadn't heard of the South's answer to Stephen King? I felt another emotional bruise from the passive-aggressive Q&A, but the woman did succeed in making me want to quit procrastinating and escape to my father's house.

"Sure," I said. "I just want to try it. I'm not going to compete with him or anything."

"He even did a holiday story." She pointed at a tall display of hardback books, green dustcovers ornamented with blood splatters, which she'd arrayed in the conical shape of a Christmas tree. Her expression showed pride in Graylee's favorite son and more than a touch of scorn, as if challenging my right to try to write anything.

So much for Shangri-La. Feeling cornered, I said in my mother's sweet Georgia drawl, "But can't there be more than one writer, even in lil' ol' Graylee?" Then I hammered her with my usual don't-screw-with-me New York accent: "Since I own this freaking town and everything in it."

Including the lease on your shop, I hoped my toothy smile conveyed.

At first I took some satisfaction at how Paulina paled to the color of her ridiculous sweater, but then I felt guilty for lording it over the woman. So this is what it was like to have power. First chance I got I'd wielded it like a club instead of an olive branch.

"Of course, of course," she replied, backing down the aisle, palms out as if to ward off another blow. "Um…you, uh, still need help finding a gift?"

"Actually I'd better go." Although the woman had been beyond rude, I added, "Sorry, I was out of line. I'm a long way from home and feeling like an exposed nerve."

That stopped her retreat. "Think nothing of it, honey. We just got off on the wrong foot is all. I hope you'll come back in, and hello me when we see each other around town."

"Count on it." We exchanged wary goodbyes, and I headed outside, sleigh bells ching-chinging behind me. The shame I felt continued to sting. I'd acted like a bully. "Benevolent dictator" would've been an upgrade.

Grimacing over my shortcomings, I checked the GPS on my phone for the drive to Dad's house and then pressed the remote to unlock the car door before remembering my "when in Rome" resolution. Of course, if Paulina's attitude indicated of how everyone in Graylee felt toward me, I probably needed to lock my doors after all. Hell, I might want someone to do a daily bomb sweep.

As I drove down Main Street, I noted two blinking caution lights at cross streets. Steering with my wrists, I took a photo through the windshield to share with my friends later: Look, there aren't even real stoplights here; three cars going in the same direction would constitute a traffic jam. However, my picture also would show them clean gutters and not a single spray of graffiti on the buildings. There were some nice things about small-town living.

The GPS stated, "Take left onto Brady Stapleton Boulevard." I was starting to get a feel for my father. Not exactly humble. And "Boulevard"—seriously?

Ahead, I spotted a Denny's Restaurant, which seemed out of place with the upscale finery. Beyond it, I turned left onto a narrow strip of blacktop instead of the usual pitted concrete. Thick woods lined both sides. Not only was the ride much smoother, but the sound of the rubber against the road was like high-pitched singing. Dad probably had kept his boulevard tuned, so the angelic choir would stay in proper voice. I wiggled the steering wheel back and forth, serpentining across the single lane, and listened to the heavenly song rise and fall.

My father had located his house on the only spot in town with any real elevation. It was just a steep hill with trees all around it, but I half-expected the GPS to announce, "Arriving at Brady Stapleton Mountain." Nothing was modest about the house, however. The sprawling stone hunting lodge covered most of the hilltop.

In the pea-gravel curve of courtyard that fronted the house, I stopped near an iron lawn jockey. The figure's face and hands had been painted bright white, but chips and scratches revealed black paint underneath. If all of this truly belonged to me, the jockey would be the first thing to go.

The granite manse boasted a deep, wraparound porch and an equally impressive balcony that bordered the entire second floor. No one greeted me. My father's lawyer had specified that, after the holidays, a "licensed, insured, and bonded" cleaning crew could tend the house and landscape each week for me. Perhaps that was in reaction to the drifter, Wallace Landry, who'd talked his way into the job of groundskeeper back in late June and thanked my father a few weeks later with seventeen bullets at pointblank range.

I called the lawyer, Mr. Pearson, who also was the executor of the estate, to let him know I'd arrived. Then I walked up the steps and followed the porch in a counterclockwise trek around the house. Clusters of cushioned outdoor furniture provided small oases on the wide expanse of wood. In back of the house, a flagstone walkway led to a four-car garage of stacked stones and slate roof that was larger than the apartment my older brother, our mother, and I had shared after she'd taken us from Graylee to the Atlanta suburbs. It was impossible not to feel anger at how he had thrived while we struggled.

Dad never once paid a dime of alimony or child support, and he'd played no role in our lives. Because Mom had refused to talk about him — other than assigning blame for my smart mouth — I was confused back in July when the Graylee police chief called with news of his murder. In my mind, Brady Stapleton had been dead for years. My brother and mother were gone as well, and here I was, the sole heir, surveying the prosperity that had been denied us.

The book I wanted to write was about Mom's life, a tribute to her strength and fortitude. I would be writing fiction because she had seldom talked about her past, so I'd pieced together fragments over the years and had to imagine the worst parts, including her marriage to the man who had come to own Graylee. I hoped to learn more about both of them, so I could do her story justice.

At the same time, I wanted to be anywhere else instead of dealing with the aftermath of Dad's violent death. Except maybe back in New York, avoiding all of my favorite places for fear of running into Andy or any of my other former boyfriends. At least I was far from all of them.

Settled in a porch rocker facing the courtyard, I finally answered the accumulated texts with as much positivity as I could muster and was moving on to Facebook when a Cadillac pulled up behind my rental car. Mr. Pearson, no doubt. He checked his wavy white hair in the rearview mirror, emerged from his Caddy, and smoothed his suit jacket. Good-looking guy, mid-sixties, with a trim build and a dedicated golfer's tan.

Out of habit, I clocked his ring finger and saw a thick gold band there. Pity, he was just my type: well-heeled and debonair, a mature gentleman. Not that I had refrained from dating a few unhappily married Baby Boomers in New York—which was how my relationship with Andy had started—but such risky behavior would be much harder to pull off in Graylee. New start, new habits, I reminded myself.

The lawyer called, "First impressions of the homestead, Ms. Wright?"

"It's big even by New York standards." I waited for him to get closer so I didn't have to keep shouting. "Are you sure my dad lived alone? He could've stashed at least four women here, and they never would've seen each other."

Mr. Pearson frowned at me, apparently still not used to my sense of humor despite six months of phone calls about the estate. "Brady only dated one at a time," he said, "for as long as I can remember."

He strode up the porch steps, cordovan wingtips glistening. When he shook my hand, I caught the flash of a chunky gold cufflink and matching watch. The lawyer was even more handsome up close, with Coke-bottle green eyes and a regal posture. I had to remind myself again to behave.

"After your mother left," he said, "Brady threw himself into his work, and then there was no time for marriage. The pressures were enormous—nearly everybody's prosperity in Graylee was tied to decisions he made."

That got my attention. I asked, "Is everyone now counting on me to do the same?"

"Not at all. I did not mean to steer us in that direction." He inquired about my plane trip from New York and my journey by car from Atlanta. The gentleman chatted effortlessly, his Southern manners impeccable. Although his precise diction and refusal to use contractions made me self-conscious about how I sounded, I relaxed into my first non-hostile encounter since arriving.

As the man continued to talk, however, I wondered if he charged by the quarter-hour and was padding his bill to the estate. And now the estate was mine. The image of a taxi meter scrolling out of control motivated me to get on with things. Interrupting him, I said, "Look, I know you're a busy man, and we've got lots to do. How do we get started?"

Mr. Pearson produced a large ring of keys from his pocket. "First allow me to give you the tour." He unlocked the front door, opened it, and stepped back. "After you, Ms. Wright."

Afternoon sunlight bathed the interior, a huge open space with exposed stone and timbers, reinforcing the impression of a hunting lodge. The cool air smelled of recently applied lemon furniture polish, leather, and old cigar smoke. Oversized chairs and couches, upholstered in maroon, navy blue, and deep green, offered plenty of seating in the great room.

Thank God there were no animal heads or taxidermied fish on the walls. Mounted there instead were large color and monochrome photographs of different portions of my dad's domain, each rendered with genuine artistry: the little town of Graylee, a light industrial center, a timber nursery with its own plant and rail yard, and plantation-style pecan groves. He'd hired a shutterbug with a great eye for details and moody lighting. Still, the images were unsettling—as if Dad had wanted to survey his whole kingdom at all times.

The central focus of the room was a gigantic pass-through fireplace, the opening roughly eight feet wide and taller than my five and a half feet. Thinking about the seventy-degree temperature a few days before Christmas, I wondered if a hearth could be useful more than a handful of days each winter. Over the piled, fresh-looking firewood, I could see partway into the other half of the room—a dining area with a table fit for a CEO and seating for about twenty.

As Mr. Pearson led me around and described the tons of stone and lumber and the Herculean efforts that had gone into the construction of the house, I verified the dining room actually sat twenty-four. I imagined the elaborate dinner parties held there while Mom worked two jobs and my brother and I babysat, mowed lawns, and did other after-school work to put a little more food on our secondhand table. It made me wonder for the umpteenth time since I was told of my inheritance why we couldn't have enjoyed at least a little bit of his prosperity. Now I could immerse myself in the whole opulent lifestyle, but had no one to share it with me: a queen in a deserted castle.

A guest bathroom, complete with walk-in shower, and an expansive kitchen took up the rest of the space on that side of the fireplace. The appliances and granite countertops looked pristine, without a smudge or any discoloring from usage. My mother's blender had been held together with duct tape, and our refrigerator had looked like tornado salvage. As for my own belongings, due to arrive after Christmas in a moving van, nothing would go with what I'd seen so far. My stuff was urban shabby chic, not gentlemen's club. How would I fit my life into this house?

"There are east and west guest wings down here," the lawyer said, "as well as two spare bedroom suites upstairs." Near both wings, wood staircases led up to the second floor, where hallway doors opposite the guest wings allowed entrance to the master suite. Mr. Pearson led the way again, resuming his tour-guide patter. The master had the same dimensions as the huge room beneath us, with the stone chimney bisecting it. We stood in a study with bookshelves crammed full of hardcovers and paperbacks—including all of David Stark's titles—a table-size TV with a manly leather recliner and a matching couch, and a computer desk that had a southern exposure, looking down on my father's "boulevard" and the town beyond it.

Mr. Pearson said, "The other side, Ms. Wright, is…well, um, I will give you a little privacy." He stepped into the hall and closed the door behind him.

I eyed the stonework of the chimney and imagined Dad's bedroom on the other side of it. No doubt the furnishings would be über-masculine. On a moonless night in July, with Dad asleep there in blue silk pajamas, Wallace Landry had inched open the door from the hallway, stepped softly over the rugs and heart-pine planks, and shot my father to pieces.

From local newspaper articles and TV reports I'd found on-line, I knew Landry had been twenty-six years old and roamed from town to town doing odd jobs. A big, fair-haired guy, hand-some in a scruffy way, with a careless kind of smile. Probably a real charmer, in addition to being a homicidal maniac. I pictured how the gunfire would have lit up the dark room and revealed Landry in brief, intense flashes, the sounds echoing around the enormous space like the end of the world.

Maybe Dad had flaunted his status in a town that depended on him for jobs. Maybe he had been a monster to Mom and totally uncaring about my brother and me. Maybe I'd even fanta-sized over the years about what it would've been like to find him alive and punish him for the ways he'd wronged us. If nothing else, I wished I'd had the chance to confront him before Landry pulled the trigger.

Likewise, I would've liked to ask the drifter why he had done it before he was gunned down in the same room. The police chief had not arrived fast enough to stop the crime, but at least he had executed the criminal.

I wanted to continue dawdling, even if it meant torturing my-self with further gruesome imaginings, but Mr. Pearson waited on the other side of the door. Rounding the chimney, I walked upon the murder scene.

2

THE CARNAGE IN THE BEDROOM HAD LONG SINCE BEEN CLEANED UP, OF COURSE, BUT THAT knowledge didn't stop me from holding my breath and clenching my fists as I shuffled in. Morbid imagination still on overdrive, I wondered if the clean sheets and comforter on the massive bed concealed bullet holes in the mattress and box springs. Idiotically, I even checked under my feet for the drifter's bloodstains, guessing I might've stood where Landry had been served justice by the police chief. Lightheaded and nauseated, I began to sway.

I stutter-stepped forward, needing to sit, but then realized I was heading toward the bed. A lurching stumble to my left brought me close enough to a padded armchair that I allowed myself to fall into it. The chair legs screeched as the furniture slid under me, knocking over a floor lamp with a crash.

Shattering porcelain from the torchiere shade brought Mr. Pearson trotting into the room. He steered well clear of the china shards. Before he could say anything, I brought my palm up and murmured, "Sorry, this is bothering me a lot more than I thought it would."

I was surprised to find myself holding back tears. Why would I cry for a man who had lived like a king while his children and former wife struggled to stay afloat? A man who meant less than nothing to me? Who had left me his entire fortune, though he had no idea what kind of person I was? I always had assumed I'd meant less than nothing to him as well. Yet he had entrusted me with his estate and the livelihoods of several thousand people because I was his only surviving child. Finally, I gave in and cried for the lost opportunity to get to know a man who, in my mind, had died twice.

Mr. Pearson pressed a white handkerchief into my hand. Thinking about my now-soggy make-up, I rasped, "No thanks, I'll ruin it."

"The least I can do." When I still didn't make use of it, he added, "To ease your conscience, I will bill you for it."

I snorted wetly, unfolded the white square, and dried my face with it, smearing what looked like ten dollars' worth of cosmetics on the carefully ironed cloth. The lawyer pointed out the master bathroom on the other side of the room. I got up unsteadily, carried my purse there, and tried to repair the damage. If I focused on one detail at a time — cheeks, eyes, lips — I wouldn't have to see my face as a whole, see my mother staring back at me as if trapped again inside the house she'd fled, with me and my brother in tow, thirty-five years before.

That thought started me crying again, so the make-up process had to begin anew. When I finally emerged, I found a sliding glass door open nearby and joined Mr. Pearson on the balcony. We propped our forearms on the railing and gazed at the pine trees enclosing that side of the hill.

"Will you be all right here?" The lawyer looked me over as if appraising my sobriety. "There is a motel out near the highway if you want someplace to stay while you reconsider living under this roof."

"I'll get used to it. It's not like I'm afraid of ghosts or anything." I glanced back toward the bedroom. "I'm just not used to being in places where violence happens."

He smiled at that. "I thought you lived in New York City for most of your life."

"It's not like it used to be, back in the day." I leaned out and inhaled the clean air. It helped to clear my head a little. "Southerners are the worst about New York prejudice. You think we have to step over fifty bodies on our way to the bagel shop."

"Point taken. I guess it is not like in the movies."

"I have to admit that Graylee smells a lot better." I eyed him, enjoying the sight of this mature, distinguished man. His presence relaxed me and even restored some of the friskiness I'd felt when I first saw him. I gave him a playful nudge with my elbow. "Besides, we don't step over bodies in the Big Apple; we kick them out of our way."

His laugh was loud and hardy, a glimpse of how he was when he let down his guard. He was making it hard for me to restrain myself. The six months since Andy ended our engagement had been long and lonely indeed—a record drought for someone who used to excel at rebound romances.

Before I could indulge in a little more flirtation, I saw movement in the trees, a fleeting glimpse of a figure who appeared to look up at me. Pale face, blond hair, a splash of color around the head that could've been a red and blue bandana. Then whoever it was stepped back and vanished.

"Did you see that?" I asked, pointing too late.

He frowned. "See what?"

"A teenager or maybe young man in the trees. I don't know—he was far away and it happened so quick. Anyhow, somebody was watching us."

"Sorry, I never was an eagle eye—your father always made fun of me when we went hunting. Perhaps the person you saw is a hunter, too, someone who became accustomed to trespassing here. I suppose he had not yet heard the news that Brady Stapleton's heir is in town."

I said, "Probably the only one in Graylee who hasn't." Scanning the woods again, I didn't see anyone and began to doubt whether I had in the first place.

The attorney glanced at his gold watch. "In order to become the actual heir, Ms. Wright, you first must get through a pile of paperwork." He returned the nudge I gave him earlier. "I have so many documents for you to sign that you are going to want to kick *me* soon enough."

I followed him downstairs and then sat at the head of the landing strip my father would've called the dining room table. Mr. Pearson went out to his Cadillac and returned with a cordovan briefcase that matched his shoes. He took a seat on my right and withdrew a sheaf of paper. About a hundred "Sign Here" Post-It flags jutted from its sides.

Over the next three-plus hours, he detailed each deed, lease, account, security code, password, and what seemed like every possession bequeathed to me, including 100% ownership of three separate, profitable businesses. I took a ton of notes on a legal pad he provided, making him pause occasionally so I could flex my cramped fingers. Just thirty minutes into the litany, I thought I would need a full-time CPA to keep up with the quarterly taxes and bills I would owe. By the end, I knew an entire accounting office would be required. Fortunately, Dad had long-since retained such a firm in Atlanta.

With relief, I signed and dated the final sheet, set down Mr. Pearson's heavy silver pen, and massaged my hand again. Glancing at the stacks of papers—a set for me and one the lawyer would file at the county courthouse—I said, "Either I've inherited a fortune or a lifetime worth of debt. Which is it?"

"Some of both." He capped the pen and clipped it inside his shirt pocket. "The good news is that the assets outweigh the liabilities." From his suit jacket, he withdrew the large ring of keys. "These now belong to you."

I flipped through them, the grip of each one tagged with color-coded plastic and labeled in tiny but neat writing: keys for the house locks, the cars in the detached garage, the industrial and timber-processing plants, a separate house that doubled as an office near the pecan groves, and on and on, down to file cabinets and foot lockers. The ring of keys felt heavy as hell, in more ways than one.

My first impulse was to fling it onto the table and tell Mr. Pearson to sell everything and give me a check for the net profits. I was in way over my head. All I wanted was a quiet place in the country where I could try writing Mom's story, get over my heartbreaks, and start doing something that mattered.

As I made a fist around the keys, though, I considered how much work and achievement they represented. My father had competent people running all three of the businesses—they could maintain their present course. If I were called on to make any strategic decisions, I would lean on the advice of those managers, at least until I learned much more about the industries.

I'd bounced around various Wall Street firms for years, chasing raises and promotions, trying to stay ahead of the ever-soaring cost of living. As a result, I could analyze financial statements, knew a lot of business lingo, and had a good BS meter. Maybe I could avoid getting snowed, but the responsibilities of even an absentee owner seemed overwhelming. My feelings circled back around to fearing I was in way over my head.

"Any questions?" Mr. Pearson asked.

I laughed. "Only a few thousand."

He made a show of checking his watch. "It is your dime, Ms. Wright."

"I wondered what your fee is."

"Well, it works out to a dime every second or so. What is your first question?"

"Doing anything for din—" I clamped a hand over my mouth as my cheeks burned. I'd been on auto-pilot, seated close to my kind of guy and feeling vulnerable and lonely in an unfamiliar place. "Sorry," I said, and wiped away the shame-sweat that had sprung out above my upper lip. "I hardly ever hit on attorneys."

"How unfortunate for the profession," he said, smiling at me. "I am flattered, of course, being noticed by a beautiful woman who also happens to be the second richest person in town. However—" he patted my hand that still clutched the keys "—I also am very married, very old, and very interested in seeing you make a positive start in your hometown."

My insides did a little flip over his compliment. I said, "You're not that old."

"Old enough to be your…well, um, what other questions do you have?"

"Who's the richest person in town?"

"That would be David Stark, the author. Maybe you have heard of him?"

"You're the second person to ask me that. Is it like his tagline or something?" I waved away the rhetorical question as he shook his head. "I guess David Stark made his fortune without taking on all the debts my father did. Maybe Dad should have tried his hand at horror fiction instead of business."

Mr. Pearson evened up one stack of documents and put it in his briefcase. "With all due respect to Mr. Stark, he employs one person to manage his schedules and correspondence, and even in these modern times he receives enough paper fan mail to help justify the local post office remaining open with a couple of staff." He pointed to my set of papers. "Your father's businesses employ 3,000, not just three. Most of those 3,000 have families, whose standard of living has benefited mightily from that employment. We love and protect our local celebrity, of course, but who do you think has been more important to Graylee, Georgia?"

I glanced at the ceiling, figuring the master bedroom was directly above us. "It's a shame Graylee didn't protect him, too."

He hung his head for a moment, as if absorbing a physical blow. I started to apologize for the cheap shot—which seemed to have become my specialty lately—but he said, "You are right, certainly. It is a shame from which we will never fully recover. But now that you are here, I hope we can make amends and put the tragedy behind us as much as possible." He cocked his head. "You still have yet to ask me a serious question."

"If you were me, what would you do first thing tomorrow?"

He nodded his approval. "Introduce yourself to the managers

at the various enterprises, who will be eager to make presentations about the products, customers, suppliers, and competitors. Get the 30,000-foot view of things."

It was good advice, and I thanked him for it. "I don't want to drop in unannounced," I added. "Do you have a list of people I can call to get on their schedules?"

"I have already made the arrangements," he replied, giving me a mischievous smile that made him look like my contemporary instead of my father's. "My paralegal, Timothy Bladensburg, will pick you up at 9 a.m. tomorrow and be your driver and escort."

"I hear the sound of dimes stacking up."

"All part of the service, Ms. Wright."

℘

After moving two large suitcases from the car into the house, I inspected the kitchen. The spotless refrigerator and freezer had been cleared out, but I found plenty of canned and packaged goods in the cupboards. I put together a small spaghetti dinner — mindful of how my metabolism had seemed to slow down the instant I'd hit the big four-oh — and ate in the huge dining room while I worked on a grocery list. Fork against plate, water glass against wood tabletop, every sound seemed to echo within the massive space and emphasize my solitude.

First dinner prepared in my new kitchen, first things to put in the dishwasher, first night in the big hunting lodge on the hill above the little town. Alone not for the first time, of course, but feeling lonelier than I had since my mother passed away when I was nineteen.

For more than two decades, a string of men had kept that feeling at bay. I'd thought each of them had the potential to be The One, and I stopped at nothing to demonstrate my worthiness. So many heartbreaks, but, when Andy had proposed, I assumed I would never be forsaken again.

Now my worst fears revisited me: lonely, abandoned, unattractive, unloved. What I jokingly called The Four Horsewomen of My Dating Apocalypse. If only they were a joke. I'd been imagining them for so long they almost had become real, stalking me with a relentless clop of hooves, creak of saddle leather, and an endless string of taunts.

Thoughts of them always made me paranoid. I recalled that glimpse of the young man in the woods, the stranger watching me. Snatching up my pad of notes from the dining room table, I found the alarm instructions Mr. Pearson had given me. I memorized the code and activated the security system. Not that it had saved my father's life, but maybe it would enable Graylee's top cop to bag another bad guy.

What I needed was to hunker down under the covers with plenty of TV and cell phone distractions. I knew which bedroom I definitely wasn't moving into; I wasn't even sure when I could force myself to clean up the smashed porcelain in the master. Since I was downstairs, I explored those guest wings first, starting with the west side. A large oak door with honest-to-God iron bands gave way to an ultra-feminine sitting area, bedroom, and bath, everything done up in pastel colors, dust ruffles, and pillows galore. In fact, if any of my dad's dinner parties had turned into an orgy, there were more than enough pillows to go around. The east wing contained a similar suite but with a floral and lace theme and doilies everywhere.

The upstairs suites featured bedrooms and living areas also heavy with chintz. It was no wonder Mr. Pearson had skipped those during the tour—most men would consider them fluffy versions of hell. They were too girly even for me. Worse, my belongings now heading South in the moving van didn't go with anything in those rooms either.

It was weird. Who had brought a woman's touch to all of the guest suites and why did that decor extend only to those rooms? It was as if Dad had hired Ernest Hemingway and Laura Ashley to decorate his house, and they flipped a coin to see which rooms they would design.

Considering the proximity of the second floor suites to the master, I eliminated those sleeping options. That narrowed my choices to the east and west wings downstairs: lace versus pillows. I had to admit I wasn't the sort of person who relished beautiful sunrises streaming through my curtains while I tried to steal another ten minutes of sleep, so my only real choice was the west wing pillow orgy.

After piling about twenty of those suckers in a corner, I had enough room on the queen-sized bed to open each suitcase and start filling the walk-in closet, wardrobe cabinets, and shelves. Cluttering the bathroom came next. I then prepared for bed and used some of the dozen remaining pillows to prop myself against the headboard so I could watch TV, exchange some Facebook and text updates with my friends, and make notes on the remaining pages of the lawyer's legal pad.

On the final sheet, I bulleted a list of people I wanted to visit after the meetings Mr. Pearson had arranged. It would be a good idea to start over with Paulina O'Shea and meet some of the other business owners before public opinion hardened against me. The post office staff might be helpful to know, as would David Stark, assuming Mister "Maybe You've Heard of Him" received visitors. I glanced yet again at the ceiling, thinking of the slaughter that had taken place upstairs. At the top of my list, I added the chief of police.

3

A STEADY RAT-TAT-TAT WOKE ME, AS IF A WOODPECKER WERE TRYING TO DISMANTLE THE house. I had slumped down in bed while watching TV and lay buried under an avalanche of pillows. As the rapping continued, I realized someone was knocking at the door.

According to my cell phone it was 9 a.m. sharp. Damn—it must've been the paralegal. I staggered out of bed, pulled on yesterday's clothes, and clipped up my hair. The polite but insistent knocking continued unabated. Time was money, and this guy was on the job. He would bloody his knuckles before long.

Blessed with a good memory, I recalled the security code and disabled the alarm system. However, I was still a New Yorker, so I also checked the peephole my father had installed. A twenty-something, African-American man in a suit stood on the other side, his hand a blur against the wood.

When I unlocked and opened the door, he took a step back. Tall but way too skinny, he would've looked better with another thirty pounds on him—and, for me anyway, another thirty years. He adjusted the knot in his already-perfect tie and checked the time on his cell phone. "I'm Timothy Bladensburg," he said with a faint Southern lilt, his voice just above a whisper. "Mr. Pearson said I should be here at nine."

"Sorry, I overslept. Can you give me maybe thirty minutes to get ready and gulp down some coffee and cold spaghetti?"

After only the briefest pause, Timothy said, "How about twenty minutes while I reschedule your visits, and then I'll take you to breakfast at the diner?" The paralegal's voice still had not become louder, so perhaps it was just the way he talked. His neck was so slender, maybe only a little air could get out at a time.

I put a hand on my hip and gave him a smirk. "Pretty cocky, making a counteroffer to the woman who owns Graylee."

"Yes, ma'am. With you being a New Yorker and all, I thought you'd appreciate a little moxie." He glanced at his cell phone again. "Nineteen minutes, or sixty seconds less for breakfast." He smiled. "Your choice."

"Give me the full twenty, and I'll skip a third refill of coffee." Remembering my manners, I added, "You want to come in while I get ready?"

Timothy took a half-step back, eyes widening in apparent horror. So much for my attempt at Southern hospitality. "No thank you, ma'am. I'll wait in the car." He indicated a blue Hyundai sedan that was nothing fancy but sparkled in the sunshine, freshly washed and waxed.

"Okay, but stop calling me that. I'm Janet." I put out my hand.

"Tim." Long, thin fingers with a warm and confident grip. Nice to see that some young people still bothered to master the art of the handshake. Before our first Wall Street interviews, my classmates and I had rehearsed ours for a solid hour.

He looked at his cell phone again, but I cut him off. "I know, I'm going to have to order my breakfast to go if I don't get moving." I waved, closed the door, and got ready for the day. Attention to hair and make-up meant just a soapy washcloth in the odiferous places and extra deodorant.

Nineteen minutes later, I was dressed for my meet-and-greets in a pantsuit and medium heels, all conservative neutrals and earth tones so I didn't scare the locals. Thinking about my encounter with Paulina, I set the alarm, exited as a warning beep sounded, and also locked the door.

Tim pocketed his cell phone as he hopped out of the sedan. He opened the back door for me, but I dodged around the hood and dropped into the shotgun seat. When he climbed in beside me, I said, "None of that chauffeur stuff."

"Yes, uh…Janet," he replied in his soft voice, mouth turned down. Clearly, I wasn't following the script he'd envisioned.

The day was going to be stressful enough without having my guide annoyed at me. Either I could keep my mouth shut—a proven impossibility—or I needed to establish some common ground. A show of solidarity. Glancing around, I spotted the awful lawn jockey and pointed it out to him. "I swear I'm going to have that thing removed ASAP. Don't you just hate it?"

He shrugged. "No more than the mammie cookie jars in Ms. O'Shea's shop."

"I didn't see those. She must've put them away to make room for the Christmas stuff. How much do the cookie jars bother you?"

He started the car and eased us across the pea gravel of the courtyard, saying, "No more than that lawn jockey."

My conversational gambits were going down in flames. I decided on a new tack. After we were heading toward town on the smooth, curving macadam, I said, "Look, I want to fit in around here, but I don't know the local customs. Can you tell me what I did wrong when I invited you in? Was it something a woman isn't supposed to do when there's a man at the door? Is it a racial thing?"

"None of that," he murmured. "The house…not that I've ever been in it, but…I'm just more comfortable in my car."

"You don't think it's haunted, do you?" When I said this, he glanced at me and I gave him wide, scary eyes and a witchy wiggle of my fingers.

Tim shook his head. "You sure are different from your old man, meaning no disrespect to him, of course."

That got my attention. I asked, "How well did you know my dad?"

"I saw him around town sometimes, but I don't think he even knew my name. Your father wasn't the kind of person who mixed with the common folk." He gestured at Main Street as the car bumped onto concrete and we coasted past the Denny's. "You weren't very old when you left here, right?"

Interesting question—it meant he knew I'd been born in Graylee. I wondered if Mr. Pearson had asked him to do some research on me. Easy enough to find out. "My parents divorced when I was five," I said, "and my mom took my brother and me to live in Atlanta."

"Atlanta?" He looked puzzled and then his mouth snapped shut, a sound louder than his voice and the perfect accompaniment to my trap being sprung.

Not letting on, I said, "Well, Acworth, northwest of the city."

He nodded, probably not even realizing he did it, as I confirmed the fact he must've already discovered. His next question sounded genuine, "Did you come back sometimes, like to spend summers with your father?"

"Nope, never saw him again. He didn't pay child support, but my mom didn't take him to court—he was out of our lives for good."

Tim signaled and pulled into a just-vacated diagonal parking space near a diner. A Christmas mural similar to the one that had drawn me into Paulina O'Shea's gift shop decorated the large front window. Judging by the number of cars and trucks out front, this eatery was at least ten times more popular than Denny's, where I'd noticed two vehicles were parked.

I unslung my seatbelt. "Do you lock up?"

"What for?"

"That's what I thought." I beat him to the diner door and held it open for him.

He shook his head. "That ain't right. What are you trying to do?"

"I don't like to be waited on. Besides, my mom taught me that the person who gets to the door first is the one who holds it." I inhaled the aromas of fresh baked goods, fried onions, and strong coffee. "Tim, I can stand here all day enjoying the smells of breakfast, but we probably only have twenty-three minutes left."

He checked his cell phone. "Twenty-four." Shaking his head, he walked past me.

Two dozen diners, all white, looked us over as Tim led me to a table along one paneled wall. The place didn't go pin-drop silent, but apparently a young African-American man dining with a forty-year-old white woman still drew stares in small-town Georgia. As soon as we sat, an old couple nearby made a big show of folding up their newspapers, slinging some money on their table, and leaving. Others examined us with unabashed curiosity.

I needed to ease off—I could afford to be the eccentric Yankee heiress who decided to move into the big house on the hill, but Tim had to live among the people of Graylee and eventually practice law for them if he planned to stick around. "Sorry," I told him. "It's not going to help you if I act out."

He ducked his head and flipped over the plastic menu in front of him. "It's not that, and it's not a race thing. I'm just used to being a pariah."

"Care to explain?"

"Not really."

A waitress who looked like she'd worked there since the Civil War came over with a glass coffeepot. Doris, according to the cursive red stitching on her uniform. A gold necklace with a dainty crucifix showed against the skin below her wrinkled neck. She said, "Morning, Ms. Wright. Hey, Tim. Y'all having a lovely day?"

It was going to be hard to get used to everyone knowing me on sight. In the Manhattan Starbucks I'd gone to twice a day for years, they always asked me what name to write on my cup. I thanked her and ordered black coffee and, reluctantly, a vegetable omelet. Damned metabolism.

Tim said, "The usual, please."

Doris filled our mugs. "Of course. Billy started on it when y'all walked in." She headed back to the fry table and chatted with the middle-aged cook. Thank goodness Tim wasn't a pariah to everyone.

I cupped the thick ceramic and took a cautious sip. Hot, slightly nutty, and electric with caffeine. If Billy made the coffee, I'd officially fallen in love with him. After taking a longer drink, I asked, "Did my father come in here a lot?"

Tim said, "I guess so. Until he brought in the Denny's at his end of the street."

Maybe he used to eat at all hours and hadn't wanted to go far for a meal. His own personal restaurant—and now mine, I supposed. "Given their history with minorities," I said, "it probably isn't your fave. They were never big on serving pariahs."

That earned me a smile at least. It looked like he wanted to talk about it, but then he stopped and cleared his throat. In a louder voice than usual, full of fake curiosity, he asked, "So, where were we? You said you were ten when you went to New Yor...." He trailed off and his eyes closed, followed by his fists. I wondered if he wanted to beat his own forehead with them.

Not letting him off the hook, I said, "We hadn't gotten there yet. I was ten when my brother, Brady Jr., died trying to outrace a train at a crossing. He was seventeen and apparently drunk." Having told him another thing he no doubt already knew, I felt compelled to add more, to get him to see me as a person, not just a research and babysitting assignment. I waited until he looked at me. "I worshipped him. It wiped me out, but it hit my mom even worse. She never recovered."

"I'm really sorry," Tim said. He looked as mournful as he sounded. At last I felt like we were talking to each other authentically. No more pretending, no games.

I said, "Thank you. It's a nightmare, one you can't wake up from. Mom and I moved to New York—Long Island to be specific—right after that."

He drank some more coffee. "Did you like living up there?"

"It was okay. The winters sucked, no surprise, but Mom slowly came back to life after we settled in, and that made it better." I put my menu back in the metal rack attached to the table edge. "She'd just started to go on dates and show her old sense of humor when cancer got her. I think it was all the stress."

"That's awful."

"I was nineteen, in college at NYU." He probably knew that as well, but he continued to look at me with such sympathy, I patted his hand and forced out a laugh. "Hey, the last twenty-one years have been pretty good." If you didn't count having your heart broken by your fiancé and more than a dozen other men before him.

Tim seemed to read between the lines. He toasted me with his coffee cup. "Here's to surviving."

I clinked my mug against his and said, "Perseverance." I took another drink, feeling much better about him. "Okay," I said, "your turn. Do you plan to stay in Graylee forever?"

His volume dropped even lower than normal, hard to hear over the clattering of plates and flatware and the conversations around us. "No chance. Even if I got a law degree and someday took over Mr. Pearson's practice, it's hard to imagine the locals coming to me to do their wills and such. Plus, the options are nil in the romance department."

"There have got to be some single women your age."

"We have fifteen black families in Graylee. The boys and girls paired off long ago. And this still isn't the kind of place that encourages mixed couples. Besides—"

"You're a pariah."

"You got it." He glanced at the time on his cell phone as Doris put our meals in front of us. I got my omelet, but it was swamped by buttery grits and half-covered by a giant biscuit that was so fluffy I could almost see the lard waiting to attach itself to my butt.

I would've done better with Tim's breakfast, which consisted of two hardboiled eggs and two strips of bacon. With a smile and a flourish, as if doing a magic trick for us, Doris pulled a bottle of sriracha sauce out of her deep apron pocket and placed it beside him.

I thanked her and forked up a bit of steaming omelet on the side farthest from the grits and biscuit. Just the right consistency: tender without being too runny, and the mushrooms and bell peppers still had some chewiness. In spite of the fatty side items, I definitely was developing a major thing for Billy the Fry Cook. Tim set about peeling the eggs with his long, thin fingers. I gestured at his plate and said, "The hardboiled paralegal."

"Tough as nails." He grinned and squirted a red pool of the spicy chili sauce beside the glistening egg whites.

"Too tough to talk about the pariah thing?"

"Too private."

"Okay, fair enough." I took another bite. "Who are we meeting with first?"

Tim dunked some egg in the sriracha. As he ate it, sweat popped out on his forehead but the burn didn't slow him down. Tough as nails, indeed. He said, "We'll go out to the light manufacturing site so you can meet the managers, get the tour. Then it's over to the nursery and wood pellet plant, then check out the pecan groves, and finish with Mr. Pearson for a debrief."

"Do you have some paper and a pen so I can take notes? I ran through the pad your boss gave me yesterday."

"Sure, but there's also a tablet computer in the car." He grinned. "Mr. Pearson wants you to know Graylee is part of the twenty-first century."

I shook my head. "Does he really think I look down on you all?"

He swirled an oval of crumbly egg yolk in the red sauce, chewed for a moment, and then chased it with a bite of bacon. "First, it's 'y'all,' Miss Forgot-Her-Roots. Also, the second richest person in town might want legal advice someday, and it'd be a good thing if she believes the local legal eagles aren't some rubes in a hick town."

I pushed away my plate with the half-eaten omelet to play up my indignation, but really because of my diet resolution. "There's no need for him to worry. Look around this place—half the customers are bent over the newest model of cell phones. It's like any breakfast joint in Brooklyn, except for the lack of diversity."

"That's where I come in," he said, and then added apologetically, "I'll quit the 'second richest person' thing if it's annoying you."

"Are you kidding? I wasn't the eight-millionth richest person in New York. I had to live with two or more roommates when I wasn't shacking up with minimally acceptable boyfriends—just so I could afford someplace that didn't involve a two-hour commute twice a day."

"I thought you had a big-time Wall Street job." Tim dabbed his last bit of bacon in the red sauce and gulped it down.

"No, I just worked at some big-time Wall Street firms. One after another. The jumps in cost of living usually stayed ahead of my pay. Thus, the roommates and the boyfriends."

"Ever get serious about anyone?"

I was tempted to continue with my "it's so tough in the big city" shtick, but he looked genuinely interested, so I confessed, "Yeah, I almost got married earlier this year."

"You get cold feet?"

"He did," I lied. The truth was much more painful. Instead, I said, "We had a big fight. Unfortunately, I lived with him, so I had to find someplace new to stay that same night." I shrugged, keeping up my other shtick: the tough big-city woman. No point in going into the agonizing details that would leave me bawling like a small-town girl whose heart still ached. "I had a couple of girlfriends looking for a third roommate, but what sucked most of all was that my new digs added almost twenty blocks to my walk back and forth to work."

He shook his head. "It's crazy, living in a place where having to change to a less-convenient address is worse than getting dumped."

"You get pragmatic, living at the center of the universe." I slugged down some coffee. "Romantic notions suffer a fast, mostly painless death." It was a good line, but I didn't think I sold it well—I definitely hadn't convinced myself.

Doris refilled our coffees, and Tim asked for the check. As they conversed, the diner door opened, and a guy came in. Everything about him was in the middle of a range, and I immediately thought of him as the Medium Man: not tall or short, not thin or thick. Even his straight, medium-brown hair wasn't cropped or worn too long. Medium Man sported a dark blue uniform shirt with a badge pinned above the left breast pocket and a black plastic name plate above the right, dark slacks, black dress shoes. An equipment-laden belt fit snug against his trim—but not too skinny—waist, including a holstered pistol on his right hip. Even the gun was medium-sized. I wondered if it had been used to kill my father's murderer.

I turned back to Tim. "Is that the chief of police?"

He nodded as he drank his coffee. "Cade Wilson."

"He called me back in July with the news about my dad."

"Chief questioned you?"

"I guess—it didn't seem like much of an interrogation, though. There were a bunch of things I should've asked him, too, but they didn't occur to me until much later." I drained my mug. "It was all such a shock. I hadn't thought about my father in years."

I looked Cade over again as he took a seat at a table beside the festive front window. He wasn't a bit like I'd pictured him during our brief phone conversation. No wedding ring and only early middle-aged, maybe five years older than me. My girlfriends would say that made him too young for my tastes, but they'd always been jealous because my Baby Boomer boyfriends had lived in nicer apartments than their Gen-Xers did.

Turning back to Tim, I asked, "When's the debrief with Mr. Pearson?"

He glanced at Medium Man and then back at me. "You should be done by four."

"And when do we need to leave here?"

He consulted his cell phone. "Five minutes."

I touched up my lipstick, walked over to Cade Wilson, and said hello.

The police chief glanced up from a coffee mug Doris had filled. "Ms. Wright?" He stood and held out his hand. His grip was medium strength and warm—not too hot or cold—and his Southern drawl was noticeable without being redneck-broad. "I'd heard you were in town," he said, taking me in with a quick down-and-up glance. Sounding far sincerer than Paulina O'Shea, he added, "I'm sorry for your loss."

It was the same way he'd ended our phone conversation in

July. Prior to his call, I hadn't heard another Georgia voice since my mother passed away twenty-one years before. I remembered how at ease I'd felt listening to him, even though he delivered shocking news and quizzed me regarding my whereabouts on the night of the murder and my relationship with one of the two deceased men. A voice from home.

"Thank you," I replied. Before I could stop myself, I added in a rush, "I know it's not proper to also thank you for killing Wallace Landry. I've been thinking about it, though, and I wanted to tell you how grateful I am. He got what he deserved."

He frowned at me, apparently needing a little time to process my comment. Finally, he said, "I just wish I got there in time to stop him." He gestured at the chair across from him. "Please have a seat."

"I don't want to interrupt your breakfast."

Cade tapped his coffee mug. "This is all I'm having, and it's still too hot to drink."

Glancing back at Tim, I saw him hold up four long fingers. I sat and then the police chief did the same. "I only wanted to say hi," I told him, "and make an appointment to see you late this afternoon, maybe 4:30?"

"Sure—assuming I'm not out on a call. What's on your mind?"

"I want to talk to you more about my father's murder. Back in July, I guess I was too stunned to think clearly and then, when I finally could, it seemed better to do this in person."

He nodded to himself and stared into his coffee for a long moment before meeting my gaze. "I reckon you've got a right to ask, but I always counsel family members that it's better to move on than hear things that'll haunt you."

I'd expected a little speech, but his words touched me. Now

that I got a closer look, Cade Wilson appeared a bit haunted himself, which made him less average and more intriguing. "Just a few questions, promise," I said.

"See you at 4:30, Ms. Wright. Tim there can show you where to find me."

I thanked him and stood. He stood as well, but hesitated as I offered my hand again. When he shook it, looking into my eyes, I felt a connection. I wondered if he did, too. Not romantic necessarily, but at least simpatico on some level. He let go before I did.

Tim climbed to his feet as I approached our table. I asked, "Did he watch me walk back here?"

"I could tell you were putting a little something extra into it, but it was wasted. He just went back to staring at his coffee."

I joked, "It wasn't wasted—you noticed."

He laughed. "Damn, you New York women know how to flirt. Maybe I need to get up there." He set down money for the bill and what looked like a hefty tip for Doris. After returning his wallet to his pocket, he touched my arm. "Hey, now the chief is looking."

I did a quick check as I slung my purse over one shoulder, but Cade was drinking his coffee and looking at the yuletide scene painted on the plate glass.

"Gotcha," Tim said in his soft voice.

"You're officially fired as my wingman."

He was smiling as I let him get to the door first and hold it open. Looking back into the diner, I caught Cade Wilson watching me. Maybe he'd felt that connection after all.

4

THANK GOD MY WALL STREET TRAINING HAD MADE ME FLUENT IN DATA-SPEAK AND BUSINESS jargon. I had no problem following the presentations by Stapleton Industries managers and even got in a few zingers to make it clear I wasn't some bubble-headed heiress they could snow.

The boardroom didn't seat as many as Dad's dining room table. Every manager at each level was a white man somewhere between forty and sixty-five. I checked out of habit, and only two didn't wear wedding rings, but even they had a married look about them: well-fed and mellow but a little bored.

Unlike my encounter with Paulina, I didn't sense hostility from the men seated around me, but they did give off an aura of wariness. Whenever I hit them with a probing question, they cut their eyes at one another as if to say, "This isn't going to be as easy as we thought."

I asked the CEO, a fifty-something named Jeff Conway, "Why not reinvest more of the profits in the business, instead of giving out such fat bonuses every December?" Especially to yourselves, I didn't add. He spluttered about how my father had made it part of the company culture and reveled in distributing those bonuses each year during the week before Christmas. I had an image of Dad dressed as the bruiser of all Santa Clauses passing out four- and five-figure checks from a huge sack.

"There's another thing," I added, and flipped through the thick handout given to each of us at the start of the dog-and-pony show. "According to Exhibit AF, revenues in June were almost non-existent and that carried over into July." I pointed at the bar graph on the screen, which showed each month of revenue with the usual fluctuations but no huge swings. "That tracks the exhibit exactly but only through May, and then nothing matches. If the exhibit is right, we actually did better than usual after a really rough midyear; if the graph is right, we did about normal throughout. Somehow, the year-end tallies line up, but what's the story?"

Conway made notes on his copy of the handout, not looking at all pleased. "It's my fault," he said, "for not reviewing the reports as thoroughly as I should have. This was sort of a rush job — Phil Pearson called me last week with news you'd be coming down before the holidays, earlier than expected, and asked that we put a briefing together." He stared at the CFO, who also was taking notes and chewing the inside of his cheek. "The accounting department will correct the errors in Exhibit AF and provide all of us with the amendment after New Year's. Sorry, it's the old 'garbage in, garbage out' scenario."

The CEO looked at me hopefully, and I realized I'd asked him the question mostly to score another point. Conway had run the company since long before my father's death and seemed to be doing a great job. Did I see him as a threat? It never occurred to me before that I might've developed an inferiority complex — and if I didn't have one, I sure was acting like a person with something to prove: Look upon my MBA and despair.

It would've been smarter to listen more, talk less, and keep some surprises in store. Now they would expect me to actually pore over every spreadsheet and map out short- and long-term strategies for the damn business. Worse, they really could apply themselves to the task of buffaloing me. I practically had challenged them to do just that, which was plain stupid.

"Okay, got it," I said, letting Conway off the hook. I stayed quiet during the remaining presentations except to compliment the managers on their successes. As they spoke I began to realize what clever manufacturing niches my father and his men had carved out. The company specialized in customized—therefore expensive—orders with computer-aided design and manufacturing tools and 3D printers that kept their efficiencies high and minimized waste.

When Tim had parked us in front of the nondescript metal building, I'd expected sweat-shop conditions inside, with unskilled, uneducated men and women plodding away in bleak, filthy conditions. On the contrary, my dad had maintained a spotless plant, trained his employees well, and paid them much better wages than they could get anywhere else in rural Georgia. Even Atlanta probably couldn't compete in terms of pay for similar work. And then throw in the annual Christmas bonus? Fuhgettaboutit! Instead of a company town where everyone scraped out a meager living, full of hatred toward The Man, Dad had bound his workers with golden handcuffs.

Not to say my father had created an industrial Garden of Eden. During the plant tour that followed the presentations, I was struck by the homogeneity of the workforce: mostly white males, with a few black men and Latinos and a couple of white women. In fact, when I asked to take a bathroom break, Conway and the other managers traded eye contact again. He said, "Uh, this way," and led me to a door simply marked "Restroom." Conway asked me to wait a moment, went inside, and came out a minute later trailing a guy still wiping his hands with a paper towel who apologized for the delay. "All yours," Conway said and held the door for me.

I supposed the few women who worked there had to do the same thing: send a man in to usher out any other guys. The women all probably went together at set times to avoid too much of this idiocy. At least the restroom didn't look as bad as I'd pictured it. I actually found one seat nobody had peed on. In January, I decided, the company would cough up the capital to add a women's lavatory.

As I walked the well-swept floor, smelling the sharp tang of hot plastic, sheared metal, and cutting oil, and flinching occasionally from a screaming drill or sharp bang, I met the employees at welding stations, fabrication hubs, and customizing pods. Watching them observe me in return—and nudge and whisper to their colleagues when they didn't think I was watching—I kept reminding myself it all belonged to me to some degree. I could do what I felt was right. If I decided to actively oversee Dad's businesses, I would make diversity a major goal.

Halfway through the tour, the shift supervisor introduced me to yet another white guy in a building full of them. The worker put aside his drill and wiped his fingers on a clean rag before shaking my hand. He said, "I hope you run this place even half as good as your old man—that'll still make it twice as good as anywhere else I've ever worked."

The supervisor clapped the man on the back and said, "Ol'

Greg here has offered more money-saving suggestions than anybody else at Stapleton in the past decade. It's Greg and folks like
him that make those Christmas bonuses possible."

A chill overtook me. I kept my face frozen in a smiling mask
while I cussed my arrogance. I knew nothing about this business
other than it was more profitable than I'd assumed a light-indus-
trial plant in Nowhereville, Georgia could be, especially given that
the people who worked there made more than unionized labor in
the high-salary North. I thanked Greg and wondered if the person I'd envisioned in his place—a Latina or African-American
woman—would've been as good at his job and so knowledgeable
about operational efficiencies. If I wasn't careful, I could destroy
a good thing with hasty decisions and unintended consequences.

At the end of the tour, Conway and his management team
stood in a half-circle facing me in the parking lot. When I'd
played fast-pitch softball in high school and college, we'd clus-
ter together that way and try not to yawn openly as our coaches
rambled. Now, with everyone looking at me, I saw dread instead
of boredom. The men seemed to be asking themselves just how
terrible an owner I was going to be. I couldn't think of anything
to say at first because my usual go-to options—smart remarks,
sharp retorts, flirty rejoinders—were inappropriate here. Those
were the tools of the sassy sidekick, not the leader.

The managers shifted and swayed and fidgeted and cleared
their throats and waited for me to lead them. To some degree. In
some way. Somehow. I cleared my throat, too, and said, "I appreciate your hard work putting together the presentations and the
tour for me. Um, to be honest, what I want to tell you is, 'I'll be in
my dad's house— just call if something comes up.'"

A few of them, including Conway, chuckled. Encouraged, I continued, "But I know I'm expected to do at least half as good as he did. The thing is, uh, I don't even know what I don't know, whereas you understand this business inside and out. You don't need some dilettante putting on the captain's hat and barking orders."

Some of their faces showed a new expression—hope—and I said with more confidence, "So here's the deal: I'm going to do my best to learn at least a little of what I don't know, a little at a time. And I'm going to rely on you to keep doing the great job you have been and to answer my endless questions…and be patient with me. Um, you've kept this place profitable for six months without the Stapleton in 'Stapleton Enterprises' calling the shots. You aren't getting a Stapleton back, but I hope a Wright won't be wrong for you." They didn't seem to get the joke, so I pointed at my chest and said, "Wright?"

Most of them replied, "Right."

That was sort of funny, so I went with it. "Right," I echoed. "I won't take up any more of your time today, but, uh, happy holidays, and you'll see me again soon as I go to school on this business. Okay?" I clapped my hands together once, as my coaches used to do when ending their pep talks. It worked. Some of the men actually jogged back inside as if taking the field. I felt great—they were my team, and I hadn't disappointed them.

Jeff Conway was the last to go. He pumped my hand and said, "That was really good—I think you've got everybody on your side. There's just one thing."

"What?"

He pointed to the top of the building where the company

name stood out in eight-foot-tall letters. "It's Stapleton *Industries*, not 'Enterprises.' Merry Christmas, boss." He grinned and headed in to work.

Tim came over, checking his cell phone for the time, and asked, "How'd it go?"

I continued to stare up at the company name. "Shit."

℘

I did better at the wood pellet plant. The operation employed almost a hundred—again, mostly white males—and the plant itself looked more like an oil refinery with its towers, tubes, and scaffolding, than the sawmill I'd envisioned. There, my father had taken a declining timber industry and found a use for all of the treetops, limbs, twigs, and other parts traditionally considered waste. The plant churned out wood pellets about the shape and color of cigarette filters that energy companies worldwide snapped up as a cheaper and cleaner alternative to coal.

After a good pep talk to that team, Tim and I had lunch in town. Though we had a number of upscale options, he chose the diner again. A few people left with cutting glances, but those seemed to have been directed at me as much as Tim this time. If I were back in the city, I would've snapped, "What are you lookin' at?" but I managed to keep my cool for Tim's sake. I think he preferred to eat there because Doris took such grandmotherly care of him.

We then drove out to the pecan groves for the final tour, where I perfected the listen-and-compliment routine and nailed my speech. Unfortunately, this management hierarchy consisted

46

of only two, and one of them had stayed home along with the rest of the crew, since the pecans were dormant for another month. Still, I was sure that Stapleton Pecans was in good hands and said as much to the lone man, who sort of gaped at me the whole time. Maybe he didn't see many women on the plantation.

Standing in the forest of leafless, skeletal trees with a guy who kept checking me out, I decided it was the perfect setting for one of David (Maybe You've Heard of Him) Stark's horror stories. He'd have to add some threatening weather, since there was nothing scary about a balmy afternoon with blue skies, but I hoped to talk to him one day about where he found his inspiration, assuming I could arrange a meeting.

On the drive to Mr. Pearson's law office, while scrolling through the notes I'd taken on the tablet computer, I asked Tim, "What was your first thought when your boss told you I was coming to town?"

"Truthfully?"

"Please."

"I thought, 'I hope she's not at all like her daddy.'"

I turned to him in my seat. "Because he wouldn't give regular people like you the time of day?"

"Uh, yeah."

"Any other reason?"

"No," he said. It was his usual soft way of talking, but there was a tremor there as well, a plea.

Still, I pressed him, "Is your feeling connected in any way to the pariah thing you mentioned?"

"I'd rather not say." His hands gripped the wheel harder, as if I were trying to seize control of the car.

I held my palms out. "Okay, fair enough." Maybe Cade Wilson would give me some answers. I checked my watch: half past three. "So, other than Mr. Pearson asking about my day and me asking about his and more dimes stacking up—sorry, that's an inside joke between us—what should I hope to accomplish with this visit?"

"The mayor and city council will be there, too. They all want to meet you."

I tossed the tablet on the floorboard. "Hey, thanks for so much advance notice." I slapped down the passenger sun visor, opened my purse, and began to repair, fortify, and freshen up in the well-named vanity mirror. Uncapping my lipstick, I said, "I don't think I've ever met a mayor before."

"Mayor McBride was a big fan of your father's. And vice versa, of course. If your dad didn't like someone running for a seat, that person didn't get in. Before each election, he sent an editorial with his picks among the candidates to the *Graylee Gazette* editor and that was about it. It was sort of funny: the following week, David Stark—" he paused and glanced at me.

I rolled my eyes and flipped open my compact. "Yeah, I've heard of him. Grew up here. Sold a few books. What is it with you people?"

He shrugged. "Anyway, David Stark would send in an editorial backing whoever your dad opposed. His open letter was always much better written, of course, but never made a difference to the voters."

"So the richest guy in Graylee," I summed up as I reapplied powder, "gets trumped by the person who employs at least one member of nearly every family. And now that person is me. It's like Paulina said: I pretty much own this town."

"Pretty much." He stopped, signaled, and turned right onto Main Street.

I whisked a brush through my hair and tried to pat down the renegade cowlick in back that I'd inherited from my mom. "Would Graylee be any different if my father and David Stark had been in each other's shoes?" Tim frowned at my question, so I elaborated. "If Brady Stapleton had been the South's answer to Stephen King and David Stark was the local captain of industry, how would the town be different?"

"Lots of ways." He signaled for another turn and parked in a diagonal space.

I read the sign above the walnut-stained door for the Law Office of Philip P. Pearson, Esq., Member of the Georgia Bar since 1974. "Would you still be a pariah?"

"Definitely not, but please don't go there. You're making me really damn sorry I said anything." He trotted around to my side so he could open my door — no doubt concerned his boss was watching. I climbed out and slowly got myself together so he'd have time to hurry to the outer office door and hold that for me, too.

Passing him, I touched his hand and apologized for being pushy. I just couldn't imagine why people would shun such a nice young man, and it made me sick to think my father had been behind it somehow. If I could gain an understanding of what had gone on, hopefully I'd be able to make amends. Assuming anyone would open up.

The entrance led to a reception area where a middle-aged woman sat at a desk. Tim introduced me to his colleague and then held open a conference room door. Once I passed through, he closed it behind me instead of going in; as with the tours, he wasn't included in the meet-and-greet.

Six men and a woman, along with Mr. Pearson, rose from their seats around a long table when I entered. I'd envisioned politicos in off-the-rack clothes two decades out of style, but they all appeared to do their shopping in New York or, hell, maybe London or Milan. Styled hair and manicures all around, even the older guys. Instead of Old Spice and Chanel No. 5, I smelled subtler fragrances—smoked herbs and exotic fruits. They would've classed up the toniest stockholders' meeting.

Mr. Pearson, looking even more coiffed and smartly attired than the day before, introduced me to Mayor McBride, four councilmen, the lone councilwoman, and the city manager appointed by the council to keep Graylee's services timely and efficient. They all greeted me with eager handshakes.

Everyone deferred to the mayor, a solemn, older man who looked more like an expensive undertaker than a political boss serving his eighth four-year term. He waited for us to take our seats. Turning to me, he said in a twang that came out as slow and thick as sorghum molasses, "I'm ever so sorry we weren't able to meet you under happier circumstances, Ms. Wright. Your father was a great man and will be remembered by countless generations to come. My dear friend Brady was responsible for building Graylee into a town that, for decades, has pleasantly surprised our state's officials with the sizable income taxes and sales taxes we contribute, given our humble size. In the vernacular of today, we punch well above our weight class."

He smiled with a full set of gleaming choppers that couldn't have been any more real than the cornpone accent he was laying on. "It's certainly not an overstatement to say that everybody at this-here table owes his position—and hers—" he added with a nod in the direction of the councilwoman "—to the stalwart support of your father."

Given what Tim had said, that sounded dead-on.

After giving him time to sit and smooth his suit and tie, I got to my feet and said, "Thank you, Mayor McBride. I didn't really know my father, having left Graylee when I was five, but I'm eager to get to know you and the council and your team of administrators. Uh, I can promise that there's absolutely no chance I'll be as important as my father was—" I paused to allow them to smile at this as circles of anxiety-sweat dampened my underarms "—but I do hope I can contribute to Graylee's continued success at least in a small way. I appreciate Mr. Pearson's efforts to arrange these introductions, and, um, I thank you all for your condolences and best wishes. Also, I hope you and your families enjoy a merry Christmas and happy New Year." Jeez, I'd given more speeches that day than in my entire life up to that point. I wondered if I'd have public-speaking nightmares for the next week.

Following polite applause, they filed out, each shaking my hand again and promising to invite me to their holiday party. After they'd gone, Mr. Pearson called Tim inside, closed the conference room door again, and complimented me on my speech. I rocked in my chair and said, "Looks like I'm going to be the toast of Graylee, at least until everyone gets re-elected."

Tim smiled and said, "All the council seats come up for a vote next November, so you'll have a lot of parties to look forward to in the next eleven months."

"Cynical, cynical," Mr. Pearson chastised, shaking his head with a mock-stern expression. "How did it go today?"

I described my experiences and went out of my way to compliment Tim for his help. I still regretted making him feel bad. The least I could do was praise him to his boss. I checked my watch and saw I had about seven minutes to get over to the police station or whatever the town provided for Cade Wilson and his deputies. I asked, "What happens now?"

"Now you live your life however you see fit, Ms. Wright. It sounds as if you have a good plan for learning about the businesses you inherited. I hope you will retain this office to provide legal services and call upon us if you have any questions or need additional advice." After I promised to do so, he added, "If you are free sometime during the holidays, I would like to have you over to the house." The mischievous smile that made him look decades younger reappeared. "My wife would love to meet you."

I wrinkled my nose at him and then stood and shook his hand. "Thanks for everything. Would you mind if I borrowed Tim a final time, to drive me home?"

"Certainly—he is all yours for the rest of the day. See you around town."

When Tim and I were settled again inside his car, he asked, "What was that all about, with the meet-the-wife thing and you making a face?"

"Just something between us, like the dimes stacking up."

"Damn, you sure make good use of your time. Maybe it's another thing y'all do better in New York. I've worked for him for six months, but we don't have a single inside joke yet." He checked his phone. "You mentioned me driving you home—I thought you had an appointment with the chief in a couple minutes."

"I do, but I felt weird about Mr. Pearson knowing I was going to visit Cade, like I was snooping behind his back or something."

He reversed out of his space, and we headed farther down Main Street, with its mix of hanging flower baskets, upscale shops, and tinsel wreaths. "Oh, but you don't mind embroiling his paralegal in your madcap schemes."

I laughed and said, "We're a good team: you with the moxie and me with the New York superpowers you keep pointing out. Anyway, I need a friend in this town, and you've shown yourself to be an able confederate."

"Whoa, 'Confederate'? Them's fightin' words." He held up one dark brown hand for my inspection. "Didn't they teach you anything in those Yankee schools about the Civil War?"

We hooted together until he pulled to a stop in front of the courthouse. It was a two-story building that took up the modest block between cross streets. "Go in through the front door," Tim instructed, "and turn immediately to your right. You'll see marble steps that go down into the basement. That's where the police station is. And the jail."

I wondered if that last bit was connected in some way to the reason Tim considered himself a pariah, but I didn't dare ask. We'd been having too good a time for me to spoil the mood again.

5

CADE WILSON HAD ANOTHER CUP OF COFFEE COOLING IN FRONT OF HIM WHEN I WALKED INTO the basement police station. A sharp disinfectant odor overwhelmed the aroma from the old-fashioned percolator chuffing on a small table near the entrance. As in the diner, Cade stood the moment he saw me, a tipoff to his upbringing. While that marked him as sexist in my mind, I also was touched he'd made the effort. It was like Tim's deal with holding open every door: I really wish you hadn't bothered, but thank you for being so sweet.

The police chief had a paper-cluttered desk at one end of the large room, with just enough additional space for his mug, a laptop, and a phone. Two other desks in similar disarray faced each other in the middle of the room—probably for his absent deputies—and the far end held three empty jail cells, their barred doors open. I found that tableau scary for some reason, as if the doors were arms extended toward me.

"We don't have many 'guests' during the week," he said, as I stared at the open cells. "Come a Friday night, we usually host one or two rowdy types who have too much to drink and get disorderly. An occasional public urination, some larceny, people trying to sell narcotics." Still standing, he took a sip of coffee and set his mug down. "Saturday night and early Sunday morning are the worst: domestic violence, a fistfight that turns into a stabbing, a shooting maybe once a month, fueled by alcohol or drugs. Sometimes both."

He invited me to use the straight-back wooden chair facing his desk. Before I sat, I turned it at an angle, putting my back to the cells to break their frightening spell. "Paulina O'Shea told me there hadn't been a murder in years."

Cade resumed sitting. He shrugged, tilted back in his office chair, and tucked his thumbs in his belt. It was a regular black number—he must've stowed the equipment belt with holstered gun because he was in the station. "Maybe she doesn't read the *Gazette* or listen to any gossip. More likely, though, she's making a distinction between an incident where someone happens to get killed and a first-degree homicide."

His discussion of violent death was so emotionless that I shuddered. What did a job like this do to a person over time? I asked, "How many first-degrees have there been?"

"Just a handful in the eight years I've worked here." His voice had thawed a bit. Then he seemed to catch himself, and the flat tone returned. "But you didn't come by to chew over Graylee crime stats. You said you had some questions about what happened to your daddy?"

"Do I have a right to see the, uh, case file or whatever you call it?"

"Case file, investigative report—yeah, that's all a matter of public record since the case is closed." He gestured at a sleek tabletop printer in the corner beside a row of battered filing cabinets. "I'll have copies made of everything except the autopsy photos. The coroner's report is a public record, too, but the pictures aren't, and—trust me—you wouldn't want to see them anyway."

Another drink of coffee. Then he lifted the mug in my direction. "Would you like a cup?"

The abrupt switch from imagining the gruesome autopsy to considering a caffeine injection made me dizzy. I rubbed my face, no doubt undoing much of the cosmetic repairs I'd made an hour earlier. "No thanks."

Cade seemed to realize what he'd done, because he waited until I looked up at him again. Though our hands weren't touching as in the diner, there was the same spark between us. With surprising gentleness, he asked, "Are you looking for answers, Ms. Wright?"

"Janet, please."

He nodded and continued in the same reassuring tone. "Janet, the case file will tell you who, what, where, when, and how, but you know those details already. What you won't find in there is the why of things."

"Isn't motive one of the most important parts of a case?" I asked.

"It is when there's an assailant who needs to be prosecuted."

I caught myself leaning toward him as he spoke. Deep voice aside, his accent sounded so much like my mother's. To remind myself where I was and what I was supposed to be doing, I glanced back at the jail cells with the barred doors like beckoning arms. Turning again to Cade, I put some steel and volume into my words. "Didn't you need to know, just for your own peace of mind? I mean, this Wallace Landry drifts into town and does a bunch of odd jobs for people. He ends up as my dad's Mr. Fix It for a couple of weeks and then guns him down—the most important man in Graylee—and you don't want to know why?"

"No need to yell," he continued softly. "I'm right here."

I didn't apologize, but I did drop my volume, saying, "Don't you want to know?"

"Of course I do."

"Well?"

"We did a background search, found an older sister who lives in California. She hadn't seen or talked to Landry since he was in middle school and she was going off to college. His mother's in assisted living in Florida with early-onset Alzheimer's. No other living relatives." He sipped more coffee. "We talked to an employer from a few years ago, the last time Landry drew a steady paycheck: there were some anger management issues, with a referral to counseling. Landry attended but quit the job shortly after he was approved to go back to work. Then apparently he hit the road as an itinerant handyman."

He held open his medium-sized hands, not too smooth but not heavily calloused either, strong without being brutal. "I've been in law enforcement going on twelve years, including eight here, as I mentioned. Even when the why of things appears to be obvious—a husband shoots his wife and her lover in bed—it never is. Why didn't the husband just file for divorce?" He shrugged again. "I've read plenty of scientific articles that seem to prove we act first and then rationalize the why."

"Do you wish you could've asked Landry?"

"You mean, before I killed him?" Both his tone and his face had become stony again, as if he were trying to mask another feeling. "Because surely you're glad he's gone after he did what he did. You said so yourself, back in the diner. Everybody around here is glad—they're always telling me how much time and

money I saved the town and the state by shooting that man dead."
He looked down at his now-balled fists and then slowly splayed
his fingers, as if letting go of something.

What would it be like to kill a man, even a bad man? What
would it do to you every day afterward? I couldn't help but reach
out and touch his arm. "You want absolution, don't you? This is
eating you up inside."

At first he shook his head like a little boy with a bad cut who
refused to admit it hurt. Then he raised his face toward mine.
"I've met veteran officers in rough places—New York, Chicago, LA—who never had to discharge their service weapons,
not even once." He took a deep breath and leaned back, pulling
away from me. "I can't tell you why Wallace Landry murdered
your father. I can't tell you why anybody does anything they do.
Folks who say they understand people are kidding themselves or
they're damned liars." He dipped his chin in a quick nod. "Sorry
for the language, ma'am."

Forcing some cheer into my voice, I gave him my best Bronx
impression: "Shit, don't fuckin' bother me none." It earned me a
smile, and I added, "Seriously, I appreciate your time, and I don't
want to take up any more of it. I can come back tomorrow for the
case file."

He checked his watch. I'd expected something militaristic
with a chronograph and lots of dials, but he wore a suave, stream-
lined model, an expensive timepiece that would've looked good
with a tux. The chief had a surprising sense of style. "One of my
deputies comes on at five," he said. "I'll have him do the printing,
and you can come back at six, or I can drop by your daddy's house
later on…um, I mean tomorrow."

I considered the implications of his stumble. My friends accused me of always moving too fast, entering into a relationship before I get to know the guy. And I could've leapt into Cade's pause, seeking a romantic rebound, if only to quiet those awful Horsewomen and their taunts. Fresh start, new habits, I reminded myself again. Trying to sound casual, I said, "I'll be in town in the morning. Why don't I stop by then and get it from you?"

He looked relieved. "That'll work. Thanks for coming on down to the dungeon."

It was my cue to help him escape from further awkwardness. I stood, and he did, too, of course. We shook hands for a beat too long—this time I let go before he did—and we wished each other a good evening. As I turned to go, the cells grabbed my attention again. I reflected on Cade's comment in the diner, his counsel to family members that it was better to move on than be haunted by the details of a crime. For a moment, I considered asking him not to bother with my copy of the case file, but letting things go was never one of my strengths.

ℰℐ

As I left the courthouse, I thought over my conversation with Cade, probing all of the nuances, interpreting every gesture, tone of voice, and length of eye and hand contact as significant. He seemed to like me, but was there something else going on, too?

Replaying moments of the encounter again and again started to make my head hurt. The sight of the blue Hyundai at the curb brought relief—I could forget Cade for a while, joke around with my new friend, and take a break from the drama.

Forearms propped against the steering wheel, Tim swiped and scrolled on his cell phone. He jolted when I yanked open the passenger door and dropped onto the seat. "Wishing you'd locked up?" I teased.

"Kinda-sorta," he said, tucking the phone in a suit pocket. "Actually, I thought Mr. Pearson came back to grill me some more. He knocked on the window about ten minutes ago."

It was a good reminder how small the town was — on the lawyer's way home, he must've spotted Tim's car and stopped to check on him. "Was he wondering why I lied to him about asking you to take me home?"

"No, he thought I'd done that already and now was hanging around outside the courthouse. He said, 'You are not still on the clock, Tim. I did not expect you to work anymore today.'" It was a dead-on impression: no contractions and the pitch just right. He'd even spoke at a normal volume instead of his usual hushed tone.

It helped to lighten my mood some more. I asked, "Did you make up some paralegal excuse about a last-minute filing or letting some cute clerk check out your briefs?"

"You watch the news any? It's never the crime that gets people in big trouble — it's the cover-up. I told him you changed your mind once we got into the car and asked me to take you here first."

"Nicely done, that bailed us both out. Did he say anything about me meeting with Cade?"

"No, he just thanked me again for helping out today." We watched a tall, thickset man of about thirty, dressed in a uniform like Cade's, stride past us on the sidewalk. Before he entered the courthouse, he glanced our way and his expression went from bland to seriously pissed. It was my turn to jump like a scared rabbit, but he was staring at Tim, not me.

After he'd gone inside, Tim said, "J.D., one of the chief's deputies."

"What's with the look?"

He only shrugged in response.

I imagined Cade asking J.D. to make a copy of the case file, and the guy talking about seeing me with Tim. Had my friend done something wrong, at least in the eyes of that lawman? I couldn't help matters if Tim refused to tell me what was going on.

Chasing it around and around in my mind, coupled with the musings about Cade, made me thirsty for a strong drink and something sinful to eat. Screw my metabolism. When Tim started the car and pointed it in the direction of Brady Stapleton Boulevard, I asked, "Would you mind assisting me one more time, with a dinner recommendation?"

"What're you in the mood for?"

"A strawberry margarita and a pork chimichanga."

"Well, there's really only one option: a little Tex-Mex joint outside of town, on the highway. We get to your father's house, I'll give you directions or pull up an address for your GPS."

"Are you hungry? I'm buying."

Tim glanced over, eyes narrowed, and I gave him my brightest, most innocent smile. Mumbling to himself, he drove onward. After a pickup passed us, however, he pulled a quick U-turn, gunning the engine so that the back end whipped around, wheels squealing. We headed back up bucolic Main Street, drawing stares from a few people on the sidewalks. He said, "You plan to liquor me up and ask me about that pariah thing."

I put one hand to my chest, "Moi? What kind of devious person do you think I am?"

"The kind who comes through town like a tornado, flipping everything over and breaking it all apart." The pickup ahead of us went down a side street, and Tim accelerated.

The sudden force pushed me back against my seat. "I just want some company for dinner—I hate eating alone. Cross my heart, I don't plan on wrecking anything."

"I didn't say that was your plan. Sometimes things just get wrecked anyway." He signaled, paused, and then screeched through a left turn onto a two-lane road that took us through the residential part of Graylee. Christmas lights brightened a number of houses. The nicest homes were close to Main Street; the size and quality of them declined slowly thereafter. However, even the worst ones looked only out-of-date, not ramshackle.

I made sure my seatbelt was secure and studied the properties to distract myself from our increasing speed and Tim's dangerous change of mood. Were the neighborhoods more evidence of Dad's higher-than-average wages, the golden handcuffs that allowed people to live in much better conditions than most small-town folks?

As if to answer my unspoken question, Tim braked, took a sudden right turn, and jounced us across the railroad tracks that led to the wood pellet plant. Soon we headed down a lane of decrepit bungalows and cobbled-together hovels with dirt yards. No Christmas cheer lit these homes.

I said, "If you don't want to come with me, just say so. No need to smash up your car just because you feel like you need to humor me."

"'Humor'?" Tim snapped. "You see anything funny here?"

We passed three young girls padding along the side of the road in bare feet and shabby clothes. Ahead of them, a boy rode a rusty bike, his feet bare as well. All of the kids were black.

Jaws clenched, Tim skidded to a halt in front of a house that had a porch built from new lumber, including freshly cut wood stairs and planks leading up to the open doorway. However, the roof shingles were dark with decay, and the overall structure looked beaten down. He said, "I'll be a minute." He swung open his door, surged out, and then paused. Turning back to me, he said, "You can lock up if you want." He shut his door—just short of a slam—and thundered up the steps. In two long strides he vanished inside.

The boy with the bike pedaled past, staring at me with an expression that was part curiosity, part suspicion. The youngest of the girls seemed to recognize the car—smiling, she waved until she spotted me. Then she dropped her hand and looked confused. She said something to the other two, who faced forward and answered her without even glancing in my direction. The little girl kept me in her sights, having to peer over her shoulder as she stumbled along beside the others, until they made another remark and she fell into lockstep with them.

Wood stairs thumped, drawing my attention back to the house. Tim approached the car, his expression having gone from angry to ashamed. Trying the door handle and finding it un-locked, he gave me a sheepish smile and got in. "Sorry," he said. "All that was uncalled for."

"What the hell did I do to set you off?"

He stared through the windshield. "I guess I was embarrassed because of the deputy. Then you gave me that smile, and I knew the grilling would start again."

"When have I really grilled you? Name one time." He didn't respond, so I continued. "You're just not used to bantering with anybody, especially women. I ask a few innocent questions, and suddenly you've got it in your head that I'm after all your secrets." With my index finger, I jabbed him hard in the meat of his shoulder, though what I really wanted to do was knock him upside his head for his dangerous driving. I asked, "Am I right?"

He tapped a quick rhythm on the steering wheel, eyes still forward. Then, he murmured, "Does it seem like we're always apologizing to each other?"

"I think I was up by one, so you owe me a 'sorry' anyway."

"Why do we keep having to say it?"

He looked pitiful now, as if he thought he'd ruined something important. "Because we want to be friends. I like you and you like me, but we're still getting a feel for each other. You know, trying to find the things we have in common and the no-go zones."

"I'm really sorry," he said.

"I accept." I let a quiet moment pass and then said, "I get that you don't have a girlfriend in town, but do you have one someplace else?"

"The grilling again." He rolled his eyes. "I drive up to Macon to see this girl sometimes. She goes to the medical school at Mercer. We were undergrads together at Georgia Southern."

"Is she fun to be around?"

"Well, she's kind of serious. She likes to call herself studious."

"But do you two—sorry, 'y'all'—have a good time together?"

"I guess. And your next question is a no-go zone." He started the car and raced the engine, a warning to me.

I held my palms out. "Fair enough. Sex lives are off-limits. Got it." I pointed to the front porch. "Why did we come here?"

"Had to tell my grandmother I wouldn't be home for supper. She doesn't have a phone."

"Do your parents live around here?"

"Not anymore." There was an edge to his voice, telling me of another restricted topic.

"So this is your home, too?" When he affirmed this, I asked, "How's it going, fixing up the place on your paralegal salary?"

"Slowly—student loans and car payments take most of it. I've still got to put on a new roof, replace the asbestos siding." He eased us onto the cracked pavement, and we headed up the road at a sane speed, dodging potholes.

"You're a good grandson, Tim."

He grunted, and then we drove in silence for a while. At some point, the residents changed from black to Latino, but the homesteads were the same kind of squalid.

Bracing for another tirade, I said, "You could've declined my invitation, you know. Just made up some excuse and had dinner at home."

He shrugged, working his jaw a little, but he didn't reply. I knew his blowup had to do with the pariah thing, in part, but there was something more, too. Clearly, he was warring on the inside, trying to decide how much to tell me and how much I needed to figure out on my own. I said, "Some part of you wanted to show this to me."

"Maybe."

"As the second richest person in town, I can help the people here a lot."

"I guess."

"So why hasn't the first richest person in town done anything about it already?"

"I don't know, but you can probably ask him in about five minutes. David Stark eats almost every night at the joint we're going to."

6

THE RESTAURANT HAD A HAND-PAINTED SIGN AT THE EDGE OF THE HIGHWAY: AZTECA, HOME OF the Bottomless Margarita. It probably meant the refills were without end, but the words also conjured a Latina undressed below the waist. I'd read in a magazine that David Stark still was something of a ladies' man, so maybe he showed up always hoping for both.

Tim parked us in a well-lit gravel lot that could've held fifty cars but currently had fewer than a dozen. I studied the make and model of each pickup and sedan, trying to decide what the first richest person in town would drive. Would he be all man-of-the-people and drive the rattletrap truck with the missing hood and dented fenders, or would he enjoy his wealth in the late-model BMW parked far from the other vehicles?

"I know what you're doing," Tim said. "You'll never clock his ride."

Glad he was back to feeling like my playful sidekick, I studied his self-satisfied expression, and then looked out at my choices again. "There," I said, pointing. "The blue Hyundai, same as yours. Or, rather, yours is the same as his. You bought this one after seeing what he drove, right? Copy the rich guy and hope some of the luck rubs off?"

He shook his head. "Damn, I hang around you much longer, folks are gonna start calling me Dr. Watson."

"Elementary, Doc. You better get those tells out of your face and voice if you want to be the next Clarence Darrow."

"I'd settle for being the next Clarence Thomas. The liberal version anyway." We headed for the front door. A cold wind blew grit at us, and Tim rubbed the outside of his suit-sleeved arms.

"Getting chilly?" I teased, immune to shivering after decades up North.

"Yeah, they say we're going to get some actual winter weather, maybe ten flakes of snow by tomorrow night. The town will probably shut down, just in case." He held the restaurant door open for me, letting out warmth, the smell of fried cornmeal, and recorded mariachi music.

I passed him, saying, "Ten flakes in Graylee means ten inches in New York, so I'm just as glad I'm down here."

"Me, too."

I smiled at that, especially touched given our recent blowup. Tim held out two fingers for the waitress, who pointed us toward a booth by the front window, a table already set with plates, napkin-wrapped flatware, and menus. The interior was lit by dim fluorescents and strings of small chili peppers that wound over the booth backs and across the walls and ceiling like a riot of red fireflies.

Some Latino couples and solo diners ate nearby. No one got up and left in a huff as happened in town—apparently Tim wasn't a pariah in these parts. On the other hand, I drew a few frosty looks, probably catching the flak for hard feelings they had about my dad.

At a shadowy table for two near the kitchen door, far from the rest of us, sat the only other Caucasian patron. He was trim and maybe sixty-five, with tousled hair that showed a lot more silver than black. I guessed the flannel shirt, jeans, and work boots were worn to make him look anonymous, but the narrow, black-framed glasses gave him away. His face had sagged a bit—he now looked like the older brother of the man whose photo graced the dust jackets of twenty-plus bestsellers. I didn't know if it was the publisher's decision to keep using a more youthful picture of David Stark or the author's vanity, but, to me, the contrast made him look sad and vulnerable.

From the basket in front of him, he selected a tortilla chip and dipped it in a bowl of salsa. As he crunched it, his eyes met mine, and he nodded. The waitress, who seemed to be working the floor alone, stopped by David's table first and exchanged a few words with him before coming over to us.

"Hello, I'm Luz," she said with a slight Hispanic accent. "The gentleman there offered to buy your drinks." She looked me over as if she couldn't believe anyone would buy me anything. I was starting to think of this as the Brady Stapleton Effect. "What do you want?"

"Bottomless strawberry margarita for me, please," I said, gazing at the menu so I didn't have to meet her accusatory stare. Tim asked for the key lime version.

Luz thanked him alone and checked on the other diners before heading past David and into the kitchen. Tim watched her go, saying, "You going to walk over now or wait a little while? Like this morning with the chief?"

Mariachi horns blared from tinny speakers, so I had to lean forward and really concentrate to hear his low voice. I grinned at him. "Talk about deductive reasoning. You should be wearing the deerstalker hat."

"Seriously," he said, "what's the plan? Are we having dinner, or are you just going to take your free drink over there and grill the famous writer about his charitable outreach?"

"Listen to you: all prickly one minute about coming out here with me and now huffy about being abandoned again so I can talk to another man?" I gave his ankle a playful kick. "I want to talk to you…and I also might take the opportunity to introduce myself to He Who Sits Apart."

"You'll see that wherever he eats out. The owners all want to protect his privacy. If someone comes in to ask for his autograph, the staff will be all over them." He set aside the menu. "Are you really going to try to help the people on my street?"

"Absolutely, and if I can enlist the local celebrity to make the impact greater, I'll do it."

Luz brought two margaritas in gigantic, salt-rimmed glasses on a tray, which also held a basket of chips and two bowls of salsa. She took our orders, a pork chimichanga for me and three chicken enchiladas for Tim, and departed again.

We each slurped our mammoth drinks. Mine was light on the tequila, but it probably needed to be from a profitability standpoint, given the size of the glass and the promise of its bottomlessness. I knew it wasn't PC to wonder if Luz and the kitchen staff had spit in mine, but the thought did occur to me. Surely they only would've done that to Dad, though, not to his innocent daughter. Pushing the slanderous image aside, I took another gulp and then dipped a warm chip and gobbled it down, pleased by the spiciness of the salsa.

Tim was doctoring his with Texas Pete. My Guy Friday probably pissed acid and shat napalm. After dunking another chip in the five-alarm concoction, he seemed happier with the burn this time. He asked me, "Why do you want to get involved?"

"Because I have the means, and because they're your neighbors, people you grew up with and struggled alongside. I think about that massive house I inherited and then the kind of place you're trying to rebuild, and it makes me feel guilty and angry."

"There are neighborhoods like mine all over the country, and most of them are a whole lot worse. Why not help some of those folks?"

"You're right, but this is personal. My father is part of the reason why you grew up the way you did, why those kids were on the street in raggedy clothes and no shoes. You said there were fifteen black families here. There are at least the same number of Latino families. But I saw only four non-white men working in my dad's businesses today, and the few women there were white." I swirled the shaved ice and sucked up more alcohol and sweetness, fueling the righteous rant building inside me. "I can't pretend to understand my dad's hatred, but, dammit, I can fix what he's done."

Tim chewed on a couple of chips as he seemed to consider my declaration. "You can't change the past," he said. "You can do things differently, try to help where there's been no help before, but what's done is done."

"What *has* been done? And what does it have to do with you and your parents?"

He smirked. "You're getting ahead of your plan. I'm not nearly liquored up yet."

For a terrible moment, I wanted to sweep my arm across the table, sending everything crashing to the floor, and then throttle Tim until he stopped being so cryptic. Instead, I snatched up my drink, bolted out of the booth, and approached David Stark. I caught myself stomping as I left Tim behind, so I focused on gentler footfalls with more hip action, and I softened my expression: sociable rather than sociopathic.

David looked up from a plate of Spanish rice and some kind of burrito. His expression started out as wary and a little hostile before he focused on my face. Thirty years of dealing with fans and autograph hounds had taken a toll, no doubt. At last he smiled and said in his famous baritone, "Welcome to Graylee, Ms. Wright."

He didn't get to his feet the way Cade had done. I supposed I approved of this, though a part of me still had a soft spot for the police chief's Old South manners. "Thank you for the drinks," I said, toasting him. It occurred to me I had no idea what else to say. I never thought I'd be the star-struck type, but I found myself gawping at him. After discarding a few idiotic lines — "I've read all your books," "Where do you get your wild ideas?" and other non-starters — I settled for, "I was planning to look you up tomorrow."

"I'm a tough man to see without an introduction. Got myself an absolute she-wolf for a gatekeeper." He eyed the huge, sweaty margarita I held and said, "Better sit down before that slips out of your hand and breaks your foot." His boot poked the chair opposite him, pushing it out a few inches.

I sat and rested the heavy glass on the table. "I just arrived yesterday, and I'm still getting the lay of the land, but everyone I meet wants to talk about you or my dad or both."

"I guess every small town has one or two centers of attention," he rumbled, his pitch so deep I felt it vibrate in my chest. No wonder he narrated the audio versions of his books—it was a voice you could imagine announcing the Second Coming or, in the case of David's novels, merely the end of the world. He said, "I'm very sorry the people of Graylee have lost their primary focus, and I'm sorry, too, for your personal loss."

I thanked him again and added, "Unfortunately, we weren't close. I was born here but can't remember the town from back then. Have you lived here all your life?"

"Most of it, with some ill-advised sidetracks to Chicago, New York, LA, and London." He shook his head. "It's been like one of my books, but with marriages getting killed off instead of wives." I expected a misogynistic remark about his exes to follow, because he'd set it up so well, but instead David said, "Fine women, every one of them—they had no idea what they were signing up for."

I didn't know if he intended to reel me in, but the comment made him appear mysterious, maybe even tragically cursed. With our age difference added in, I could feel my old habits come to life as an antidote to my worst fears. My body settled in to its favorite posture: leaning forward to show interest, arms crossed under my breasts for added lift, mouth slightly open as if breathless with excitement. I heard myself murmur, "Can I ask you something?"

"Certainly." His free hand swept through his hair in an attempt to comb it into shape, and he canted toward me as well, a well-practiced partner who recognized the invitation to dance.

It was just as Cade had said: we act and then we try to rationalize that action. What the hell was I doing? I hadn't come over intending to seduce or to get sucked in. Sure, I was frustrated with Tim's stubborn moodiness, uncertain about the spark between me and Cade, and uneasy about my father's impact on the town and my ability to make things better. And, yes, those damned Horsewomen were galloping across my battered heart. However, I reminded myself, I'd had a plan when I sauntered over. And becoming another notch on the bedpost of Mr. Maybe You've Been Laid by Him was not it.

I ducked my head and drank some margarita. A drastic change in the conversation was needed. To undo the message I was projecting, I slumped back in the chair, re-crossed my arms so they covered my chest, and said coldly, "When you look around at the place you've lived most of your life, what do you see?"

David narrowed his eyes. The spell clearly broken, he no longer looked at me as if I were dessert. Now I had become a nuisance. He said, "It's a town—hell, a village really—just like any other. Mostly good, decent people, some bad. In general, folks have an okay life."

"Lots of people getting by, some not so much?"

"I s'pose. What are you driving at?"

"Look, my ideas aren't even half-baked yet, but I was hoping to talk to you about some charitable projects we could collaborate on."

Frowning, David dug into his burrito and ate a hunk of it. The rudeness seemed intentional, as if to repay me for my mixed messages. He swallowed, pointed his fork at me, and shook it, as if wagging a finger. "Helluva thing," he growled, "telling somebody else how to spend his money."

I wasn't about to back down, but I also didn't want to piss him off. Giving him a genial smile, I persevered. "Like I said, I'm just spit-balling here. But I think we can do some good."

"What I think is your dinner companion is getting peeved that you left him to talk to another guy."

I didn't bother to glance over my shoulder. "Poor Tim's used to it by now. I know this isn't the right time or place, but can you tell me when and where it would be right?"

"What's right, Ms. Wright, is for you to dig into that steaming meal Luz just put on your table, and let me get back to mine. I was just being neighborly, buying y'all some drinks. It wasn't a come on or even an invitation to chat." He began to eat again, staring down at his food, dismissing me.

I gave it one last try. "Who do you like in the city council election next year?" He paused in his chewing, so I pressed ahead. "I understand you've had quite a losing streak, but you might find me to be more progressive than my father. I'm not saying the influence I inherited is for sale, but maybe I can be...persuaded."

The fork started to wag again, but then David set it beside his plate. He looked at me with renewed interest, but now I was an intellectual puzzle to solve rather than a sexual conquest.

He withdrew his wallet. I expected him to toss some money on the table, but instead he handed me a white, triple-thick business card that bore only four words: David Stark, Admit One. He said, "You'll recall what I said about the she-wolf and the introduction. That'll get you past my gatekeeper. Timothy can tell you where I live. Be there at 10:15 tomorrow morning—it's when I usually take a break from writing, depending on how the work is going."

I fingered a corner of the heavy paper, amused by the paradox it implied. "The only way to get this introduction to meet with you is by...meeting with you?"

"Controlling access is the key to maintaining a sane life for the likes of us, living in high cotton. You let in every sumbitch off the street, you'll never have any time for yourself."

"What if you don't like being alone?"

He snorted. "Then get used to not getting anything done. You start throwing money around, it's for damn sure they'll be lining up for miles with their hands out."

"But there has to be a way to help people without making them dependent."

"In the morning. Right now, you best attend to your meal and Timothy over there. Your date looks like he's ready to bolt."

"He's my friend, not my date. I only just got here—you think I'd pick up a guy that fast?"

He gave me a look through those narrow, iconic glasses that was pure judgment and sentencing, as if I were a character in his current manuscript and he'd just decided my fate. "I think you do whatever you have to, relentlessly, to get what you really want. Have a good evening, Ms. Wright."

Dismissed, I retreated to my seat opposite Tim, setting down my drink between us. My first reaction to David's comment was that he didn't know me at all. I'd never thought of myself as a go-getter, someone so driven that I'd do whatever it took to achieve a goal. Maybe I had it wrong, though. Looking back at my career and student days, and the way I acted around men, there had always been an element of ambition—and obsession. Unfortunately, that same obsessiveness also had driven away Andy and my other boyfriends before him. How amazing that David could peg me so quickly and explain me to myself.

As I stared past Tim, sliding my fingertips over the thick edges of the Admit One card, he said in his near-whisper, "You look like this woman who got saved in my church one time." He didn't sound peeved, only relieved I'd come back. And more than a little tipsy. "She was just sittin' there beside me," he continued, "listenin' to the preacher, and—just like that!—she was struck by this... epiphany, I guess they calls it. Like a angel done whispered in her ear and made it all real."

It did indeed feel like a revelation. I shook my head in wonder. "He's a complex man. Part angel, part devil maybe. He was rude to me, but he also gave me this amazing gift."

"That card you playin' with?"

I tucked it into my purse. "No, the card gets me in to see him tomorrow morning. The gift was much more personal."

He'd been waiting, food untouched, until I returned, but I noticed Luz had freshened his key lime margarita at least once. After a deep drink, he said, "You gonna make me gesh? I mean, 'guess'?"

"No, I'm gonna make you eat. Seriously, you need some solids—it sounds like you've been trying to find the bottom of that glass."

"Jess hastenin-in'...hastenin'...your plan." His eyes seemed a little shiny, as if he were about to cry.

"Fork in hand, Tim. I'm starving." The fried shell of the chimichanga crackled as I cut into it, and steaming aromas of cooked pork and molten cheese bathed my face. I waited until Tim had started in on his chicken enchiladas and then began to pollute my body in a most delicious way.

We ate in silence, other than making sounds of pleasure. Halfway through the meal, David paid his bill and left. He gave me a polite nod in passing but nothing more, and didn't wait for my reaction. The other diners watched him go, obviously aware of who he was. As the front door closed behind him, I overheard conversations in Spanish rise around us, probably of the "if I had his money" variety.

After Luz swung by to check on us, making a point of not looking at me as she spoke, I asked Tim whether he felt better. He said, "I never said I didn't, uh, not feel good."

"Well, you still sound pretty drunk. I'll drive us back." I braced for outrage, but he seemed to appreciate the permission to get hammered. He pushed his keys across the table to me, warm from his pants pocket, and slugged down more margarita.

Between mouthfuls, I warned him, "You're going to feel like crap in the morning."

He pronounced his words very carefully, as if walking a tight-rope of letters. "That assumes I don't feel like crap normally."

Though I was dying to explore that confession and find some way to make things better, I said, "Eat, and I'll quit the third de-gree. No more questions tonight, promise."

"I has a question for you," he said, still a man swaying on a wire. "What if you find out something bad about your daddy, something that'll make it awkwe...hard...for you to show your face in town? Will you pack up 'n' go?"

"Never," I said. "I'll just have to show everyone I'm different from him."

Had Dad swindled people in town? Gotten a married woman pregnant? Maybe killed someone? Horrible possibilities swirled like the shaved ice in my glass.

"Tha's good, tha's good. I'd mish you." He tried to lift his drink but it—or something inside him—seemed too heavy and he merely rotated the glass inside a ring of condensation. "I ain't had a friend in a long time," he said. I stayed quiet, but I guess he saw the question in my expression and plowed on. "Ain't seen the Mercer girl in months. She won't answer my tests…texts-s-s… my calls, nuthin'. Even before that, she wasn't never really a friend. Somebody to go out with, yeah. Somebody to stay in with—" he appeared to blush, his gaze lowering to his glass again "—but not somebody I could really, like, *talk to*, y'know?"

I placed my hand over his and said, "I know. You just described my love life since I was fifteen."

7

I PARKED TIM'S CAR IN FRONT OF HIS GRANDMOTHER'S HOME, KILLED THE ENGINE, AND RE-leased my seatbelt. Moonlight made the lumber of the new porch gleam like white gold.

During the short drive, I'd made the mistake of turning up the heater for his comfort, and it finished the job the margaritas had started: he was dead to the world. "Tim? Timothy?" I shook his shoulder and spoke louder. "We're at your grandmother's. Come on, you don't want to embarrass yourself in front of her, right?"

He didn't respond other than to turn his back to me. I had visions of having to drag all six feet, two inches of him out of the car, up the stairs, and into the house. Even as skinny as he was, I didn't think I could manage it. I hoped I wouldn't have to. One positive about being in a lot of relationships was that I had accumulated all sorts of experiences, including dealing with drunks.

I'd taken mixed martial arts classes for years at a YMCA in Manhattan and could think of about twenty-five ways to get Tim's attention. Too bad a number of them would've made him vomit. On the plus side, he had taken a bathroom break before we left the restaurant, so some options were wide open to me.

I said, "Sorry about this," and jabbed four stiff fingers into his left kidney.

Tim jerked upright while he sucked in a deep breath. His left arm slid back to cover his wounded side. He gaped at me as if I were something from a nightmare.

"You're thinking, 'Who's this crazy bitch and what the hell did she do to me?'" I spread my hands. "I don't want to hurt you, but I also don't want you to shame yourself in front of Grandma."

He whined, "Why'd you have to poke me so damn hard?"

Matching his tone, I replied, "Why'd you have to drink so damn much?"

"Lemme sleep it off in here." He smiled and nodded at that irrefutable logic, as if he'd just scored a key point with a judge, and closed his eyes again. His left arm continued to guard his side from further assault. Of course, that exposed his entire front and gave me lots of choices.

I settled for a sharp elbow to his ribs.

Tim grunted and covered the spot with his right hand. He looked fearful now: he had no way to protect himself from a third blow. I curled my left fist into what my instructor had called a "cobra strike" and slowly drew back my arm.

He blurted, "Shit, all right, okay. I'm awake for fuck's sake."

"I never heard you swear before." I lowered my fist. "I'm getting all kinds of good stuff on you. Need help getting out?"

"You mean like a kick in the ass? It's about the only thing you ain't done."

Actually, he'd gotten off easy, but now I felt sorry for him. I'd had my share of bleary nights. My friends claimed I was a nasty drunk: the cussing, kicking, hair-pulling kind. Lots of pent-up anger, apparently. Tim was of the sleepy variety—bless his heart, as Mom would've said. Before I exited the car, I jabbed the seatbelt release near his hip, causing him to flinch away in panic.

Although the dashboard thermometer had shown thirty-five degrees, and I only had my business suit for warmth, the air didn't feel that cold. Of course, I was conditioned to far worse winters, and I'd drunk my share of alcoholic insulation as well.

I took deep breaths of the piney fresh air to clear my head a bit. After opening Tim's door, I offered my hands. Mercifully, he allowed me to help him to his feet.

He steadied himself on the door frame and then took a few short, tottering steps. I stayed close by, ready to grab him if he stumbled. Maybe I should've put my arm around his waist and helped him more, but I knew how that would look to his neighbors and his grandmother. She probably watched us from behind one of the lace-curtained windows.

Tim gripped a handrail and pulled himself up one porch step at a time. It worked for two stairs, but then I needed to steady him with both hands so he didn't topple backward. Together, we made it up to the planks that led to the maple-stained front door, which also looked newer than the rest of the house.

It opened as we approached, and a short, squat woman with fluffy white hair and huge glasses shuffled into the moonlight, bundled beneath two sweaters and a hand-stitched quilt draped across her shoulders. Her face crumpled in grief. She said, "My Lord, was there some kind of accident?" Then air hissed through her nose, and fear settled into her elderly features. "What's that smell?"

I said, "Tequila, ma'am." Patting Tim's back, I asked him, "You good, big guy?"

"I'm going to bed," he mumbled. His right hand rubbed his chest and side. "Gotta nurse my wounds."

His grandmother looked even sadder after his last remark

and glanced down at her hands. They were curled into rigid claws, as if she wanted to punch someone.

Hoping Tim wouldn't get a further beating, I asked, "Would you mind if I go in and make sure he gets settled?"

"Of course. Where are my manners? Please do come." She led the way into the dark house and snapped up a wall switch with the side of her fist.

A couple of table lamps lit the small living room. On the yellow walls and on every horizontal surface, faces peered back at me from countless photographs in simple frames. Maybe five generations of an African-American family, from an unsmiling, formally dressed couple in sepia to five-by-seven color shots of grinning toddlers and babies.

Dozens of other pictures showed a short woman in white—a nurse's uniform—posing with people of various races and ages in medical settings, from modern hospitals to Third World clinics. The woman in the photos seemed to age as I turned clockwise around the room, scanning them, until I looked again at Tim's grandmother in person. I now realized arthritis had crippled her hands: a nurse who literally couldn't lift a finger to help her grandson.

"My name is Janet Wright," I said. Automatically, I started to put out my hand to shake but then pulled it back, cursing myself.

"Abby Bladensburg," she replied with a curt nod. The oversized glasses pressed in her small, wide nose, which twitched again. I wondered if she'd caught a whiff of strawberry-scented tequila from me.

Tim scuffed toward the back of the house. He bumped an end table, knocking over some frames. I said, "I better help him."

Abby only looked at her hands again. I caught up to Tim and held his right arm above the elbow to give him some stability. We walked past a cramped kitchen and the aromas of ginger-bread and fried pork chops. That she could overcome her arthritis enough to cook was a minor miracle and probably scary as hell to watch.

Tim's bedroom was one of two at the end of the hall. "I'm okay," he mumbled. "Don't need you to tuck me in. Or sing me a song. Or beat on me no more." He snorted, then sat hard on a single bed in the dark and groaned.

Before he could protest, I untied his shoes and pulled them off his feet. Then I gripped his ankles, lifted his long legs, and swung them onto the mattress. He was a slumped-shouldered silhouette. I asked, "Need help taking off your suit jacket or tie?"

"Unh-uh."

"I have to borrow your car to get home. I'll bring it back in the morning. When do you go to work?"

"Before nine. Lest I'm going to the diner."

"I'll be here at 8:30 and take you to breakfast. Get you some hardboiled eggs, bacon, and sriracha."

"Okay."

I turned to go, but he added, "Thanks."

"For what?"

"Y'know…not grilling me tonight. The whole pariah thing."

I reached out carefully to find his shoulder and gave it a squeeze. Then I left him, closing his bedroom door behind me, and walked back down the hall. I found Abby in the kitchen drinking water from a straw, her fists pressing two sides of a plastic cup to get it close to her mouth.

"He's a great guy," I said. "I'm sorry I brought him home to you that way. It was a long day for him, driving me around, suffering my questions, and I just wanted to take him out to show my thanks."

She set down the cup. "Praise Jesus, Timothy's been good to me. I don't know why he stays here—it takes a toll, for sure. Can I get you coffee or something else?"

"No thanks. I better go."

"Sit with me a spell."

Although I was beat, I thought it might be a rare opportunity to learn some things about my new friend. I had to come at it indirectly, though. My Yankee style of going right to the point would make her clam up. Stifling a yawn, I perched on a rickety wooden chair and said, "In those photos, it looks like you've been all over the world. Have you lived here long?"

"This was the old home place. My mama and daddy lived here, grandma and granddaddy, and the ones that came before them. I moved around a lot, yes, but Graylee always meant coming home."

"Was your husband in medicine, too?"

"A doctor. Graduated from Shaw University, up in Raleigh. It was a calling for us both. Traveling the world, tending to those that God led us to care for."

"Was your husband in any of the shots?"

"He was always taking them. Handsome man but real camera shy." She pushed out of her chair, knuckles on the tabletop, and led me back to the living room. Her thumbs had enough mobility to clamp two sides of a large, framed wedding photo against her curled fingers and slowly heft the black and white image for me to examine. "This is the only one I have of him."

Her husband posed in a tuxedo, a slim mustache curling up above a gentle smile, with Abby beside him, slender and lovely in white lace. I said, "You two made a beautiful couple."

She thanked me, replaced the frame with care, and gestured at nearby monochrome photographs of young boys and girls. "Hard life for our children, traveling, so my folks ended up doing the raising, and this became the kids' home, too. Every time we'd come back, the house would rock with laughter and stories and carrying on until we had to go again. Then, my folks said, it was tears and sniffling for weeks after. The going-away was always hard on everybody."

As her gaze roved over the images, I asked, "Why didn't you go away with your family when they left?"

Abby kept looking at the pictures, as if searching for something. Finally, she said, "I spent forty years wanting to get back here. Buried my husband at the old AME church up the road, and God told me I done enough healing and could rest at last." She gestured at the room with a fist. "This is home."

Before I could chicken out, I held her gaze and said, "I got the impression from Tim that something happened, something to make your family sort of like outcasts."

I held my breath, thinking the question would take us in one of two directions—the big reveal or a polite ejection from her house—but Abby chose a third path. She said, "Something's always happening in families. Whatever became of your mama?"

Her question was the perfect way to get me sidetracked. I said, "Cancer got her when she was in her forties. I was nineteen."

"Mm-mm-mm, I'm sorry to hear it and sorry for your loss." Abby lowered herself onto a floral loveseat, so I sat in the matching armchair facing her. "You got Mary Grace's eyes and nose and cheekbones. She even had the same cowlick at the back of her head. I remember she wore one of those hippie headbands but that hank of hair always managed to poke out in a little flip. Like a smile."

I touched the back of my head and felt that rebellious curl. "How'd you know her?"

"Saw her a few times here in the neighborhood, between our trips. Late sixties, before she married your daddy. I reckon she was in her teens. Used to run a sort of bookmobile out of the trunk and backseat of the fancy car her folks bought her."

"She never told me about that."

Abby smiled. "She was a pistol. Decked out in those peasant blouses and bell-bottoms, the headband on or a scarf tied up like one." She swiveled her gaze, searching the photos again. "I wish we took a picture. You should've seen her, handing out the paperbacks she and her friends had read, children's books she'd grown up with, putting in handmade due-date cards as bookmarks. She could talk to anybody: old men, young mothers, little kids. Black, brown, yellow, or red. Always knew the perfect book for everybody." Abby laughed and tapped her knee with a fist. "I'll bet her people had no idea what she was up to, hanging out in the 'colored' neighborhood."

Though I managed to smile at the image, I felt sad—I only could remember the woman who had struggled just to stay afloat, not someone determined to change the world. Wanting to hear more about that side of her, I said, "I think she married my dad just out of high school. You see her much after that?"

Abby shook her head. "If she still came around, it was when

we were away, but I remember folks talking about her, about them. Nowadays, your parents would've been what the TV people call a 'power couple.' They were from the two richest families in the county. Your daddy started learning their businesses, and I reckon your mama began keeping house."

"You're right—she never went to college. My brother was born the first year they were married." Before we went too far down the rabbit hole, I needed to get back to my original focus. "I appreciate you telling me all this," I said, "but what does my mother have to do with your family leaving?"

"Only that she made a difference back then. It was a small thing, of course, handing out books, but it's not about the size of the gesture—it's all about how you make people feel. We mattered to her."

I thought about the neighborhood she and Tim lived in and my determination to change things. Following in my mother's footsteps—who knew? "After Mom got married, something went wrong with them," I said. I spoke to myself as much as to Abby, as I reasoned through what must've happened. "My father probably exerted more control over her than her parents had done. I came along in '76, and she packed us up and left town in '81. By then he pretty much owned Graylee and did whatever he wanted. From the little Mom would say, it was clear her parents sided with my dad, most likely because he was running their businesses better than they ever did. They disowned her."

Abby stayed quiet, looking at me as I continued to think out loud. I said, "Finally, with my father not hiring people from this street, and backing local politicians who couldn't care less about your community, it took its toll. Just like with my mom, my brother, and me, your family needed to find opportunities elsewhere, right?"

She glanced toward a frame on the mantel displaying a family portrait: a black couple in their forties—the man taking after Abby's husband—together with a lovely late-teen girl and her older brother, Tim. They grinned at us, but my hostess was not smiling. She said, "'Took its toll' is mighty right anyway."

Obviously, I'd missed something, but I could always revisit that. I returned my focus to my original goal, saying, "It still doesn't explain why some people treat Tim like a pariah."

"Is that what he told you?" She snorted. "That boy is so melodramatic."

I shook my head. "No, I've seen it. At the diner some people got up and left as soon as we sat down. It wasn't about me and who my father was—they were looking at Tim." Even if he hadn't passed out already, there was no way he could've heard me from the back bedroom, but I still lowered my voice and chose my words carefully. "He's a great guy, and I want to be his friend, even mentor him if he'll give me the chance. But I need to know if he's done anything that, you know, he now regrets."

In an instant, her expression changed from amused to stricken, as if I'd slapped her. I added quickly, "So I can help him through it…whatever it was."

"Raped a white girl, you mean?" She practically yelled it, eyes flashing behind the huge glasses. I cringed as her volume rose even higher. "Sold drugs? Shot somebody?"

Her voice reverberated with accusation, and I was guilty as charged. I had considered every stereotype I'd seen on TV and applied each one to Tim, deciding the shoe could fit. Ready to forgive him, of course, but not rejecting any of those scenarios as patently ridiculous and totally offensive. Somewhere along the line, somehow, I'd become a bigot. Abby had cut through all the crap and showed me what I was, though I'd never thought of myself that way. So, it was really my dad I took after, not Mom.

Abby hissed, "You best be going."

Hanging my head, I apologized and left her fuming on the loveseat. Outside, I pulled my suit jacket tight around my shoulders and chest. Even with the heat cranked up in the Hyundai, though, I couldn't get warm.

Instead of having answers about Tim's life, I only had more questions, plus the new feeling that I didn't deserve to call myself his friend. I drove back through the sad little neighborhood, across the railroad tracks, and past the white-owned homes that were increasingly grand and draped in more and more opulent displays of Christmastime as I approached town. I turned onto Main Street. No one was outdoors, not even driving around. The phrase "I own the road" slipped into my mind before I realized it was pretty much true. A bitter taste at the back of my throat accompanied the knowledge.

Cruising by the courthouse, I considered stopping to get the investigative report Cade had tasked his deputy with copying for me. It could've been a welcome distraction. However, I was too worn out to delve into those details. Besides, collecting the file in the morning meant another encounter with Cade. Even in my depressed state I was curious to see where that would lead.

My consideration of a potential new romance so soon after the humiliating episode with Abby left me feeling unworthy and dirty, on top of everything else. What the hell had I become?

I lost myself so completely in these churning thoughts during the drive up Brady Stapleton Boulevard that I missed something strange about my rental car when I parked beside it. Not until I had to return to Tim's Hyundai to retrieve my purse—forgotten in my fog of recrimination—did I notice how much lower my sedan sat. All four of the rental car tires lay puddled on the pea-gravel drive, as if the intense moonlight had melted the rubber. Someone had slashed them.

I flashed back to my brief glimpse of the blond guy watching me and Mr. Pearson from the woods as we leaned on the second-floor balcony. Whirling around, half-expecting to catch the SOB sneaking back into the stand of trees with his switchblade still out, I noticed the depth of the shadows around the house. If not for the moon, the hill would've been in total darkness. And there I stood, totally exposed and vulnerable. I hopped back into Tim's car, locked the doors, and kept pressing that switch to ensure they stayed locked. Who would do such a mean, crazy thing? If someone were still pissed at Dad, even after his death, why take it out on me?

No way was I going to stay in the house overnight. The day before, about the time my stalker had shown himself, Mr. Pearson mentioned a motel out on the highway. I did a jittery Internet search on my phone, finally found their website, and called them to confirm they had a room free. While I talked to the desk clerk, I watched through the quickly fogging car windows, dreading an attack. After I entered the motel address into my GPS, I fired up the engine and switched the defroster on full blast.

The whole way back through town, I expected a maniac with a knife to appear in my high beams. I realized I was picturing

Wallace Landry, except with a blade instead of his gun. Was it possible he not only hadn't been killed by Cade but now was coming for me, too?

A ridiculous notion, but I couldn't stop my imagination. Or my shaking.

8

THE UNSHAVEN MOTEL CLERK SOLD ME A FLIMSY, CELLOPHANE-WRAPPED TOOTHBRUSH AND A small tube of toothpaste and took down my credit card details before handing over a key. Then I shuffled back out into the cold and re-parked my car in front of the room I'd been assigned.

Once inside, with the locks and chain in place, I set the alarm on my phone to wake me at 6:00 a.m. so I could return to my father's house. I would need to see if any other damage had been done, and then get cleaned up and put on fresh clothes. For a quiet town, Graylee was wearing me down fast.

After a lukewarm shower with not enough water pressure, I hoped sleep would come, but the bed smelled of mildew and cigarettes—despite the "No Smoking" sign—and my nerves were still jangled because of the tire slashing. Turning to Facebook for solace, I shared that experience along with the few positive highlights of my day, trying to avoid a totally doom-and-gloom tone. However, my pessimistic New York friends seized on the vandalism and once again begged me to "come home."

The trouble was, I wanted to make Graylee my home, at least for a while. Even if I liquidated all of my new assets, somehow managing to find buyers for everything, the cost of living anywhere in New York—hell, even New Jersey—would gobble up my after-tax wealth in a matter of a decade or two. In Graylee, I could live in comfort for the rest of my life. I could make a difference in the community, write my mother's story, and hopefully get to know someone who would make me forget all about Andy and the other men who'd made New York radioactive for me. I didn't want to consider that place as "home" anymore.

Recalling David Stark's surprising insight about me, I typed my reply to them: "I want to make this work. I might be screwed up in a hundred different ways, but one thing I'm NOT is a quitter. Once I decide on an action, I stick with it until I get what I want." I posted the rah-rah pep talk, written mostly to reinvigorate myself, and waited for the "likes" and the "you go girl" words of encouragement to pour in.

A few thumbs-up appeared from people I didn't even know but who somehow had become my Facebook friends. They were the kind of people who clicked "like" no matter what someone posted, from stirring declarations to suicidal pleas for help. My real friends didn't respond. It was just after 10 p.m., but maybe all of them had early-morning meetings and decided to go to bed even before their kids did. Yeah, right.

The stupid tally by the stupid thumbs-up icon stayed fixed at a stupid three, plus a "YGG" reply from some twit whose profile selfie looked like a mugshot. Grumbling, I set the phone on the scarred nightstand, killed the light, and waited for sleep.

To-Do lists immediately sprang to mind: take Tim to breakfast and help him through his hangover, see Cade to collect the case file and dictate a vandalism report—how romantic!—and visit David to turn him into an eager philanthropist while his muse took a coffee break. Then I had to talk to the rental car company about the tires, learn my father's businesses in detail so

I could be a responsible owner, help those who Dad had disen-franchised, improve the other townspeople's opinion of me, and begin to write that book about my mom. Somewhere in there, I also had to buy groceries.

∽

Six in the morning came way earlier than it should have. I slapped the chiming phone onto the stained carpet. Having to go after it to silence the alarm finished waking me up. Because I had to put on my stale clothes from the day before, I didn't bother with another mediocre shower.

Outdoors, the temperature had dropped further overnight. I puffed out clouds of vapor as I stared at Tim's frosted-over car. Friggin' fabulous. I had to use my credit card to scrape enough of the windshield and back and side windows to see ahead and check the mirrors. The process soaked my hands in ice shavings, and I shivered all the way back to the threadbare lobby, where I turned in the room key and collected my receipt. So much for my Yankee resilience to winter.

After the short drive back to Graylee and up to my father's place with the heat at maximum, I did a walk-around of the low-riding, frost-covered rental car to see if the maniac had in-flicted any other damage. Nothing else was apparent. When I unlocked the house and opened the door, the security warning beeps startled me. I managed to recall the code before the unit could summon the police. A careful check of the other doors and the windows confirmed everything was safe and secure.

Relax, I told myself. Maybe the tire-slashing was just a quaint ritual for newcomers, what the locals did instead of bringing over a homemade pie. Or maybe I was whistling past the graveyard. The conjured image of Wallace Landry brandishing a knife haunted me again.

I found the thermostat, got the heat going, and prepared for only my second full day in Graylee. If it duplicated the first one in terms of the emotional rollercoaster ride, I'd be ready for an asylum by Christmas, only two days away.

Due to the cold snap, I chose a black wool pantsuit and ankle boots. Thank God I'd needed a heavy coat when I took a cab to LaGuardia. I retrieved it from the front closet and set the security alarm. Before heading back out, I noted the wood pile in the fireplace and decided to light that sucker in the evening.

As I eyed Tim's car from the front porch, I half-expected to see his tires slashed as well, but everything seemed okay. However, the lawn jockey now listed forward a bit, as if to get a better look at the deflated rubber under my rental. The gravel and earth around the base had been scraped away, revealing a poured concrete footing. Dad had been serious about making sure his little bit of racist nostalgia stayed put. Taken together, the iron figure and the concrete must've been heavy as hell: the nut who'd stabbed my tires obviously had given up on whatever insane scheme he'd hatched. Probably, he'd planned to throw it through my windshield.

As scared as I'd been the night before, and as addled as I felt when I drove up a short time ago, it was possible I'd overlooked the condition of the lawn jockey. Surely the damage hadn't been done while I was showering and dressing only a half-hour before. I walked to the side of the house and confirmed the drapes were closed in the downstairs west wing. At least no one could've watched me through the windows. Cold comfort.

Furious at this bizarre war someone had declared on me, I kicked the lawn jockey upright. It took several tries. I finally stomped to the Hyundai with new scuffs on my boot and bruised toes.

I arrived at Tim's home well before 8:30 and stayed in the driver's seat, telling myself I ought to check e-mails, texts, and Facebook. In truth, I wanted to avoid Abby after my shameful screw up. I'd just pulled out my phone when she opened the front door and beckoned me inside. Her expression seemed friendly enough—hopefully she wasn't the kind who baited a trap with a smile and a wave.

After clomping up the stairs, I said, "You're sure you want me to come in after last night?"

"As a Christian, I'm a great believer in second chances."

"Forgive and forget?" I asked.

"No, ma'am," she replied, her fist pushing shut the door behind me. "I'm 'all about' forgiveness, as the young people say, but I don't never, ever forget."

Maybe it was only a reaction to her frosty statement, but the interior of her home felt just as cold as the outside air. I heard a shower gushing from a bathroom in the back of the house as Abby led me into the kitchen, where the stove had warmed up the room enough for me to open my coat. She struggled with a coffee pot, sloshing the steaming contents both in and around two chipped china cups. I hurried over to help before she scalded herself.

With both of us back in the same chairs as the night before, she said, "It's mighty nice of you to want to help Tim, be his friend and all."

I sipped the coffee and noticed how my hands made the cup rattle against the saucer when I set it down. Get a grip, I told myself, she's not judging you. At least not until you say something else that's stupid and offensive. Weighing each word carefully, I replied, "Something definitely is going on, though. Pariah or not, and melodrama aside. Can you help me help him?"

Down the hall, shower knobs squeaked and the water stopped running. Abby lowered her voice to Tim's normal level. "I was taught not to speak ill of the dead."

Okay, so this had to do with my dad. I'd have to play Twenty Questions with her and extract one clue at a time. "Did Tim work for him before going to work for Mr. Pearson?"

"Good heavens, no."

Of course he didn't—it was a dumb idea. The few blacks and Latinos Dad had hired looked like they'd been there forever. Come on, think! I recalled the family photo on the mantel. "When did your family decide to try their luck elsewhere?"

"Middle of the year—June, it was. They went up to Atlanta."

"Tim's sister, what's her name?"

She busied herself with tearing sugar packets between curled thumbs and forefingers to sweeten her coffee. Finally, she said, "LaDonna."

"Pretty name for a pretty girl. Had she graduated already?"

"No, she was between her junior and senior year." She looked at me over her cup. "It was hardest on her, of course."

"I'll bet, enrolling in a new school with just a year to go." Knowing she wasn't going to answer any direct "why" questions,

I considered what could've happened to drive them from the old home place.

Behind me, Tim called, "Can I help with the coffee, Grandma?" He came into the kitchen knotting a green and red paisley tie over a starched white dress shirt. My new friend was bare below the waist except for Superman boxer shorts and socks that matched his tie. His legs were even skinnier than I had imagined. Meeting my eyes, he hollered, "Shit!" and then covered his mouth. He turned and fled down the hall.

I leaned through the doorway to watch him go. He had a surprisingly supple backside under those kid shorts. "Hey, Clark Kent," I called. "Lois Lane will be down there in thirty seconds with a cup, so leap over a tall building and into some pants, will ya?"

A slamming door was his only reply.

Looking back at Abby, I saw she was shaking with laughter, clearly no longer in the mood to discuss the breakup of her family. I fetched a cup and saucer, poured the coffee, and excused myself before I clomped to Tim's room.

I knocked and asked, "Are you decent? *The Daily Planet* has a scoop they want you to cover. Something about a streaker with Tourette's."

Through the door, he said, "I thought it couldn't get any worse with you."

"It can always get worse with me. Ask any of my ex-boyfriends." I tried the knob and opened the door.

He shrugged on a charcoal suit jacket that went with the pants now covering his lower half. Glancing at me, he said in his soft voice, "My headache had just started to back off, and then you made me run the fifty-foot dash in my drawers."

"I didn't make you do anything. You could've joined us for a civilized conversation at the table. I would've taken off my slacks to make you feel less self-conscious, but it's cold in the house and friendship only goes so far. Besides, I forgot to wear my Wonder Woman panties."

Tim laughed and then winced and rubbed the skin between his wide-set eyes. "Did you even go home last night?"

I held my arms out, careful not to spill his coffee. "You tell me, Dr. Watson."

He buttoned his suit jacket and yanked an overcoat from his small closet, setting a thick plastic hanger swinging on the rod. With a check of the time on his cell phone, he said, "I need to apologize to my grandmother about last night and just now. In private. Can you wait in the car?"

"Sure, but she's not upset with you."

He tapped his chest. "I'm upset with me. Don't you get it? I haven't done anything to disappoint her for…well, a while. And now I feel that same, deep-down shame."

I'd felt something similar with her, but I decided to keep bantering instead of making my own confession. "Wow, you've led a pretty boring life if having too much to drink and shouting a swear word are your worst sins."

Instead of replying, he started for the doorway, and I side-stepped to block him. I knew I was being my usual pushy self, which could be a bit much even when someone wasn't nursing a hangover, but I didn't want to see my new friend beat himself up over such small things.

However, trapping him there was a mistake. His face hardened; his mouth became a slit as straight and narrow as a chisel mark in a block of mahogany. He muttered, "For half a year I prayed about getting back my old, boring life—and now you show up. God's a funny dude."

He took a long step toward me, and I yielded, barely getting out of the way as he brushed past my shoulder. Rather than shadow him and add to the tension, I studied his room while drinking his coffee and mentally kicking myself. So now we both were beating ourselves up. Nice going, Wonder Woman.

His walls were bare. Not one framed photo stood on his nightstand or desk either. Maybe he was a pariah to the rest of the family as well, or he had shut them out. Whatever the case, it must've been a trial for him to walk through the house each day, surrounded by the faces of the people who had cast him away or whom he had forsaken.

I heard his hushed tone and Abby's reassurances. What had happened half a year ago besides my father's murder? Or had Tim been involved in that somehow?

Chair legs scraped on the linoleum floor. As he left the kitchen, I headed up the hall. I rinsed his now-empty coffee cup at the sink, shared a goodbye with Abby, and exited as Tim held the door for me. We pulled our coats closed on the way down the porch steps. Each breath came out in a feathery puff. He said, "Sorry for snapping at you inside."

"It was my fault for teasing you. You're like the kid-brother I never had. Whenever we get together, there's something that brings out an urge to needle you and joke around. I have to learn when it's not the right time for that."

"Friends again?"

"Friends always, promise." Not caring what his neighbors

thought, I hugged him, and he returned the embrace. The way Tim clung to me felt desperate rather than platonic, like a drowning man wrapping his arms around a buoy.

Once we were in his car with the engine running and the heat on, he adjusted the driver seat for his longer legs and said, "One other thing. You go snooping through my drawers?"

Remembering his surprising underwear, I made a calculated guess. "Not much," I said, "although I love your Hulk and Spider-Man boxers, too."

"Oh, man, you did look!"

ത

At the diner, we sat at what I was starting to think of as "our table." No one got up and left, but maybe that wasn't a surprise. In a small town, people would learn each other's routines and schedules—those who were offended by Tim for whatever reason would know he'd be in the diner between 8:30 and 9:00. They would eat there before or after. We'd caught them by surprise the day before because of my tardiness.

Doris hustled over with a fresh pot. All she could talk about was the larger snowfall now forecasted for the afternoon: a quarter-inch at least. Maybe it would even stay around, and we'd have a white Christmas! I put on a worried expression and asked for a bowl of oatmeal, adding, "Something to stick to my ribs in case we all have to stay indoors until New Year's." Tim had his usual. We both wrapped our hands around mugs of hot coffee.

I said, "How are you feeling, Captain Underpants?"

He rolled his eyes. "I definitely prefer 'Watson.' Actually, I'm doing a little better. The aspirins are kicking in."

"You recall much from last night?"

His expression turned wary, as if he were bracing for the worst. "What'd I do?"

I wanted to run with it, tell him he'd put a drunken move on me, but I reminded myself not to tease so much. "Nothing bad," I said. "But do you remember me going over to talk to David Stark?"

As he nodded and stared at his coffee, I took the Admit One card from my purse. "He said you could tell me how to get to his place. I have an appointment with him at 10:15."

Tim drew a map and jotted directions on a napkin and slid it over. "I had to drop some documents there a few times; he's a client of ours. The man likes his privacy—he's way out in the country, a good twenty minutes from here." He glanced at the time on his phone. "After we eat, I'll take you home so you can get your rental car."

"Well, there's a problem with that. Fortunately, I've got my dad's cars." I told him about the vandalized tires and lawn jockey.

"Damn," he said, "that's cold. I hope it's not because we've been hanging together."

Again with the persecution complex, but I knew I'd run into a brick wall pursuing that comment, so instead I asked, "After I get back from David's, can I take you to lunch?"

"Normally I'd say yes, but Mr. Pearson needs me to handle some filings—including all that paperwork you signed—up at the county courthouse today. It's not exactly walking distance from Graylee, and I gotta get up there and back before the snow comes." Even he looked a little panicked by the impending "snow-pocalypse." A quarter-inch must've been a huge deal if one had never seen more than a few flurries.

Envisioning the population of Graylee at their windows, counting every icy flake, I said, "I guess the town will shut down by noon, so I better file a vandalism report ASAP. Cade can drop me at home before I head to David's."

Tim paused until Doris set down our meals and then departed. Squirting a lake of sriracha onto his plate, he said, "You going to tell him about your appointment with David Stark?"

"I guess so. Any reason why I shouldn't?"

"No," he said. "It's just going to be an interesting conversation is all."

"Why?"

"You'll see."

9

AFTER BREAKFAST, TIM DROPPED ME OFF AT THE COURTHOUSE. HE SAID, "GOOD LUCK."

"Come on, give me a hint at least." He merely grinned in response, so I said, "Okay, but just remember who has the kryptonite, Man of Steel."

"Jesus, I'm never going to live that one down."

"So spill."

"Nope—can't wait to hear about it."

I shut the passenger door and headed up the concrete stairs. The clouds had thickened and lowered; it looked more and more like a snow sky. A cruel wind played havoc with my hair just before I made it inside, and I had to pat it back into shape—except, of course, for Mom's renegade cowlick. Then I descended into what Cade had called the "dungeon."

The police chief was standing beside his chair when I entered, dressed again in a dark blue uniform shirt with black slacks. He must've heard my boots on the steps. "Morning, Ms. Wright."

"Janet," I reminded him. "Good morning." I made steady eye contact, partly to avoid staring at the open cell doors.

"You have a good evening?" He indicated the chair across from him.

"Just awesome," I said. After draping my coat across the chair back, I sat and waited for him to do likewise before I added,

"Someone jabbed a knife into all four tires of my car. I'll need a police report to send to the rental car people."

With a grimace, the chief opened a file on his laptop. "I'm real sorry. This is the first vandalism problem we've had since the Zabriski twins graduated in May."

"Either they're back or the property is cursed."

My joke fell flat as Cade continued to frown at me. "It's hard for me to not take these things personally—like I told you yesterday, Graylee's usually a safe, peaceful place to live." He typed a few things into the form on his screen.

"You need the address?"

"Kind of hard for me to forget that one. I only had to type it about fifty times in July." He clicked more keys and then pointed out a bulging manila folder on the corner of his paper-strewn desk. "That's your copy of the case file."

He quizzed me about the timeline and details of my discovery. His questions were delivered gently, as if he understood how upsetting the incident had been. I appreciated the serious attention he gave something that, were I in a Manhattan precinct, would've been regarded as trivial. "Just kids screwing around," they would've said before shooing me out the door.

When I mentioned meeting David Stark at Azteca, Cade only grunted. Maybe he actually didn't have any feelings about the author, and Tim was just getting back at me for teasing him so much. I downplayed how drunk my friend had gotten, but the police chief still made a point of thanking me for not letting him drive.

As I continued to dictate my statement, Cade rapidly clicked keys, never once glancing at his fingers. When he wasn't checking his screen, he was looking at me. I noticed details about him I'd overlooked in our two previous meetings. What I'd dismissed before as average brown eyes really were more complex: cappuccino blended with a stippling of olive. He had a generous mouth, and his nice smile revealed white teeth. Not so much of a Medium Man after all. Of course, there was his whole big-guy-in-charge vibe—strong, capable, powerful—but I also liked how his touch-typing and sensitive interviewing style punctured that cliché.

He saved the file, printed two copies, and handed one to me. "Normally I take my coffee break at the diner now," he said, glancing at his watch, "but let's go up to your father's place instead so I can see the car and that jockey statue."

"The scene of the crime?"

"I was trying not to sound like a TV cop. Do you still have Tim's car, or do you need to ride along with me?"

I said, "I'm on foot patrol this morning. Walking the beat."

He shook his head, grinning. "Okay, you get one more of those but that's it."

I stood and pulled on my coat. "I don't want you to miss Billy's coffee. We could stop by the diner first—I'll spring for the donuts."

"Couldn't resist, huh?" He got up and patted his stomach, which looked flat to me. Rock-hard, in fact. "Sorry, no more donuts for this fella." He strapped his equipment belt with holstered gun around that trim waist, retrieved a leather bomber jacket from behind the door, and locked up behind us.

From his jacket pocket, he withdrew a plastic placard with Velcro backing and tapped it in place against a strip on the door.

The sign provided his cell number and a reminder to call 911 in case of emergency. As we walked up the stairs, I entered his information into my phone and saved it. Just in case. There were some emergencies 911 wasn't meant to address.

Though I once lived with an NYPD detective, I had never sat in a police car before. Cade's was surprisingly clean and modern, each window meticulously scraped free of the morning frost. He drove a Chevy Caprice with what I assumed was the full police package, including a push bar in front and a light bar on top. When I climbed into the passenger side, I half-hoped I'd find a wet bar, too, but instead I saw a swivel-mounted laptop on the dash, a riot gun clamped upright between the front seats, and a plastic barrier sealing off the rear passenger compartment.

The clear shield reminded me of New York taxis, but without the little pass-through window for cash and receipts. Probably no tiny TV playing back there either.

I set the case file on the rubber floor mat and tried to get comfy. My shoulder blades found the cushion but there was no support for the lower part of my spine, which soon started to ache. "Fancy," I said, wriggling my butt against the plush upholstery, "but my lumbar can't quite settle in right."

"The seats are scooped out to make room for all the gear on our belts. It's a nice touch—when I was a rookie in Atlanta, I couldn't ever get comfortable in those old patrol cars." He pointed at the purse on my lap. "Tuck that behind you. I bet it'll hit your back just right."

I did get some relief that way, though the cosmetics, emergency phone charger, and all of the other stuff crammed into my purse made it feel like I'd propped myself against a jumble of building blocks. When I was younger, I never even noticed my lumbar. Welcome to forty.

Gesturing at the laptop and the grime-free dash, I said, "This looks a lot better than I thought a small-town cop car would."

"Picturing that old Ford from *The Andy Griffith Show*?" He whistled a bit of the theme as he strapped in. I hoped he hadn't noticed when I flinched at the mention of "Andy." His gaiety seemed forced, so it wasn't a surprise when his next comment came out much more somberly. "Actually, it was a gift from your dad. He didn't want me and my deputies driving around in dusty rattletraps. Thought this would reflect better on the town, give people a sense of pride."

"Yeah, I'll bet the drunks you haul to jail on Saturday night comment about how proud they feel." I turned sideways so I could face him and also peer through the plastic into the back. It looked as bland as the passenger compartment of any sedan—contoured fabric and seatbelts—but something about the barrier made it exotic and dangerous, like a cage at the zoo.

Cade checked his mirrors and reversed out of the diagonal parking space. We headed up Main Street at a funereal pace—I could've jogged alongside and kept up with him. In a weary voice, he said, "The answer is 'no.'"

"About the proud drunks?"

"I reckon, but mostly about your next question: 'Have I ever sat back there, can you sit back there, has anyone ever thrown up back there, have I ever had sex back there?' Take your pick. Everybody asks at least one, sometimes all four."

I couldn't help envisioning some backseat gymnastics with Cade—it was like being told *not* to think of a pink elephant.

Playing the innocent, though, I said, "Surely no one really asks about, you know, getting it on."

"More than you'd think. I guess it's the uniform, the gun, the badge. You know, power and authority." He shook his head in dismissal of those things that, I had to admit, were part of his growing attraction to me. "Even as small as Graylee is, we've still got some groupies. 'Hands off' is the first thing I have to tell a new deputy."

"So much for the perks of the job."

The surprising sex talk made me want to wriggle again, but I contented myself with watching him and how carefully he drove. Slow and steady—I checked out the back seat again and wondered if he'd do everything that way.

As if realizing he'd lingered on a taboo topic, he added, "Civilians ask about a lot of other things, too. 'Have you ever pinned the speedometer, can we turn on the siren and lights, can we call someone on the two-way radio, can I touch your gun?'" He shook his head again.

"Is it mostly the groupies who ask that last question?"

"Very funny."

I summarized, "Pretty much, your answer to every question we 'civilians' ask is 'no'?"

"Yes."

He said it so deadpan I had to laugh. I liked this guy more and more. It must've shown on my face, because when he glanced over and met my eyes, he flushed and turned back so fast I heard his neck pop. A good sign.

I asked what I'd thought was an obvious follow up, "Don't you think we all wonder the same things because most people are fascinated by cops?"

Cade turned the car onto Brady Stapleton Boulevard, and his demeanor changed back to all-business again. "These days, most folks are more afraid of, than 'fascinated by,' the police. What they see on the news is a handful of officers gunning down the innocent and choking unarmed people to death. They never see the rest of us helping anybody or having to deal with idiots, the insane, or plain ol' bad guys. Nobody can imagine what we really do or why we do it."

Wanting to get us back on happier footing, I said, "I think most cops are awesome. You're doing a job the rest of us would be too scared to try."

Cade didn't appear to notice the compliment. He plowed on, almost as if he were talking to himself. "Nobody likes to think about it, but there are evil people out there, and we're the ones who have to deal with them." His face had gone gray and a muscle now twitched beneath his right eye. "Sometimes that evil rubs off—I've seen it. Mostly, though, it just leaves scars."

He stared through the windshield as we approached my father's house. His eyes seemed to be scanning the second floor, where he'd had to confront that evil six months earlier.

My attention drifted to the rental car, settled on the gravel over its flattened tires. Sunshine had warmed the air a little, but frost still covered the back window of the sedan. On that glittering white backdrop, sometime in the past few hours, the maniac had returned and carved a single word there with his fingertip: "MURDER."

Cade stopped behind my rental, his gaze still fixed on the upstairs windows. I touched his arm and pointed at the word. We stared at it together. I couldn't hear anything but the humming motor, the vents breathing heat on us, and the rapid thumping of my heart.

The gritty city girl I so often tried to be would've trotted out some brassy quip, but I couldn't find my voice. Fear and anger battled inside me again. Who would be so hateful that he'd want to remind me about Dad's fate? Or was it a threat from a second killer, now coming after *me*? This time would Cade be able to stop him?

He shut off the engine. "Stay here," he commanded. Besides the no-nonsense tone, there was something else in his voice, a slight quaver. Was he afraid, too? He climbed out, removed his cell phone from a pants pocket, and took photos of the window.

I expected him to walk around the vehicle and photograph every tire, but his attention shifted to the ground. It was a crime scene, I reminded myself; the car with its flat tires wasn't going anywhere. Better to look for something dropped or another sort of clue before trampling all over potential evidence.

Watching professionals do whatever they were good at always had appealed to me, from brokers to bricklayers. As Cade took his time, squatting often to examine patches of pea gravel and the skewered tires, I quelled my own fear and banked my anger. I didn't have to deal with this alone. My father's avenger would become mine as well.

After taking pictures of the tires and the lawn jockey, the police chief moved to the rear of the sedan again and got some close-ups of the frost-writing. He was about to slip the phone back into his pocket when he froze. Then he backed off, peering at the horizontal surface of the trunk lid from different angles. Finally, he captured more images. A notebook and pen soon replaced the phone in his hands, and he filled three pages.

Cade returned to the car and climbed in beside me. His bomber jacket radiated cold, making me shiver again. He said, "Whoever it was wanted to be sure you got that message, in case the frost melted before you came back. The same thing was scratched on the trunk."

"Like with a knife?"

"Or the tip of a flathead screwdriver."

"But we know he has a knife, because of the tires."

He shook his head. "We don't even know if it's a 'he' or a 'she.' Someone could've used a screwdriver on the valve stems — pushed in the tip and let out the air from each one, then put the cap back on. Until we take the tires off and test them for cuts, we can't say for sure."

I wanted a decisive sort of lawman, someone who would eagerly corroborate the drama I'd sketched out in my mind and plot a way to catch the creep. Instead, my avenging angel was indeed the slow-and-steady, deliberative type. Never enough data, always wanting one more piece of evidence before drawing what should've been an obvious conclusion. I snapped, "Why are you arguing with me about technicalities? Someone's throwing 'murder' in my face."

My yelling didn't appear to bother him — no doubt dealing with emotional citizens came with the job. Keeping his voice even, he said, "I'm not trying to start a fight with you. It's just important that I follow the facts instead of jumping to conclusions."

I jabbed my index finger toward the hateful word carved into the frost. "What does that fact tell you?"

"Not much, only that the person who did it knows how to spell." He snorted at his attempt at humor, but I didn't even crack a smile, so he added, "I don't know the reason, the why. Yeah, it could be a threat. On the other hand, it might be a heads-up, a warning. Maybe it's a sick joke about your dad. We can't say."

He was so goddamn calm, I wanted to slap him. Instead, I whipped off my seat belt and bolted from the car. Glaring back inside, I said, "It's a wonder you killed Wallace Landry—even with that smoking pistol in his hand. I'm surprised you didn't ask him to stand there so you could fuck around with some test to see if he'd really pulled the trigger. Seventeen times." I slammed the door and marched to the back of my rental car.

The day had warmed a bit, and the frost was melting, slowly erasing the word. On the trunk lid, the maniac had scored "MURDER" deep into the black paint. The block letters glinted as silver as the knife blade that must've carved them. I scanned the trees ringing the hilltop, feeling someone watch me. Maybe laughing to himself and biding his time.

"Come out," I shouted at the pines. "Show yourself." My voice echoed mockingly, making me feel even more ridiculous.

Gravel crunched from behind, startling me. Cade murmured, "This is what I mean when I say nobody can imagine what we really do or why we do it. We solve puzzles, sift evidence, and analyze. We're truth-seekers and keepers of the peace. We don't go off half-cocked." He stopped alongside me, my copy of the case file in hand. "Here you are, yelling at the woods, daring someone to show himself—or herself—knowing this person is armed with something sharp."

I pushed my fingers through my hair and blew out a frosty breath, embarrassed and upset with myself. The tantrum definitely had made me look bad in his eyes. Wanting to sound tough, though, I quipped, "I figured you wouldn't hold my tirade against me if some madman ran out with a knife."

"No, I reckon I wouldn't. Not even if it was a crazy woman with a screwdriver." He shifted, and I hoped he wanted to give my shoulders a comforting hug—I needed it. Instead, he said, "I've gotta get back to the station. After I log the photos, I'll add to the report for your rental car company. I hope you went for the insurance coverage—the damage claim keeps going up."

I glanced at my watch. It was nearly 10:00. "Oh shit, I'm supposed to be at David's in about fifteen minutes."

"Who?"

"David Stark."

He scowled. "What business do you have with *him*?"

Again I remembered Tim's "this will be interesting" comment. It turned out he hadn't been jerking my chain. "Saving the world," I replied, "or at least our little part of it. Do you know how to get out there?"

"Yeah, I suppose I do."

"By the time I find the code to open the garage door and the keys to one of my father's cars, I'm going to be way too late." I gave him my helpless look, which had been working on boys since I was fifteen.

He sighed and said, "Come on, I'll drive you."

"Can we put on the lights and siren?"

"No."

10

MERCIFULLY, CADE COULD DRIVE FAST WHEN HE WANTED TO. HE STILL LOOKED EASYGOING AND unhurried behind the wheel, but he revved up the Chevy and had us through town and on the highway in no time.

I wanted to repair his opinion of me as much as possible, so I asked questions to give him a chance to talk about himself. A man always felt better about the woman he was with when encouraged to do a little bragging. However, he played the humble sphinx, just like Tim had. What was it with these Graylee guys?

Over the next ten minutes I only learned that he'd grown up nearby in Thomasville, close to the Florida border, his parents and siblings still lived down there, and he'd played football, baseball, and basketball in high school but none of them while at the University of Georgia.

"Wow," I said, "a three-sport man. I bet the girls loved you."

"Maybe some did for a while." He shrugged as we shot past an eighteen-wheeler and returned to the right lane. "They set their sights on better men when they went off to college."

"Don't you mean better athletes?"

"I meant what I said." The edge was back—I needed to remember he didn't like words being put in his mouth. "I was an average student and not as good in sports as I thought I was, once I got a taste of real competition. Just a good ol' boy with delusions of grandeur, getting his butt kicked during tryouts." Another shrug, another big rig left in our wake as he went even faster. "I wasn't much fun to be around." Then he laughed at himself. "As if I'm the life of the party now."

Taking a risk, I murmured, "I think you're fine."

A glance my way, a hard swallow. Maybe I was back in the game. Checking the dashboard clock—10:09—I asked, "Did you graduate?"

"Yeah, a business degree, marketing major, like a million others. Did some jobs I hated and wasn't much good at."

"What made you want to get into law enforcement?"

"My uncle on my daddy's side is a Statie, meaning he's a trooper in the state patrol. He'd suggested it."

I waited but he didn't say anything more, so I decided to get down to it. "Ever been married?"

"Once, about fifteen years ago. My business career and marriage sort of tanked at the same time." He glanced at my hands, possibly to reassure himself he hadn't overlooked a ring. "You?"

"Close but no cigar."

"Anybody waiting for you back in the big city?"

"Oh, countless anybodies. Hearts broke all over the five boroughs when I left. In Jersey, too."

"I'll bet." He said it in that deadpan voice, not a trace of sarcasm. No telltale smile when I checked his expression.

I realized how much I was trying to start something with him. Those old fears of being alone and unwanted urged me to keep pushing. He was far from the urbane, sophisticated guy I usually gravitated toward—plus we'd been born in the same decade—but there was a deep calmness about him I found comforting. If I could avoid having another meltdown, I thought we might progress to a dinner date that night. And then a drink at his place. No way did I want to sleep at my father's house with the "MURDER" stalker still on the loose.

Switching over to safe small talk, to let the chemistry between us percolate, I asked, "How much farther is it?"

"A few miles," he said, and then added, "So, exactly what are you up to with Stark?"

Suspicion, jealousy, maybe something more. Fear? Interesting. Possibly he saw David as a romantic rival, given the author's wealth and his reputation as a sort of redneck playboy. Hoping to reassure Cade, I replied in a light tone, "Like I told you, I want to talk to him about philanthropy. I think we could do a lot of good for Graylee and the whole area." I watched his face as I said, "You keep calling him by his last name—don't you like him?"

The chief gave away nothing. "He's okay, I guess. How'd you manage to wrangle an invitation?"

"I can be very persuasive when I want something." Nothing wrong with stoking that jealousy and fear of a rival. Hopefully that would keep him from hesitating later on. I took out the Admit One card from my purse. "He said he has 'an absolute she-wolf' for a gatekeeper."

He grunted. "That she is."

"Oh, did you try getting past her one time?"

"No, I'm not exactly a fan of Stark...can't say I like his books. But Bebe and I, um, have had some interaction." He didn't elaborate, adding one more mystery to the pile I wanted to unravel.

The police chief signaled, braked hard, and turned us onto an unmarked drive. We followed a winding path through a dense grove of leaf-bare oaks and tall pines and then emerged in a clearing.

If my father's house was the solid, hulking hunting lodge of a man's man, David Stark's estate was the hodge-podge sprawl of an eccentric genius. The central portion, a craftsman bungalow with mission-period accents, looked the oldest. From both sides, and probably the back, other styles had taken shape.

A wing on the right echoed Dad's stone manor, while one on the left would've looked at home on Cape Cod. Maybe living in solitude with an ever-growing fortune meant he could experiment without caring what other people thought. His novels reflected the same attitude, never giving his fans the same kind of scare from book to book.

The driveway curled behind the house, presumably ending at a garage, but Cade parked near a walkway of multicolored glass bricks that led to the front door. He'd gotten me there with a minute to spare.

"I really appreciate this," I said, giving his thick bicep a squeeze through the leather jacket. "I know I'm getting in the way of a hundred important things you need to do. You want to come in?"

He tapped the dash-mounted laptop. "I can work from here."

"Hiding from that nasty old she-wolf?" I teased.

Cade gave me a tight smile and busied himself with his computer. I closed the passenger door much more civilly than earlier and went up the walk. Catching my reflection in the narrow, mission-style sidelights that flanked the front door, I finger-combed my hair. The cowlick rebelled as usual. After a fruitless search for a doorbell, I rapped on the cold wood. No response from within.

I squinted through the column of wavy leaded glass and

knocked harder, stinging my knuckles. Finally, a person-sized blur of red appeared, and the door unlocked and opened.

The she-wolf was drop-dead gorgeous, only a few years older than me, and somewhat familiar. Creamy skin with a light spray of freckles across her cheeks and nose, violet-blue eyes, and a classic heart-shaped face. Red, red lips, tumbles of wavy auburn hair, and a scarlet dress that her bust distended dramatically. She wasn't heavyset—the woman's waist was smaller than mine—but "curvy" didn't begin to describe her. I couldn't help but wonder about Cade's "interactions" with her, and, of course, what she did with David Stark all day, every day, out here in the secluded woods. It was a wonder he got any writing done.

Her familiarity turned to recognition when she said with an Irish brogue, "Right on time, Ms. Wright." The name Cade had referenced now fell into place. It was impossible to believe she'd aged two decades since I'd seen her on TV—if anything, the faint lines at the corners of her eyes and mouth made her more beautiful than when she was the twenty-something star of a few sitcoms in the 1990s.

"You're Beatrice McLaren?"

"I am indeed, and how grand of you to remember my old shows."

"Of course—you're what made them great."

"Thanks for that. Please call me Bebe."

"Janet." We shook hands briefly. Mine was unforgivably cold against her warm touch.

She stepped back so I could enter, and then she looked outside before closing and locking the door. "I see you travel in style," she said, that voice so lovely she could make a speech on tax policy riveting. "With a police escort no less." Her face betrayed nothing regarding Cade. Perhaps their interactions hadn't been of the sort my mind was conjuring. Or maybe she still was a terrific actor.

"It's a long story," I told her and held up David's Admit One card. "Can I keep this, or do I have to earn each invitation?"

"I'm afraid it's the latter. Mr. Stark does so guard his privacy." Crimson nails plucked the card from my fingertips before she helped me off with my coat and hung it in a closet. "This way, if you please."

She led me through the lemon-custard foyer and down a hall with framed photos of David posing with presidents, celebrities, and famous fellow writers, all of whom held up one or two of his hardbacks for the camera. The display reminded me of Abby's home, but with the great and powerful instead of family and fellow healers. It was a good distraction from Beatrice, whose perfect bubble-butt and elegant stride in high heels made me even more envious. Clumping behind her on the hardwood, I felt as ugly and ungainly as a zombie in snowshoes.

Before reaching the kitchen at the end of the hall, we turned right and entered a study done up in red-flocked wallpaper, cherry furniture, and cordovan leather. If Bebe weren't so pale, she would've been perfectly camouflaged in there. A fireplace contained a minor inferno that blazed and popped, scenting the air with wood smoke.

"He should be with us momentarily," she said, "depending on the mood of his muse. May I get you something to drink while you're waiting?"

"Coffee would be great—black, please—but only if you'll have something with me."

"Certainly—I'd love a wee chat." Pivoting as gracefully as a dancer, she exited.

It was hard not to hate someone so beautiful, poised, and honey-voiced, but I told myself to give her a chance. Maybe she had terrible table manners or fits of farting or something else that made her more human. Otherwise, if she and Cade were an item, I didn't stand a chance.

While I waited for my caffeine injection and for David's muse to release him, I checked out the study. Floor-to-ceiling bookshelves on two walls contained hardcovers and paperbacks of David's novels, each in a dozen or more languages, along with autographed first editions from all of his contemporaries: King, Koontz, Straub, and other greats. I flipped to the title page of a few of these and read the compliments written there:

To David, I wish this one was half as good as your latest.

D, The only reason I keep churning out these damn things is so you'll have the illusion of competition.

C'mon, Stark, ease up. If you set the bar any higher, it'll decapitate me.

From the doorway, Bebe said, "Don't you believe a word of those now. Mr. Stark swears they hate his 'redneck guts.'" She came forward and bent down to set a tray with two large, tapered mugs on a coffee table, giving me a view of more cleavage than I could've mustered with a bustier and hydraulic jacks. I was surprised the momentum didn't flip her onto her pretty red head.

Be nice, I reminded myself. It must've been hell to haul around those soccer balls. She probably couldn't see her shoes without looking in a mirror. Bless her heart, as Mom would've added.

I thanked her for the coffee and tasted it. Not as good as Billy's at the diner, but it would do. We sat in matching leather club chairs, facing each other over the table. Beneath the tray were several large art books devoted to the golden age of horror movies, from Boris Karloff to Christopher Lee. I gestured at them and the bookcases. "Does being surrounded by all this scary stuff ever get to you? I mean, does it make you want to curl up with a trashy romance or watch a funny show like the ones you used to do?"

"Good heavens no. I much prefer having my blood curdled than my funny bone—or anything else—tickled. It's why I went after this job in 2000. My Hollywood agent knew his literary agent and told me Mr. Stark was looking for a new assistant and did any of my out-of-work actor friends want to apply?" She sipped her coffee. "He had no idea I was Mr. Stark's biggest fan—I jumped at the chance. When he found out, he wanted to box my head off."

"Did you miss acting, at least at first?"

"A bit, but it's for sure I didn't miss the lifestyle. Paparazzi stalking you, tabloids calling you fat one week, pregnant the next, and then jilted and then stealing someone else's man. My ma and da didn't know what to think. It got so bad I couldn't go outside unless the studio sent a car for me."

"But doesn't it get lonely out here with just you and David?"

I'd tried to make the question sound innocent, but she gave me a knowing smile and said, "Sure and now you sound like one of those Hollywood reporters. I'm Mr. Stark's assistant. I'm also his first reader. And that's the end of it." Bebe nodded once in emphasis with her sweetly dimpled chin. Then she asked, "Are you a fan of his books?"

"You could say that. I've only read everything he ever wrote, including the short stories."

"Then can you imagine being the very first one to see his manuscripts? And what's more, he asks for my opinions. He's changed character names, paragraphs, and whole scenes based on my comments. Why, the ending to *Scatter the Remains* was my idea! 'Tis a dream job and no mistake."

She sounded so earnest, almost breathless. However, I had to remind myself again she used to be a professional actor. Possibly she was playing me, to undermine my naughty imagination.

Before I could reply, she said, "Enough about me. Here you are now, a woman of leisure, a fortune fallen into your lap. That must seem like a dream as well."

"Or a nightmare, if you think about how that fortune came to me." I managed to catch myself before I added "soaked in blood." My smart mouth was primed and ready to let fly, but it didn't pay to piss off the gatekeeper. Softening my tone, I added, "You're right, though. I'm lucky to have so many choices now about what to do with my life."

"Then why stay in this tiny town and run your da's businesses?" She snapped her fingers. "No, that's not what I heard; you want to be 'a benevolent dictator.'"

So word indeed had gotten around. I began to protest, but Bebe cut me off, saying, "You didn't know your da at all, am I right?"

Warily, I answered, "That's right—I really can't remember him."

"And I heard he didn't pay a penny of alimony or child support, even though he sat on a pile of money almost as high as Mr. Stark's."

I wondered where she'd heard that particular fact, but I only said, "Right again."

"So that man Wallace Landry really did you a great favor, didn't he? Did the same for all of us, in fact—your da had his boot on Graylee's neck since long before I got here."

I took another drink of coffee to try to get myself under control. Making sure my voice was steady and civil, I said, "It sounds like you're actually celebrating my father's death."

"Not at all. A tragedy it was and that's for certain. I'm—" From somewhere nearby, there was the sound of wood sliding on wood, like a chair scuffing across a floor, and then it came again. Before I could look around, Bebe added with a double dose of friendliness, "I'm merely pointing out some good can come from it: you can afford to live anywhere in the world, do anything you want."

Close behind my chair, David Stark said in his deep Southern rumble, "But if I recall correctly—" he paused while I jolted and twisted around in my seat "—what you want to do is give that fortune away. Mine as well." He smiled and put out his hand to shake. "Sorry for the delay. The scene I was writing was just too much fun to abandon."

I held his cool, strong fingers for a moment while I recovered and took him in: the iconic narrow glasses, rumpled hair, and salt-and-pepper stubble, as if he'd only made time for writing since he woke up. He'd cloaked his lean torso in a fisherman's sweater

Bebe's ancestors might've knitted. Tight jeans and scuffed loafers completed the picture. Maybe it was just because my heart continued to gallop from him startling me, but I thought he looked delicious. Much better than in the restaurant.

"Something scary?" I managed to say.

"A love scene actually. There's usually only one or two per book, but it raises the stakes for the main characters — horror works best when there's a lot to lose."

Bebe stood. "Coffee?"

"Yeah, thanks," David said. While Bebe exited with lots of hip action, he lounged on the sofa to my left that completed the U-shape of furniture around the low table.

I asked, "How did you manage to sneak up on me?"

"I wasn't sneaking. The wall behind you conceals a pocket door that leads into another wing of the house. That's where I do my work." He settled in, hands behind his head, elbows jutting out. "Your father gave me the idea, actually. I was at his place one time, and Brady rose up through the floor like a vampire in a haunted house. Scared the shit out of me."

"So you like to scare your guests, too?"

"Of course, they expect it. Do you like a good scare, or do you prefer the love scenes?" He gave me a rakish smile that suggested bedrooms rather than dungeons.

I gulped some coffee. "In your books, um, like you just said, there are way more scary scenes…and they're really good."

"There are more of them because they're a snap for me to write. I like doing the love scenes best — they're a lot more challenging. If they came easily, I guess I'd be a romance writer instead." His grin widened.

"But you never had any doubt you'd be some kind of author?"

"It's all I'm good at." He gave me a playful shrug. "Well, that's not entirely true."

I could tell he knew exactly what he was doing to me. However, before I could cool his jets so mine could settle down as well, I heard Bebe in her heels coming down the hallway. For her benefit, I said, "I appreciate you spending your morning break with me. Is it hard for you to stop and then get started again?"

As soon as I'd said it, I winced at the double entendre, but he didn't run with it. Instead, he replied, "I do what Hemingway did: always stop at a place where I know what's going to happen next."

Bebe entered with a matching mug of coffee. She set it before David on the tray, bending over more deeply than she needed to: bombs away.

Despite the flesh show only a few feet from him, he still was looking at me. Maybe he knew what was going to happen next, but I had no idea.

11

BEBE STRAIGHTENED AND GLANCED FROM DAVID TO ME AND BACK AGAIN. HER BROGUE CAME out a little thicker, as if to draw his attention. "May I do anything else for you now, Mr. Stark?"

David said, "I'm good." He looked at me. "You?"

"Fine, thanks." The coffee had cooled, and I'd guzzled most of it already. If I asked for a warm-up, though, Bebe would never leave us alone.

He smiled up at his assistant. She nodded and withdrew, again taking her time to exit, like an actor eager to hold the spotlight for as long as possible before leaving the set.

My host bolted some coffee and said, "I never do this, but let me show you the slaughterhouse."

I almost dropped my mug. "The what?"

"You know, the chamber of horrors: what everybody conceives of as my work area." We set down our drinks, and David took me over to the wall of cherry paneling behind my chair. "See this?" He tapped two fingers against a faint rectangular outline in the grain and pushed. The cutout depressed a quarter-inch. What looked like a mere seam between panels edged back, and a floor-to-ceiling section slid to our left with the sound of a chair sliding across hardwood.

The door-wide gap revealed an airy space that would've suited Andy, who was an architect. In addition to a plain pine standing desk with a high-end laptop, the only other furnishings on the caramel-colored floor were a lounge chair, footstool, and lamp. Huge windows in the back showed the trees that shielded David's home, and overhead lights suspended from exposed beams brightened the room—necessary because a low, dense cover of snow clouds had made the morning already look like dusk. Aromas of coffee and vanilla-scented floor wax replaced the smell of burning firewood from the other room.

Once inside, he showed me the doorbell-like button on the crème wall and used it to close the panel. Beside the button was a set of wall switches for the lights and the automated window blinds that nestled against each of the wood beams.

I pictured the outside of the house again so I could get my bearings. We now stood in the stone manor wing. It was as if David had aped the exterior of my father's place but instead of continuing that theme within, he created a work area that better reflected his personal interior. His "slaughterhouse" comment now made me smile. He wanted to show me his true self. Just as I'd loved the spaces Andy had designed, I adored this room, too. I could've stayed there forever.

As I reveled in the bright, spacious simplicity, he pointed to a hallway on the opposite wall. "The manacles and iron maiden and all are in the other rooms. Shitload of bats, too."

Laughing, I asked, "Gifts from your fans?"

"You have no idea. If you ever need a coffin, just call. Some guy shipped me three he'd made by hand, with custom carvings inside and out and hand-sewn linings." He shook his head. "That probably used up all his savings, so I'm sure he'd appreciate a handout from you."

I pushed him playfully, in part because he deserved it, but I also wanted to see how he would react. Some guys hated physical contact unless they were doing the touching; that always spelled a quick end to my interest. Not that I was really interested. Just keeping my options open.

David staggered back into the wall and made a big deal out of rubbing his shoulder, but he smiled as he did it. "Never mind," he said. "It looks like I'll be suing you for your entire inheritance. Sit down over there and let's talk about money."

I headed to the standing desk instead. He had a thick leatherette mat over the hardwood, which I guess would make the hours of standing tolerable. Having spent my teenage and college years doing jobs on my feet, though, I couldn't imagine wanting to go without a chair by choice. The laptop screen was black, so I brushed the touchpad. Nothing happened.

"What are you up to?" he asked, walking over.

"I wanted to read that love scene that was too much fun to abandon."

"Goddamn, you're brash. No one sees my work until it's ready."

Testing limits. He'd pegged me again—it definitely was part of my MO. I shrugged and said, "Can't blame a girl for trying. Why so secretive?"

He shot back, "Have you ever done any kind of art?"

I looked at my boots. "Well, actually I always enjoyed writing. Or at least the thought of writing." I looked up at him and confessed, "I haven't managed to do any of it yet."

"If you ever start, you won't want anybody to see it for a long time."

I snorted. "Because it's going to suck so bad? Thanks a lot."

"All first drafts suck. Mine do, everybody's does. It's the nature of the beast. You have to write in order to rewrite—that's where the real art comes in." He shooed me away. "Sit down—you're making me nervous over here."

I dropped into the lounge chair and put my booted feet up on the stool. "Tell me more about writing," I said. "How do you do what you do?"

David relaxed a little. He leaned back against his tall desk and tucked his hands in his front jeans pockets, a professor warming to his subject. "A beginning writer is the sorcerer's apprentice," he began.

Not understanding, I frowned and shook my head. He tried again: "Writing well is like doing magic. Look at this." He pushed a button on the laptop and it came to life with a symphonic sound and a lit-up screen. Pointing at the manuscript on the display, he said, "What we call letters and punctuation are just abstract symbols—meaningless pixels or ink on a page. It's all made up. When we come into this world, we don't understand any of it."

He patted the area over his heart. "The only things we understand as little kids are basic emotions: mad, sad, glad, and scared. We have to be taught everything about language, the alphabet, what all these letters mean, because they don't have any inherent meaning. You need to learn how each one sounds and how the combinations of them form words, each of which has a definition you also have to learn. Again, because it's all made up. Are you with me now?"

I said I was, and he continued, "None of it means any-thing—and yet…." He let that hang there a moment and gestured at the screen again. "And yet, if you take these abstract, meaningless marks and string them together in just the right way, you can make someone feel rage or cry or laugh or piss their pants in terror. These made-up symbols can cause a genuine, deep down—*real*—emo-tion." He tapped his heart again. "At our best, writers use some-thing completely artificial and false—a lie—to produce an actual, true feeling in you. That, my friend, is doing magic."

I was impressed by his speech. However, the act of writing sounded even harder than I'd imagined, and I was glad I'd put it off for so long. I said, "You're not giving me much hope of ever succeeding. How does the apprentice learn to be the sorcerer?"

"You want to create magic tricks? You study magicians. When-ever you're reading along in a book and catch yourself feeling something, one of the basic, deep-down emotions—mad, sad, glad, or scared—stop reading." He clapped his hands once and then spread his fingers wide, as if he'd made a dove vanish. "You stop because right there the magician has done a trick. Go back and figure out how and why the trick worked: what combinations of words did the author use to establish the characters, action, di-alogue, setting, and mood such that you actually felt something?"

"Then what?"

"You go to school on it, keep studying the tricks. Learn them so you can put a spin on those things and make the tricks your own. You're smart, quick-witted. It'll be a snap for you."

My stomach flipped as we looked at each other. Cade still had a lot going for him, but David definitely won in the charisma department. Finally, I said, "You're a good teacher."

He shrugged. "I'm glad you think so, because now I'm going to piss you off. It's time you learned about people and money."

That broke the mood. I sighed and asked, "Is this where you tell me about the error of giving fish to a man instead of teaching him to fish for himself?"

"No, that's bullshit. If you give a man a fish, he'll ask you why you didn't give him a bigger fish. If you teach a man to fish, he'll demand that you give him your favorite fishing spot. To ask him to find his own damn spot is to deny him an opportunity. To 'disenfranchise' him. What I'm saying is, no matter what you do for folks, it's never fucking enough."

"That's a pretty cynical view of people."

"It's based on experience." He crossed his arms and went on. "Years ago, right after I started to hit the bestseller list, I volunteered to teach writing at the high school here and the nearby community college. Pay it forward, you know? I taught them how to fish, but the little bastards always wanted more: 'Would you rewrite my story to make it better?', 'Can we work on a book together?', 'When will you introduce me to your agent?'" He made a sour face, eyeglasses flashing. "Everybody looking for an angle, so they wouldn't have to work hard."

"That's the way of the world," I said. "It's not what you know, it's who you know." His expression turned even surlier, but I settled in for the argument. "Can you blame them for trying to get a leg-up and not have to rely on luck or fate or whatever?"

He threw up his hands. "Yeah, I guess earning your way is too old school."

"In a bunch of interviews, you said your first manuscript was plucked out of the slush pile and given to an editor by a summer intern—some girl who went back to school without realizing you owed all your future success to her. You expect everyone to be that fortunate?"

"I expect people to try and fail and try again until they succeed." He pushed off the table and started to pace. "I know the young guy you were with at Azteca. I've been down the street where Timothy lives. It's a slum, but it doesn't matter how much money you give those people—it'll never be enough to save them. They'll just develop more expensive vices or find other ways to self-destruct. Because that's what's keeping them on that street. They're comfortable in failure; they like feeling sorry for themselves. It suits them."

There were so many fronts I wanted to fight David on, but I still really liked him despite his attitudes. Maybe I could change his thinking if I stayed level-headed. Keeping my voice even, I told him, "I didn't say I'd give them cash. I said I want to help them. My dad controlled this town and seemed to go out of his way to keep them down; I want to rectify that."

David seemed to struggle with what he wanted to say next. His expression softened, and he braced himself as if he were about to deliver a confession. Then his defenses kicked in and he replied, "I gotta tell you, Brady was a rat-bastard in many respects. We grew up together, so I know everything about him—I mean *everything*—but the man understood money. He also knew what makes people tick and how to motivate them."

The abrupt change of topic threw me, and David's implication that he knew some secrets about my father made my mind race. Abandoning the philanthropy discussion, I blurted, "Can you tell me why so many people around here seem to hate me? Someone even carved 'MURDER' on my rental car."

He frowned at me, walked over, and sat beside my boots on the footstool. "What was that last part again?"

I told him about the flat tires, the tipped statue, and finding the word written in frost and gouged into the trunk lid.

He asked, "What did the police chief think?"

"He has no idea. Do you?"

David shook his head. "You're not going to keep sleeping there, are you? You might wind up like a victim from one of my books."

"Believe me, I've thought about that, but I don't like the motel out on the highway, and I don't know anywhere else to stay around here."

"I've got plenty of space." My jaw dropped, and he started talking fast, "I mean, you could have a whole wing to yourself—we'd never even bump into each other. Until Cade gets this situation sorted out, it's not safe over there."

"Before, I couldn't even get in to see you without a literal engraved invitation. Now you want us to be roomies?"

He stammered, "Well, you only just got here but you're already running into all kinds of shit. It reflects badly on my hometown, and I'm in a position to help, so...."

I stared at him. If he'd set his sights on me during our encounter at the restaurant, he could've staged the whole thing. He left ahead of us and could've driven straight to my dad's place to wreak a little havoc and in the morning returned to gouge "MURDER" in the frost and into the trunk. Then I'd come running to him like some damned damsel in distress, our meeting time already set. He'd know those incidents would be weighing on my mind, and he would provide the perfect solution to ensure my safety.

Viewed that way, it looked like a plot from one of his novels: scare the girl and have her run into the arms of the monster posing as her savior. On the other hand, maybe I was being paranoid and suspicious of a perfectly innocent offer. He did look concerned about me.

Probing for flaws, I asked, "Won't Bebe mind?"

"Why would she?"

I laughed. "Oh, please. You invite a single woman to stay here, and she's not even going to bat those long lashes?"

David was shaking his head before I'd finished. "We're not a couple," he said. I sneered at that, and he started his verbal tap dance again. "Not anymore. I admit we had a thing years ago, when she first came to work for me. I was newly divorced, and Bebe...well, hell, she was even hotter back then. But now it's strictly business, I swear."

"You're full of it," I said. "I'm as straight as they come, but with the way she looks and that accent? Even I'd fall for her if we stayed cooped up together all alone in the woods."

"She's got a thing going with Cade, okay? Happy now?" He stared at his shoes. "She tossed me aside for a younger man. Someone who can keep up with her."

David looked plenty fit to me, so the "interactions" Cade had alluded to must've been extra-vigorous. Why hadn't the police chief come in with me, then? Get a little morning loving while I had this meeting? I wanted to think it was because Cade liked me and maybe was hoping for something deeper. No way could I compete with Bebe, though, in any department.

Just my luck—she'd been with both guys who'd caught my eye, and maybe she still switched between them whenever it suited her.

Giving my booted ankle a squeeze, David said, "Hey, it's a free country—girl's gotta do what she's gotta do. Anyway, don't worry about Bebe. Just think about my offer, okay?" He glanced at his watch. "I've got to get in another thousand words today. Come back and stay for a while, at least until Cade catches whoever's trying to scare you."

I freed my leg and set my feet on the floor. "No promises. Even if I decide to come back, though, I can't get in: Bebe took my Admit One card."

He reached into his wallet and handed over a solid black card bearing only a phone number and e-mail address. "Just flash this at her. It grants you permanent access. Text me first though—I'll let you know when I'll be coming up for air next."

I thanked him, tucked the card into my purse, and let him lead me back through the secret door, across the smoke-scented study, and into the main hall. I opened the closet to retrieve my coat. No sign of Bebe anywhere, not that I was disappointed. Given our tense encounter, and David's obvious interest, I could picture her ready to ambush me. With an axe.

"We're not done discussing my project," I told him as he helped me into the sleeves. "Or my dad."

"Looking forward to it."

Me, too, but all I said was, "I'll talk to you later."

"Thanks for coming over." He smiled and gave me a quick hug, which I returned.

The sudden contact felt nice. I definitely could end my six-month drought that night if I wanted to. David certainly seemed willing, but Cade wasn't out of the running yet.

"Better go back to your dungeon now," I said. "You got your love scene in, so we're all counting on a 24/7 fright-fest until the end." Not wanting to give him the last word, I stepped out onto the front walk and closed the door behind me.

The inside of Cade's police car was red. A quarter of the interior anyway, specifically the front passenger seat. It wasn't blood — it was Bebe.

She was talking to the police chief. Her hand gripped the shoulder of his bomber jacket, as if she were about to pull him into a kiss. Or maybe they had done that already and were coming up for air.

Not the ambush I'd envisioned. An axe would've been preferable.

12

BEBE MET MY GAZE AND SAID SOMETHING TO CADE, HER HAND DROPPING FROM HIS SLEEVE. AS I approached the car, he turned to glance at me and then looked back at her. She gave him a huge smile—a Hollywood red-carpet stunner—and took her time exiting. Somehow she could even make clambering out of a bucket seat look sexy.

I said, "Warming it up for me?"

"Just getting reacquainted with my dear old friend, don't you know," she replied, really turning on the brogue. "But I do think you'll find it quite toasty in there." She looked me over, maybe searching for clues about how David and I had spent our time together. The woman fought fire with fire; that was for sure.

"I enjoyed meeting you," I said, trading places with her at the open passenger door. "I'm sure we'll see each other again soon."

"Oh, that'd be grand—he gave you another Admit One card then, did he?"

"The black one," I said and paused to enjoy the look of surprise on her gorgeous face. "I promise to call first—I don't want to drop in and interrupt anything."

An arctic gust of wind rocked us and swirled our hair. "Certainly," she said, rubbing her bare arms. "Excuse me now—it's getting brisk."

I rippled my fingers in a little wave and watched her scurry up the walk. Then I slid in beside Cade and closed the door. The fabric beneath me felt as if it had been baking in an oven. I snapped, "Jesus, Chief, turn off the seat warmer."

"It's not on," he said. "What's wrong?"

Bebe did promise that I'd find it "quite toasty" inside. I prodded the cushion and said, "That woman puts out some major body heat. She's a furnace."

"Red hot," he agreed and then laughed when I shot him a look. "My God, are you jealous of her?"

I crammed my purse into the scooped-out lumbar section, eased back, and felt a trickle of sweat edge along my hairline while my bottom and shoulders roasted. My temper had heated up, too. "What would I have to be jealous about?" I asked. "You can have all the 'interactions' you want, with her or anyone else. I'm just a citizen filing a vandalism complaint." I cracked the window to let in a little cold air and stared straight ahead.

He sighed. "Okay, where to now, citizen?"

"I've taken up way too much of your time already." I jabbed a thumb at his dash-mounted laptop. "You probably weren't nearly as productive as you hoped to be, what with the distractions."

"I got a lot done before Bebe came out, and she was just one distraction."

"Just one? Then you weren't paying close attention."

He laughed again and put the car in gear. "Nothing there I hadn't seen before." As I sputtered, he added, "Look, we dated for a while, and then she broke it off. I was as surprised as you were that she came out to see me."

"I can't remember touching any of my exes that way. If I ever put my hand on them after a breakup, it was preceded by a decent backswing."

Cade chuckled some more as he turned around on the driveway and got us moving down the winding road through the woods. The air blowing through my window chilled my front while Bebe's residual heat continued to plague my back. Combined with Cade laughing at me, it was a special kind of hell.

We drove in silence until he got us onto the highway, heading toward Graylee. He asked, "So how'd it go with Stark? Ready to save the world together?"

"The plans are still on the drawing board, but there was a new development: he invited me to live at his house—at least until you catch the vandal." I kept my face pointing forward but watched his reaction.

He kneaded the steering wheel. All he said was, "That was mighty generous of him."

"I'm sure he has only my best interests at heart," I deadpanned. "No way am I going to stay at my dad's place now, and the motel is kind of a dump."

"I've got three empty jail cells."

"Ha ha. I'd sooner sleep in the backseat of this car."

"Cindy Dwyer runs a B&B in town. She's the go-to person when folks come here for weddings, funerals, and such." He slapped the wheel. "Nope, scratch that, bad idea. I'll put you in touch with some widows and empty-nesters who take in boarders."

"What's up with Cindy Dwyer?"

He chewed the inside of his cheek but finally replied, "She was the one who put up Wallace Landry, so I'm thinking you'll want to stay someplace else."

My booted foot tapped the case file while I recalled his comment the day before about the paperwork offering every detail but "the why." I wondered if Cindy would have some insights about that missing piece, some bit of random conversation with Landry she forgot to tell the police. "She'll do," I said. "Graylee is so small, if I try to avoid everywhere he went I might as well leave town."

"You sure?"

I wanted to tell him to make me a better offer and see where that led, but I was already falling back on old habits—the jealousy and neediness that had infuriated Andy and my other exes so much. It would be easy to scare Cade off before we even got started.

"Sure I'm sure," I said. "She's someone I should meet anyway. If you'll drop me off at my dad's house and give me Cindy's number, I'll introduce myself, pack up, and head over to her place."

"Sounds like a plan."

He didn't sound particularly pleased about that plan. At first I thought he was hiding something and afraid I'd learn it from Cindy. Then I noticed how long it was taking to return to Graylee. Pretending to work out a kink in my back, I stretched in his direction so I could see the dashboard. According to the speedometer, Cade was keeping the Caprice a good five miles an hour below the speed limit. He was drawing out our time together. Not the most romantic gesture ever, but it was sweet, like a boy dragging his feet while walking his date up to her front door.

Testing my theory, I asked, "Can I stop by later today to get the updated vandalism report from you, for the rental car company?"

"Definitely," he said. "When do you want to come by?"

Yes, there was that eagerness again. I thought about what I

needed to do that day and replied, "How about 4:30 again? That's becoming our regular time."

"Uh, sure, I guess so. 4:30…our time." He frowned.

I thought about the luscious smile Bebe had given him. Maybe it signaled "See you later" instead of "Goodbye." In as casual a tone as I could muster, I said, "If that's going to bump up against a dinner date with Bebe, I can come by earlier."

This produced another head snap. "What?"

"It looked like you two—*y'all*—were getting reacquainted, 'interacting' nicely, so I thought you might be going out later."

"But how'd you know she suggested supper?"

She'd probably suggested way more than that, but I said, "It's what a woman does when she's interested in a guy. Or, in her case, re-interested. Graylee might be the last bastion of Southern manners, but surely the women here don't wait until Sadie Hawkins Day to ask a guy out."

"I reckon." He glanced at the dashboard clock and asked, "How about lunch instead? Give me an hour to take care of some things. You can stop by—or we can meet someplace if you want—at, say, 12:30?"

There it was: the first-date invitation. However, I didn't see any advantage to doing lunch if Bebe already planned to do "supper" with Cade and no doubt have him for dessert. Better that I waited to see whether my competition stayed in the picture or was the one-and-done type. "Another time, promise," I said. "I've got lots of stuff piling up. Is 4:30 okay?"

"Yup." He signaled and turned us off the highway, heading for town. After a few blocks, he said, "Have you ever carried a gun in your purse?"

Not the follow-up I expected to the postponement of our first date. "Come again?"

"I've been thinking, whoever did that to your car might not restrict activities to your father's property. Brady had a couple of pistols—we found a gun safe in his bedroom." He looked at me and then made another turn. "I know some people at the county probate court and could have a Georgia Weapons License fast-tracked for you, but that'll mean getting your fingerprints and such. In the meantime, my boys and I will look the other way if you want to conceal and carry."

"You're telling me to start packing heat?"

He shrugged. "You don't have anything against guns, do you?"

"Not unless I think about my dad being shot to death."

"And what about his murderer being shot to death?" Cade touched his holster, as if to reassure himself he still was armed. "Doesn't that balance things out?"

I pitched my voice low and tried to get his accent right: "I reckon."

A smile quirked the corner of his mouth. "Look, I can show you how to shoot if you've never done it, and I'll teach you about gun safety if you're worried about that."

The NYPD detective I'd lived with had taken care of those things, but I was willing to play dumb. Would shooting be part of our first date, or was he now proposing a second date? I imagined us out in the country, facing a kudzu-covered fence topped with old cans and bottles, his body enveloping me from behind as he held my arms out and showed me how to aim and squeeze off shots. A little kinky, but it could lead to some interesting developments.

"Okay," I said. "Assuming I can cram a pistol into my overloaded purse."

"It's just until we can get whoever's messing with your property."

"No, you're right. My mixed martial arts instructor warned me that my brown belt would be no match for a punk with a .22 and a steady hand."

He glanced at me when I mentioned the brown belt, maybe with some new respect. "He was right."

"She." That earned another look. "You ever spar?"

"Not since the police academy."

Another fantasy sprang to mind. "Well, I'll trade you shooting lessons for some moves on the mat. Deal?" When he looked at me, I gave him my best smile. Not in Bebe's league, but it had the desired effect.

"Uh, I'm sure Bebe just wants to talk," he babbled, driving even more slowly. "We haven't seen each other in a month of Sundays, what with her out there in the country with Stark. It's not like it's a real date or nothing."

"Maybe for you, but I think she looked pretty serious."

"I'll call her, tell her we can get supper some other time."

"Hey, don't do that on my account. I'll be out of your hair by 5:00 at the latest."

"No, no, this is much more important. There might be some new developments today, maybe find a resolution to our problem. Who knows?"

I didn't want Bebe to declare all-out war on me—I already had to watch my back—but now Cade might decide to call it quits before she lured him into dessert. Mission accomplished,

I punched his arm and said, "Jeez, go have supper with your old girlfriend. We'll have lots of chances to go out."

"Oh, okay. Good." He relaxed as he drove us down Main Street, waving at the few pedestrians brave enough to be outside when the forecast called for an impending quarter-inch of snow.

We turned toward my dad's house and headed up the glass-smooth road. Cade parked again behind the rental car. Less than two hours had passed, but it felt much longer. Sunshine had melted the frost, erasing one version of the "MURDER" message. I checked Cade; he seemed to be holding his breath, same as me, while we scanned the scene for signs of new damage.

"Think it's all right?" I asked him, fingers on the door handle.

"Let me do a walk-around first." He climbed out, resettled his equipment belt and holster, and did a loop around the vandalized car and statue. Apparently seeing nothing of interest, he inspected the house, checking the front door and testing the windows as he followed the wrap-around porch out of sight. In a minute, he completed the circuit and gave me a thumbs-up.

I headed to the rental car trunk to see the threat again, the hateful word scored deep into the black paint. A vivid reminder that, somewhere in town, a sicko was getting his rocks off by scaring me. Suddenly I didn't feel like flirting anymore.

Cade came over and said, "I've asked my second-shift deputy to get out here with a fingerprint kit. You'll see B.J. this afternoon."

He lifted his arms a bit, and I got ready to return his embrace. I needed a little comforting. However, he only stuffed his hands into his jacket pockets. He nodded to me, cop to civilian, totally professional and completely unsatisfying.

13

BEFORE HE HAD DRIVEN OFF, CADE CONSULTED HIS CELL PHONE AND COPIED CINDY DWYER'S number for me. She answered on the second ring and told me what an honor it would be to host me for as long as I needed. The cost was only forty dollars a night, which was even cheaper than the motel and included breakfast. Despite her breezy tone, I sensed underlying uneasiness and maybe some hostility, too—the Brady Stapleton Effect again—but at least she didn't say no.

I took down Cindy's address and entered her information into my phone. Remembering David's black card, I also put in his phone number and e-mail.

Surrounded by repacked luggage in the pillow-orgy bedroom, I wondered what else there was to do before leaving again, maybe for a while. I came up with two items to locate: a gun and the hidden trap door David had mentioned. The latter could wait, but Cade's idea to arm myself had been a good one.

The police chief didn't tell me exactly where Dad had kept his gun safe, but, if it held only pistols, there was a good chance he'd stored it under his bed. Within easy reach, he would've thought. I took a few deep breaths and tried not to think about the slaughter that had occurred there as I forced myself to march into the master bedroom.

After kicking aside some of the larger fragments of the porcelain shade I broke when I had my meltdown during the tour of the house, I planted my boots wide, squatted—very much aware of the white shards and china powder just under my black-wool-clad butt—and peered beneath the bed. On the hardwood floor sat a dark plastic case about the size of a laptop bag.

The case was heavier than it looked—maybe twenty-five pounds—and had a brand name, logo, and the words "Gun Vault" stamped into the top. Beneath the logo was a chrome lock. After searching among dozens of choices on the massive key ring, I spotted "GV" on a small label. Unless it unlocked a cache of Givenchy haute couture, I figured I'd found the right one.

Still in my squat, I inserted the key into the lock and pushed up the lid. Two pistols nestled in gray foam molded around their contours. One gun was black and bulky, with a trademarked laser sight below the barrel; the other one was pocket-sized and chrome-plated. A spare magazine for each gun had its own rectangular cutout in the foam, as did two boxes of .38 caliber bullets. Home defense for the anal retentive.

During my relationship with the NYPD detective, he'd taught me the basics about guns. I dug out the shiny pistol, surprised by its lightness—just a pound or so. While I weighed it in my hand, I saw a switch above the grip labeled "Safe." I thumbed it down, which revealed another word stamped into the metal: "Fire." Before inspecting the gun further, I flicked the safety back on and then double-checked it by aiming the barrel at the side of the mattress. I cringed as I tried to pull the trigger. It didn't budge.

Another switch at the bottom of the grip released the rectangular housing for the bullets, which were copper-tipped and stacked to the top. I pushed the magazine back in until the switch clicked. In countless movies and TV shows, they used the phrase "locked and loaded," but someone always said it after cocking his gun. My pistol didn't have a hammer, but the top could slide back if I forced it. After a little struggle — the spring mechanism was tight — I slid the U-shape toward my shooting hand and a bullet fell out from the side and bounced on the floor. That meant it had been ready to fire, and now I was short one bullet. Afraid that one shot would make all the difference, I pocketed the spare magazine and put the loose bullet in its place in the foam.

I pushed the gun vault back under the bed, pocketed my keys, and retreated to the study on the other side of the fireplace. At the desk, I set down the pistol and then dumped the contents of my purse beside it. Tossing out a surprising number of balled tissues, mostly empty cosmetic cases, pen caps with no pens, and other detritus, plus sorting and stacking the rest, gained me enough free space for the firearm and spare ammunition. However, reaching blindly into the purse, there was no way I'd manage a quick-draw.

Another concern was the added weight. The gun and extra bullets were only a few pounds, so it must've been psychological. I knew I was carrying a deadly weapon. Still, the purse now felt like a bowling ball in a sling when I hefted it onto my shoulder.

Armed with so-called peace of mind, I decided to head to Cindy Dwyer's. On the way downstairs, I flipped through the key ring to select my ride, noting three options: Mercedes, BMW, and Jaguar. I had to admit again that inheriting Dad's estate didn't totally suck.

I retrieved my two large bags and rolled them past the front entrance on my way to the back door and detached garage.

Chimes sounded. Three descending notes. Gulping, I dropped the luggage handles and clawed at my purse. Then I stopped and told myself to calm down. Would a killer really ring the freaking doorbell? It could've been Cade, Tim, another friendly face, or someone with a surprise Christmas delivery. Still, I dragged out the pistol and put it in my coat pocket. What to do: switch off the safety now and jack-in a round or ask the maniac to wait while I did it literally under the gun?

The chimes sounded again, the sinking tones matching my falling confidence. Right hand gripping the pocketed pistol, I peered through the peephole my father had installed in the heavy front door and saw a young woman of twenty or so. She'd streaked the ends of her blond hair with a raspberry dye and painted her bangs turquoise to match her fingernails. I decided to keep the safety on.

Looming behind her head was a puffy, green bedroll. Straps from a backpack creased the insubstantial jacket covering her shoulders. She rotated in place, looking left and right, as if expecting me to come from either side of the wraparound porch. Her movements swayed the camping gear that dangled down past her denim-clad knees.

I unlocked the door and eased it open so I didn't startle her. "Hi there. Are you lost?"

My visitor stood maybe five-foot-four, discounting a couple of inches for her hiking boots, and was slender and pretty except for the funky hair colors. She laughed. "Yeah, no. Actually I was hoping to see you."

"Oh?"

"So, I totally get that this is, like, out of the blue, but, you know." Her pitch rose at the end of every statement, as if she were always asking a question.

I waited for more, noticing her petite nose ring and an eyebrow stud. Her clothes probably hid a canvas of tattoos.

She added, "Um, we have this, like, really major thing in common, and I think it's time we clear the air or whatever."

"Whatever?"

"So, what I mean is, you sort of have blood on your hands, and it's totally cool if you don't get it, but it's, like, crazy, and I thought we should, you know, bury the hatchet." She frowned at my lack of response and said in a loud, slow voice, "Talk or whatever?"

As I continued to work through her verbal cul-de-sacs, she said, "You know, it's really rude to leave a person standing on the porch like this. I'm just saying."

Part of me wanted to shoot her, for her own sake, but I muttered, "Thanks for pointing that out." I backed up and stood clear so she could enter.

"No problem." In the foyer, she dropped the REI shopping spree from her shoulders. It sounded like a body smacking the floor.

I closed the door and put out my hand. "I'm Janet Wright."

She pumped it enthusiastically, apparently not minding the blood she claimed it was soaked in. "Tara Glenmont," she said. "Everybody calls me Tar."

Unfortunate nickname. I would've expected a "Tara" to be really Southern, but she didn't have a regional accent. Instead, she sounded like the Millennials I'd worked with in Manhattan. However, those young people had bathed every day, whereas this girl reeked of dried sweat and the other body odors that came from camping in the wilderness for a long time.

She released my hand and looked me over. "So, are you, like, the trophy wife?"

"I'm not married."

"The girlfriend then, or whatever? Someone he met up North? You don't sound like you're from around here."

"New York," I confirmed. "But who are you talking about?"

"Well, duh—you."

I rolled my eyes. "Okay, but who else?"

"Him." She gestured at the room around us. When I didn't respond, Tara frowned, lifted some raspberry-dyed hair off her shoulder, and held it in front of her eyes, as if to confirm she was still herself and the world hadn't gone nuts. She said, "So, maybe you're like a squatter here?"

I put on my icy expression, usually reserved for guys who hassled me on the subway. "Okay, that's enough. You need to leave, Tar. Right now."

She crossed her arms. "No need to go all super-witch on me. I'm just saying."

"Well, I'm just saying you need to get out of my house."

"So, I'm only trying to get, like, some answers or whatever."

"You're done asking questions." I yanked the door open.

She walked toward the fireplace in the great room and dropped onto the leather sofa. Bits of dried mud marked her trail.

Amazed by her chutzpah, I grabbed her backpack by the straps, intending to heave it onto the porch, but I could barely lift it off the floor. Hard to believe she'd been lugging it around without apparent discomfort—the girl was much stronger than she looked.

She glowered at me through turquoise bangs. "I can't believe you're treating me so crappy, after what I've been through."

"Look, I don't know who you are or what you've been through. And I don't care." I wondered if I could shoot her and claim justifiable homicide because she wouldn't leave.

"You should care, since you're living in the House of Death, or whatever."

I stomped toward her. "What do you know about this place? First it was blood on my hands and now it's the goddamn House of Death." I stood over her, hands tucked into my coat pockets. My right hand gripped the pistol, just in case. "Come on, spill it."

"Or what? You'll, like, make my head explode with your evil glare?"

"No, I won't give you the answers you want. Besides, I don't think you'll miss your head, since you obviously don't use it."

"Super-witch." She folded her arms and stared straight ahead, which happened to be level with my midsection. After a moment, she blinked and looked up at me. "Is that, like, a gun in your pocket?"

I glanced down at my coat—sure enough, I was pressing the barrel hard enough against the fabric to create a noticeable outline. "Yes," I said, "and you're tempting me to use it."

She snorted. "That'd be just my luck—shot to death in the same house as Wally."

I staggered back two steps and had to pull my hands out of the coat pockets for balance. Good thing a chair was behind me. My knees folded, and I dropped onto the leather cushion. "You knew Wallace Landry?"

"Well, yeah. He was only, like, my boyfriend or whatever." Her defensive posture vanished, and she leaned forward as if sharing a secret. "So, we were kind of engaged, but he couldn't afford a ring. He was trying to earn enough money to buy one."

And just like that, I knew the missing motive, "the why" Cade had said I wouldn't find in the case file: a poor boy who wanted to start a life with his wife-to-be and targeted my father's fortune. The reports would tell me whether Landry's pockets had contained a lot of stolen cash, but I bet my father hadn't cooperated when threatened, so "Wally" murdered him. Despite the alarm going off, Landry probably figured he would have plenty of time to search the house and escape, long before the police arrived.

Tara's face had taken on a reverential glow as soon as she started talking about Landry. Wanting to slap away that expression, I snarled, "Your fiancé shot my father so he could rob this place and buy you a goddamn ring."

"He was your father? So, he really is, like, dead?"

"He's not 'like dead'—he is totally, thoroughly dead. Thanks to your Wally."

Tara popped off the couch, shouting, "Wally's dead thanks to your dad." Her left hand disappeared into the pocket of her jacket and emerged less than a second later with a gun even smaller than mine. It was a revolver, with a cylinder of bullets pointed at my face.

No way could I have drawn my pistol that fast. However, my self-defense classes from the Y flooded back even as I wondered what to do. I slid down on the chair seat, moving below her aim, and kicked upward with my right boot. The toe punted the gun from her hand. As my foot descended, I chopped it sideways, scything Tara's legs from under her. She fell full-length, gasping as she hit the slate floor, and rolled onto her back.

Off-balance myself, I allowed my body to continue to slide out of the chair. I ended up with my knees planted on her chest, making her exhale in a whoosh of stale breath. If we were in a movie, I would've caught her revolver in mid-air, but it struck the fireplace mantel about six feet above us, bounced once, and stayed there, out of sight.

My martial arts instructor had been wrong—it turned out I was more than a match for a punk with a gun and a steady hand. This punk anyway.

While Tara squirmed under me, I took out my own gun and jabbed it toward her face, yelling, "What the fuck are you doing?" Belatedly, I remembered to thumb-off the safety and cock it.

She looked much more like a pitiful kid barely out of her teens than a cold-eyed killer. "Jesus," she groaned, then looked past the barrel and met my eyes. "Oops, sorry. That's a dollar for the swear jar."

I had to laugh. "You feel bad about that but not for pointing a gun at me?"

"I guess I'm feeling bad about everything." She sipped air, eyes wide. "Look, you're not, like, fat or whatever, but can you get off? Please? I can't even breathe."

I eased into a crouch above Tara, mindful of her fast reflexes, and then sat down in the chair again. The adrenaline boost began to subside, leaving me weak and shaky. My pistol quivered even when I used both hands to aim it. Being this close to her, I couldn't avoid smelling the intense body odor. Hopefully there would be a shower and washing machine in her near-future. Unless I shot her first.

She took some deep breaths while rubbing the fingers I'd kicked. After a moment, she rolled onto hands and knees and hauled herself onto the couch opposite me. Amazement had re-placed anger on her face. "So, your daddy trained you to be, like, a ninja?"

"I didn't really know him. The 47th Street YMCA in Manhattan taught me self-defense."

"Awesome." She looked like she meant it.

"Are you going to be good, or do I have to shoot you?"

"Yeah, no, I'm super-cool. Sorry for going all psycho on you."

I lowered the gun but continued to grip it. "What the hell was that all about?"

"I sort of lost it. I've been thinking that Wally was murdered but Brady Sta—your daddy—like, faked his own death to get away with it. Then you showed up, and I thought maybe you were in on it."

"What would be the point?"

"One of those thrill-killings? Or maybe Wally stumbled on some dark secret and had to be dealt with? Or maybe *he* had a dark secret *I* didn't know about and was killed for it. Or—"

"Wait. Stop. You're making me want to shoot you again." Reining in my anger, I paused and then tried again in a calmer tone. "Wally murdered my dad, and then the police had to kill him. Those are the facts. Your theories all hinge on my father being alive, but he's not."

"How do you know?" She narrowed her eyes under those turquoise bangs. "Did you, like, see his body?"

I hadn't, of course, but I wasn't about to let that tiny detail get her going again. Better to keep punching holes in her ideas and start getting answers from her. First though, I thumbed on the safety for the pistol and pocketed it so I wouldn't give in to temptation. Scary how merely having a gun at hand made using it seem—if only for a moment—the most reasonable course of action. Maybe I needed Cade's firearm lectures after all.

"Look," I said, "I need your help to understand Wally. What he did changed my life forever, too."

"You're being, like, totally sincere that you're not in on his death?"

"There's no conspiracy. No cover up. No deep, dark secret people are hiding from you."

"Yeah, no, I guess the theory was sort of crazy." Her voice thickened. "Kind of out there." She looked around the room, everywhere but at me, as she pressed her hands together and squeezed them between her knees. Her face reddened, and she began to rock in place. I knew the signs of a dam about to burst—after Andy kicked me out, I had done it a lot.

As her first tears began to trickle down, I hurried to my purse atop the luggage and fished out a package of tissues. I put the packet in her lap as she continued to rock and cry. By the time I came back from the kitchen with a glass of water for her, the rivulets had become a stream.

I faced her again from my chair. When she'd finished wiping her face, I said. "I know it's hard to stick to the facts when your heart's involved. When you know, deep down, the guy you love has done something wrong." She didn't seem to hear me. My language was too analytical—no way would I reach her.

Trying again, I said, "It totally sucks, okay? But we need to man up and get on with life or whatever." I raised my fist in a power salute, gave her what I hoped looked like a brave smile, and said, "YOLO, right?"

With that quick left hand of hers, she threw the tissue packet and hit me dead-center in the chest. "Could you be any more, like, patronizing?" she sneered.

Cheeks burning with embarrassment, I said, "You're right—I'm sorry. Let's start over. Tell me about Wally."

Tara blew her nose. After stuffing the used tissues in a jacket pocket, she cleared her throat and peered at me shyly through her dyed bangs. "So, he wasn't my first boyfriend or whatever," she said, "but he always felt more real than the others, you know? Sort of like he was The One, the dude I'd been waiting for. How old are you?"

I frowned at the sudden shift in focus. "Uh, I turned forty this year."

She nodded, as if I'd confirmed a suspicion. Did I really look forty? Maybe I needed some of that neon hair color.

"So, like, you've been with some boys?" When I didn't respond immediately, she added, "Or girls or whatever. It's all cool."

"Boys. A few," I deadpanned.

She checked out my ring-less left hand. "I don't want to go all woman-of-the-world on you, but have you ever been, like, engaged at least?"

"Once. Didn't work out. Your point?"

"Well, you thought he was The One, right?"

I finally saw where this was going, and I was relieved to shift the conversation back to her and Landry. "Of course. Same as Wally was The One for you."

"Totally. He was awesome."

"And he was trying to earn enough money to buy you a ring," I prompted, "and start a life together."

"Yeah, so, after he lost his job, which was this total miscarriage of justice, he told me he was hitting the road to find work. He texted me all the time to say what town he was in and, you know, if he was having any luck. Then he said he couldn't afford his cell phone anymore—they were, like, cutting him off from the world for not paying his bills—but he'd write postcards. I didn't even know they still made those."

Her fingers busied themselves with the zipper on her jacket, moving it down and up, revealing and then hiding a wrinkled, stained tee shirt over and over. "So, like, months go by and I don't hear from him. I wondered if he'd found another girl or maybe got into some kind of trouble, because he did have this, you know, sort of a temper or whatever. He always kept a lid on it, except for sometimes. So, out of desperation, I Googled his name, and up pops these stories about Wally shooting your daddy and getting shot by the cops."

"What'd you do?"

"So, I kind of lost my mind for a while. Couldn't focus at my jobs. I just kept zoning out and getting fired. Finally, I decided I needed to come up here and sort of unravel the mystery."

"But that's what I keep trying to explain," I said. "There's really nothing to unravel here. Wally needed money, my dad was loaded, and it was a robbery that went wrong." Tara started to protest, but I overrode her: "Or maybe it was an argument that got out of hand. Things happen."

Wanting to distract her, I decided to share my real concern. "I *am* stuck in the middle of a different mystery, though. Did you notice the flat tires on the car parked out front, and the jockey statue some guy tried to uproot? He also carved a threat on the trunk lid."

Tara dismissed me with a wave. "It's, like, a totally bogus mystery. I did all that."

14

GOOD THING I'D PUT AWAY THE GUN.

Back when I'd stood on the balcony with Mr. Pearson, I must've mistaken Tara's hair dye for a red and blue bandana and assumed a man was watching me from the woods. The damage and threats had been so easy to pin on some mythical, sinister guy. Cade had been right about the danger of making assumptions.

Gaping now at this girl who had provoked so much fear and anger, I snapped, "Why did you want to scare the shit out of me and vandalize my fucking property?"

She shook her head, mouth turned down in disappointment. "So, do you know you have this total potty mouth? I'm just saying. Granny Hazel would've collected, like, ten dollars in her swear jar from you already." Her face brightened again. "Oh, I haven't told you about Granny. She's totally awesome, but she didn't care too much for Wally. He accidentally dented her Pontiac one time by sitting on the hood. It's a red Grand Am, but she doesn't want anybody thinking she's cussing—like, saying 'Gran Damn'—so she always calls it her 'Grand A.M.' Isn't that the best?"

Fighting to regain control, I said, "I'm going to do more than swear at you unless you explain why you've been terrorizing me."

"Hey, don't go all ninja on me again. You're worse than Wally. I was just trying to get your attention."

"Mission accomplished. Can you think of any reason why I shouldn't call the police and have them throw your ass in jail?"

She cocked her head. "Seriously?"

"You also pointed a gun at me in my own home. I think the cops and a judge would take a dim view of that, too."

"So, where'd you kick that gun anyway? It's my daddy's — he'll, like, kill me if I lose it."

The rejoinders were too easy. I settled for, "Focus. Why did you want to scare me?"

"I was trying to call you out or whatever. Tell you I knew something sketchy had happened here."

"My God, why didn't you just leave a note?"

She gestured at her backpack near the front door. "I didn't bring anything to write with."

"Just a knife," I said, "to carve 'MURDER' on my trunk and slash my tires."

Tara patted her jeans pocket. "Daddy's Swiss Army knife," she said, confirming one of my assumptions had been right anyway. "He said it would come in handy. Same as his camping stuff."

I stood up to give me a height advantage and also to be prepared in case I needed to get physical again. "You sound pretty proud for someone who's in big trouble."

"You can't throw me in jail," she said. "I don't have any money for, like, bail or anything."

"Don't do the crime if you can't do the time." I pulled the cell phone from my back pocket.

She shook her head. "So, if you want to find out about Wally and why he did what he did, you need me. I'm the only one who really knew him."

161

I thought I could live with that ambiguity, not knowing all of "the why." But…my life had changed so completely because of my father's murder. Wouldn't turning my back on that key event haunt me? In fact, hadn't I become a little bit obsessed with finding out the whole truth? Guilty on both counts, dammit. Another dollar for Granny Hazel's swear jar.

Tara had done a lot of things wrong, but she didn't seem to be evil. Anger and grief over Landry's death obviously still clouded her judgment. When I'd been engaged to Andy, had he murdered someone and been killed afterward, I would've gone to any extreme to get to the bottom of it. And flattened anybody who got in my way.

I paused with the phone in my hand long enough to make Tara appreciate my control over her fate. She didn't appear contrite exactly, more like a girl struggling between guilt and defiance. However, I understood that as well: it pretty much summed up my emotional life until my mid-twenties. With an exaggerated sigh, I returned the phone to my pocket and sat again.

Tara slumped into the couch cushions. Between the tears and tension, she looked even younger, like a runaway teen who'd been living on the streets. Or in the woods.

I glanced at her muddy boots and then the pile of gear beside the front door. "Where have you been camping?"

"There's this sort of tree farm close by—I've been putting up a tent there at night for the last, like, three weeks and then hiking up here to scope the house. But that gets boring, so I mostly wander around in the woods."

"Do you go into town for food?"

She shook her head. "I packed a bunch of dehydrated food

Daddy and I take on long hunts, and water purifying tablets and stuff like that. Plus, there's a really deep stream where I catch fish. The only time I, like, go into town is late at night, to charge my phone at this outdoor outlet I found."

I certainly couldn't have survived that way for three weeks. The girl was tough, and she also was in distress. Despite our many differences, I could empathize. "Okay, here's the deal," I said. "As long as you help me understand Wally and what happened here, I won't turn you in. We'll talk, I'll even spring for lunch, and then you go home. Is it far?"

She laughed. "Yeah, no. It's only, like, fifty miles. I can hike that in two days easy."

I shook my head in wonder. "Change of plans. After we're done, I'll drive you home—but only if you cooperate fully."

The indignant look returned. "I'm not hiding anything or whatever."

I put up my hands to stop her before she got going again. "You'd probably like to freshen up. There's a full bath down here. Then we'll talk while we get something to eat."

She shrugged and retrieved a less-grimy tee, wadded underwear, and wrinkled jeans from her pack. I led her to the bathroom door, which she closed in my face without a word.

Listening to the shower run, I consulted my To-Do list. Driving her home would kill the rest of the day—and postpone my follow-up visit with Cade—so I reprioritized based on what I thought I could get done on Christmas Eve. I wondered whether the chief would be free that night or if Bebe would try again with him.

Tara emerged in less than twenty minutes, with her hair still wet, but she looked and smelled cleaner. Then she donned her ripe jacket, undoing some of those hygienic efforts.

Massive key ring in hand, I returned to my decision from what felt like hours ago: which car to drive? Jag, Beamer, or Benz. Any of the three options would rub salt into a wound for Tara, as if I were saying, "Look at all I got from my dad's death. What'd you get from Wally's?"

If she made a remark, I'd just have to remind her we could've taken my modest rental had she not disabled it. I gestured toward the back of the house. "The garage is this way."

She looked around again. "My daddy's gun—I need to find it."

"We're going to Denny's, not the OK Corral. You don't need the gun now."

"I just don't want to, like, forget it."

"We'll search the room when we get back. Promise."

She scanned the floor and furniture as we walked into the dining room. From the table, I lifted my yellow legal pad of notes and flipped to the page where I'd written the code to open the garage door. Turning away from Tara, I memorized the digits and set the pad facedown.

Out back, we went down the steps and followed a flagstone walkway to the huge garage. Screening Tara again, I tapped in the code, and the overhead door scrolled upward, revealing four wide bays. The rightmost one was empty except for a mottled collection of oil drips. In the other three, cars had been backed in: a low-slung Jaguar roadster in British racing green, a black BMW sedan, and a boxy silver Mercedes SUV that resembled a miniature armored car. I sorted through my keys and confirmed there only were three for automobiles, but maybe my father had wrecked a fourth vehicle or merely sold it.

As Tara gaped at the shiny showroom display, I asked, "You have a preference?"

"The green one. Oh, yeah."

The Jag had caught my eye, too. I opened the driver door and was about to climb in, but then I noticed the stick shift between the front seats. "Sorry," I said, "I don't know how to use a clutch."

"That sucks." She eased her hands over the curve of a fender, as if petting a wild animal. "My daddy's pickup had four on the floor. I learned on it."

As empathetic as I was to her emotional pain, no way was she getting behind the wheel. She'd pulled a gun on me not too long ago—I wouldn't become her captive again. I shook my head and tried to look regretful. "Sorry, you're not on my insurance, of course, and if something happened...."

"So, do you always, like, play by the rules?"

I wasn't about to let her goad me into giving her the keys, but I also couldn't let the challenge go unanswered. "Definitely not," I said. "But this time it's for the best."

She stroked the roadster some more. "Can we go in any of the others, or do you need, like, a Georgia driver's license first?"

I'd forgotten her wit was as quick as her hands. She was pushing me, trying to rebalance the power between us. I would've done the same in her position, but it still pissed me off. Through the side window of the Beamer, I saw a five-speed automatic. "My New York license is good enough. Let's go."

She gave the Jaguar a farewell pet and muttered, "Whatever."

After she climbed in beside me, I guided the sedan out of

the bay and found the garage door button on the visor to close it behind us. I drove around to the front of the house, where we passed the crippled rental car and jockey statue in the courtyard, and headed down the boulevard.

The enclosed space made the odor from Tara's jacket even more evident, and the interior was musty from disuse, so I turned up the fan to vent in some fresh, cold air. I'd barely had time to appreciate the leather seats and smooth ride before we arrived at the Denny's that my father had opened on Main Street near the turnoff to his house.

Apparently, it really had been his personal eatery because there were no other diners. The lone server, mid-fifties and heavy-set, even held the door for us as we entered. "Hey, Ms. Wright," she said, "I'm Gloria. Thanks for coming in." She led the way to a booth that literally was spotless. In fact, the whole place looked new.

Trembling with obvious nervousness, Gloria seemed anxious to make herself useful. She hung up my coat alongside the booth and then went to pour our requested glasses of iced tea. I had to make do with the sweetened kind—apparently no self-respecting Southerner asked for sugar-free, so she didn't have any prepared, nor had a fresh pot of coffee been brewed.

On her return, she recommended several items on the menu as her favorites. I pictured her and the cook eating there alone every day since my dad's death. No doubt she had a good idea of the house specialties. We ordered based on those, and Gloria hustled back to the kitchen.

Tara had slung her jacket beside her on the padded bench seat. Her short-sleeved pullover showed off bodybuilder arms.

No wonder she could carry that camping gear with ease. She crossed them on the tabletop and said, "So, you've eaten here lots of times?"

"Never, why?"

"She, like, called you by name."

"Everyone's been doing that. They all know who my father was, and word got around fast when I came to town two days ago. You're probably the only one in this part of the county who was in the dark about that."

The kitchen door opened again. Instead of Gloria making another appearance, a lumbering, bearded man in a John Deere ball cap and clean apron waved a spatula at us, as if we were family who'd come into his back yard for a cookout. He shouted over the vacant booths and tables, "I'll have it right out, Miz Wright. Don't you worry none."

"Thanks," I yelled and waved back before the door closed again.

Tara shook her head. "This is crazy weird."

"They've got to be worried about their jobs. My dad probably kept the place open for his use. They're hoping I'll do the same."

"Why not just hire a personal chef, or whatever, instead of wasting a ton of money on a whole restaurant?"

"Maybe he thought he was providing another option for the town — though everyone else might've seen it as his place, not theirs." I sipped my achingly sweet iced tea. "Lots of people here are resentful of my dad: happy to have good-paying jobs, of course, but apparently they didn't like being beholden to the guy who controlled nearly everything."

"And now you control nearly everything?"

"I guess, but I haven't really thought about that," I lied.

She folded her straw wrapper over and over onto itself and then drew it out and pushed it back together, a paper accordion. "If it was my money," she said, "I'd, like, give it all away. Do some good with it."

"I might."

"Yeah, right."

"Hey, what's that supposed to mean?"

She slurped some tea. "In the car, you kept rubbing your butt cheeks on the leather seat like you were coating two ears of corn with butter."

I was about to retaliate, but goading me was just another way for her to reclaim some control. Plus, she probably was right, even if I hated the image—the leather seat had felt great. I let my temper settle and said, "Tell me more about Wally. What was he like?"

"So, he could be, like, really sweet, you know? Considerate, loving. He cooked me meals sometimes, gave me breakfast in bed or whatever." She looked away, and her face flushed so much it matched her raspberry highlights. "It's not like we were living in sin or anything. I just mean—"

"Tar, I don't want to go all woman-of-the-world on you, but I've slept with men. There's nothing to be embarrassed about."

She relaxed and took another long pull of her drink. "He was funny, too. Had this really warped way of looking at the world. I laughed, like, all the time."

I thought about the details Cade had shared with me and some earlier comments she'd made. "All the time?"

Staring into her glass, she murmured, "He did get angry, you know, now and again. Like any dude. Shouted and swore. Threw stuff when things weren't going his way."

"Did he ever get physical with you?"

"Unh-uh." She looked relieved when Gloria came over with a pitcher to top off our tea and promised our meals would be out shortly.

After the waitress returned to the kitchen, I leaned forward and asked as gently as I could, "How many times did he hit you?"

Tara swallowed hard. "He never did, I swear." She played with the straw wrapper again, glanced up and then back down at her hands. "So, how'd you know? Was your fiancé that way?"

It was an obtuse sort of confession, but probably all she'd allow herself. I said, "No, but I've had friends in similar situations. I usually go for older men. If they're assholes, it's because they're emotionally abusive, not physically."

"Wally was older than me by a few years."

"I mean a little older than that."

"Ah."

Tara stared at me in such a frank, appraising way, it was my turn to look relieved when Gloria backed out of the kitchen door with two large plates. The waitress said, "I hope that didn't take too long," and set meatloaf with mashed potatoes and white gravy in front of Tara and grilled chicken with steamed veggies before me. Tara's meal looked much tastier.

After we'd promised Gloria everything was perfect and nothing more was needed, she left us again, and Tara asked, "So, why do you go for the oldsters?"

"Hey, it's not like I've dated any grandfathers." Another lie. I couldn't help it if some men had children early in life and their kids followed suit.

"I'm not, like, judging you or whatever."

I put down my fork and knife. "Not that I owe you any explanations, but I've always found older men to be more interesting. They're better read, well-travelled, and have had fascinating life experiences. And they're usually more mature and good conversationalists." She was sculpting the mashed potatoes with her fork, practically ignoring me, so I added, "They can be much more considerate lovers, too—focusing on your needs first, if you know what I mean."

She blushed again and hid her face by taking another slurp of tea. Gloria opened the kitchen door once more, but I waved and said we were fine. When I turned back to Tara, she'd set down her glass and was gorging on meatloaf. I asked. "Were you two together a long time?"

"Like forever, practically a whole year. Was your fiancé older?"

"He was fifty-five." To keep from thinking about Andy, I focused on my meal, which wasn't half bad: moist chicken with just enough char from the grill, steamed, buttery carrots, and green beans that weren't too soggy.

"Oh," she said, "I'd pictured you with some, like, ninety-year-old dude."

I snorted. "Now that's gross."

"Totally. Still, you have major daddy issues. I'm just saying."

"I do not." It wasn't the first time I'd heard that, but I wouldn't put up with being psychoanalyzed by a fetid, fluorescent Freud-wannabe.

She shrugged. "So, if he was this mature, globetrotting, intellectual love machine, why'd you two split?"

"Let's keep the focus on you and Wally."

"Come on, why?"

I finally saw the tit-for-tat game she was playing. She wouldn't give unless I did, so I replied, "Things he never mentioned when we were dating seemed to get on his nerves more and more after we got engaged."

"Like what?"

"Like everything. He said I was clingy and needy and jealous all the time. And insecure and every other damn thing. He kept calling me out, and we fought a lot."

Time had lessened the intensity of my feelings, but anger, humiliation, and heartbreak still roiled together inside me. I wanted to stop, but Tara had primed the pump, and it had been forever since I'd talked it through with anyone. "We'd picked the church and set the date, but I came home from the office one day in July, and he met me at the door and said it wasn't going to work out. He'd packed my things already—they were all waiting for me in boxes and bags. When he asked for the ring back, I threw it down the hall."

As I relived the scene in my head, sweat popped out along my hairline and across my chest and back. "Keep in mind that this was *after* what happened with Wally and my dad, which means Andy knew I was coming into a big inheritance. And still he told me to find another place to stay. That night." My voice echoed across the empty restaurant. "I'd become so repulsive to him that the sonofabitch wouldn't even marry me for my money."

My eyes burned, and I balled my hands into fists to stay in control. Tara reached over and patted my wrist, but somehow that small bit of sympathy made things worse. I was not going to cry. Absolutely not going to give in to self-pity. I was over him.

Done. And abandoned and ugly and unloved and completely, hopelessly alone.

The kitchen door opened and Gloria asked, "Sorry, were y'all hollering for me?" I didn't look up, and Tara didn't say anything, and the door closed again. No doubt word would spread immediately and morph into something like: "Did you hear about Brady's daughter having a meltdown at the Denny's? Bless her heart, folks are saying she might go back to New York City as soon as tonight."

15

I WANTED TO COLLECT MYSELF IN THE RESTROOM, BUT NO WAY WOULD I LEAVE TARA ALONE. She'd probably hustle up to my dad's house, break in to grab her camping gear, and disappear. To show that I was calm and cool, I choked down some chicken and carrots, tasting nothing. I said, "Anyway, as soon as the estate cleared probate, I decided to move down here."

"So, I guess you don't have to, like, ever work again?"

"Tell me what kind of work you did."

She smiled, as if my attempt to redirect the conversation actually was a point in her favor. "Babysitting and part-time grocery stuff."

"What do you do for fun?"

"Some art—metal sculpture—but there's no money in that."

"Sculpture? Seriously? Show me some pictures."

Rolling her eyes, she tugged a cell phone out of her back pocket. After a few taps and swipes, she slid the screen beside my plate.

The first photo showed a large sand and grass yard that had been invaded by an iron menagerie: people with wings, creatures with the heads of animals and the bodies of men, a few robot-looking figures, gigantic mechanical bugs, and other fantastical beings. I scrolled through a number of close-ups of complex individual features and panoramic shots showing dozens of sculptures in rust brown. The ability to weld and shape them explained her strength and also showed that quick, creative mind at work. Given an opportunity, she could go far.

Looking through the plate-glass window beside her, I saw a police car make the turn onto Brady Stapleton Boulevard. Probably the second-shift deputy on a mission to collect fingerprints off the rental car and statue. Tara's fingerprints.

I slid the phone back across the table. "Those are amazing. I've never seen anything like them—where'd you learn to do that?"

"So, my daddy's this, like, welder and ironworker."

"What's your mom do?"

She began to sculpt the remainder of the mashed potatoes with her fork. Finally, she said, "She sort of took off a while back, when I was a little kid."

"I'm sorry. When my mom left my dad, she took me and my brother with her."

"Your mother get remarried or whatever?"

"No, she never did."

Tara said, "So, no mom for me growing up, no daddy for you. We both did okay."

I wondered if either of us did. Though smart and talented, she had some major anger issues, and apparently I had my own baggage. At least Andy and my other exes had thought so. "I guess," I said. "Can you get a job where your dad works?"

She jabbed the fork into her meatloaf and left it there. "Why are you, like, all concerned about how I make money?"

"In New York, you're what we call a 'tough cookie.' I like that, and I just want to make sure you have something to go home to."

"And if I don't, are you going to set me up for life or something?"

David's warnings came back to me, along with his image of an endless line of people with their hands out. I replied, "I'm sure I can get you work in any of the businesses my father built. There's a fab shop where your welding skills would be a good fit. If you like the outdoors, there's the tree nursery you've been camping in, plus a wood pellet plant and seasonal work in the pecan groves."

"So, you kind of feel guilty about what happened to Wally?"

"No, but I feel bad about you heading back to a place with only limited options."

"Uh-huh." She wobbled her embedded fork and then pushed her plate aside. "Okay, I want a welding job. When can I start, and how much will you pay me?"

Grinning at what Tim would call her moxie, I wondered if they'd make a good couple. "I'll talk to the CEO and let you know," I said. "There's a B&B owner in town named Cindy Dwyer—she rented a room to Wally, and I'm sure she'll have space for you."

"I don't have any money. How long will you pay for my stay there?"

"Wow, you don't hold back. Are you gonna hit me up for a clothing and toiletries allowance, too?"

"That was, like, my next question. I'm sort of your personal makeover project, right? Rehabbing the poor but talented hick girl who fell into a murderer's clutches or whatever?"

"The way you put it makes me sound awful." I slid my plate out of the way, my temper rising again.

Gloria must've been eyeing us through the kitchen door. It

opened, and she headed toward us. "Y'all didn't eat that much," she said. "Wasn't it any good?"

Tara replied, "Yeah, no, definitely. It was the best. Can I get a to-go box?"

"Make that two," I said. "Thank you."

"Dessert for anyone? No? Okay, I'll be back in a jiffy." She departed with our plates.

I turned back to Tara. "You're doing your best to keep me seriously pissed off at you, but I know what it's like to have my heart broken. The anger you can feel at the world."

"But you're still going to rat me out in case I go all ungrateful on you?"

I shrugged. "You haven't exactly given me a helluva lot of 'grateful' yet, but, yeah, if you make any more trouble for me, I'm afraid I'd have to get the police involved."

"There's no proof I did anything."

"They're collecting your fingerprints at the crime scene right now."

She shook her head. "That's bogus — I wore gloves. It'd come down to your word against mine."

Before we could go at it some more, Gloria returned with takeout boxes. She said, "Thanks for coming in, Ms. Wright. And for bringing a guest," she added without turning to Tara. "We hope to see you again real soon. I'll have some unsweet tea made from now on."

I reached for my purse, but Gloria said, "There's no charge. Mr. Stapleton owned this franchise, so I reckon you do now."

"Yes, but don't I have to pay for her meal?"

Gloria shook her head. "Mr. Stapleton paid a lump sum at the first of the year that was good through December to cover him and anyone he brought in."

"Oh, that's kind of a relief. I pictured him eating here all alone."

"Good gracious, no. Other people eat here sometimes, out-of-towners mostly. And he was in lots of times with, um, a guest." She glanced at Tara with a critical eye, but then she seemed to catch herself. Looking back at me, she touched the padded leatherette near my head. "We saved this-here booth for him—he always sat just where you're sitting."

That gave me a creepy feeling, as if I were becoming my father. Plus, the look she'd directed at Tara started my mind churning in unsettling directions. I shivered and slid to the edge of the booth to retrieve my coat.

Gloria retreated a few steps to allow me to stand. She handed over my to-go box, letting Tara fend for herself. We exchanged holiday wishes, and I put a twenty on the table for her and the cook and headed to the door before she could protest.

Outside, the temperature hadn't budged. The thick gray clouds looked lower and darker than earlier, definitely promising snow. "Door's unlocked," I said.

"Why wouldn't it be?" Tara got in and set the box between her feet.

I put mine on the floor mat behind my seat and slipped behind the wheel. Crazy theories crowded my thoughts, based solely on Gloria's "guest" comment and the hairy eyeball she'd given Tara. What if this girl knew my father, had hung out with him? Maybe she convinced him she was his daughter from a long-ago love affair and teamed up with Wally on his murder, hoping to discover tons of money stashed in the house. What if she really *was* his daughter — making her my half-sister — and knew something no one else did about his murder? What if... what if....

As I guided the car up the boulevard toward the house, I asked in a conversational tone, "How long did you know my father?"

"What are you talking about?"

"How many times did you eat at the Denny's with my dad?"

She turned in her seat to face me. "So, I never even heard of your daddy before he got Wally killed. Why would you go all accusatory on me?"

I let the "got Wally killed" comment go, deciding to focus on the new mystery. "Gloria seemed to know you. Why?"

"She was giving me the bad eye since we walked in. That was the first time I was ever there." She pulled her bangs lower and stared at them, as if to recheck the color. "Maybe she's not a fan of, like, individualism."

"Maybe."

"Can I relax now, or is the inquisition going to continue?"

Rounding the final bend, I noted the police car stopped behind my rental and a thirty-something deputy huddled in a massive coat with a badge pinned to the outside. Despite being encumbered by thick gloves, he delicately skimmed a brush over the trunk lid. At his feet were a Styrofoam cup and a plastic case the size of a tackle box, which probably held his fingerprinting kit. I glanced at Tara and said, "Hey, it might just be getting started."

"Are you, like, kidding?"

"Yeah, no, maybe." I stopped behind his vehicle and shut off the engine.

We left the car with our takeout containers in hand. I approached the deputy while Tara hung back. "Thanks for coming out," I said to him. "I'm Janet Wright."

"Yep, I know." He set his tools on the pea gravel and straightened. Behind him, the black rental car trunk bore over a dozen pale ovals, as if I'd sped in reverse through a cloud of moths. "B.J. Tindale," he said in a twangy tenor. A wad of chewing tobacco pushed out the skin under his lower lip. B.J. pulled off his right glove, shook my hand, and then quickly covered up again. He probably regretted not wearing earmuffs under his Smokey Bear hat.

When the deputy looked past my shoulder, I introduced Tara to him. She merely waved from where she stood and called, "Finding anything?"

"I got a bunch of prints, yeah, but who they belong to is anybody's guess. You a friend of Ms. Wright's? I ain't seen you around town."

"We just met," I answered for her, "but we know some of the same people." Despite her lack of gratitude, I really did want to help Tara. Hopefully, she'd appreciate the good-faith effort I was making to keep her in the clear.

B.J. shook his head. "Nobody comes to town for months, then all of a sudden we got not one but *two* new folks—and trouble again." He tilted his face down and to the side, hollowing his cheeks as if about to spit, but then seemed to remember whose courtyard he was about to deface. After depositing a stream of brown goo into the Styrofoam, he tipped his hat to me and said, "'Scuse me, ma'am. I ought to get back to this so I can report to the chief." He cleared his throat. "Before I go, would you mind if I got me a set of your prints for comparison purposes?"

"Of course not—I'm sure most of the ones you found already are mine."

He looked past me again and asked, "You touch this car at any time?"

She held up her hands as if in surrender and laughed. "Yeah, no, I never laid a finger on it."

"Mind if I print you, too, just in case?"

"No problem."

"All-righty then." He crouched, lifted the bottle of fingerprint powder and its brush, and resumed skimming the trunk lid.

Tara and I walked up to the house. I unlocked the front door and stood aside so she could enter first. No way could I focus on any of the things I needed to get done until she was somewhere else. I said, "Have a seat while I see about a welding job for you. Then I'll call Cindy Dwyer to get you situated."

"While you do all that, I'll look for my daddy's gun."

I resisted replying, "You're welcome," as I carried the to-go boxes to the kitchen and stored them in the fridge. Then I tossed my coat over the luggage I'd left near the front door and opened my purse. There was still plenty of time to thank me after everything was squared away. I found Jeff Conway's business card and called the CEO. He didn't respond at his office number, but I got him when I tried his cell.

We exchanged greetings while Tara checked behind sofa cushions and crawled around, looking under furniture. I said, "This is my first chance to make a pain of myself, but I'm sure it won't be the last time."

"Anything, Ms. Wright. Just name it."

Thinking about the culture at the plant and the scarcity of

women, I said, "There's someone I met today who's an exceptional welder, a real artist, and is looking for work. I'm hoping you—I mean *we*—have an opening."

"Uh, sure, I reckon our payroll could take a hit for this friend of yours."

"I promise I wouldn't ask if this person wasn't well-qualified. You won't be sorry."

"I'm sure he'll be great."

I let that pass. "Thanks. What does the job pay?"

"Starting salary is thirty-five."

"Hold on." I tapped the mute icon, walked into the great room, and asked Tara, "How does thirty-five thousand dollars a year sound?"

She popped up behind the chair where I'd sat during our confrontation. "Forty."

"You're negotiating? Seriously? What chance do you have to make even thirty where you come from?"

"Forty."

I sighed and unmuted the phone. "Sorry," I said, "could we go as high as forty?"

"He must be really good," Conway said loudly and slowly, as if for the benefit of others nearby. "Yeah, I guess we could survive having a new welder start at forty."

I imagined the eye-rolling and muttering around him. No doubt I just lost any good will I'd generated the day before. "I really appreciate it," I said. "What would be a good start date?"

"We're closed between Christmas and New Year's, so why don't we say January 2nd?"

"Okay, that'll work."

"What's his name?"

"It's Tara Glenmont. Thanks again!" I ended the call before he could respond.

From her knees, Tara said, "So, I can't figure out where it went."

"I just got you a job that pays more than all your previous work put together. You can go home for the holidays and then start work on the 2nd."

"I'm, like, totally grateful." She looked at me for a beat and then went back to scanning the room again.

My conversation with Cindy Dwyer wasn't a negotiation but merely canceling my reservation and holding a room for Tara starting on January 1, with me footing the bill for the first thirty days. I didn't bring up Tara's connection with Wallace Landry—I figured she'd do that on her own, after she burrowed in like a tick.

Tara wasn't bad, I reminded myself, just self-absorbed and irrational, like any young person. After searching around and within the fireplace, she stood, wiped her hands on the seat of her jeans, and studied me. I must've glanced above her head, because she turned and looked up at the mantel. Without a word, she grasped the lip of the wood ledge and did an effortless pull-up to peer along the top.

After dropping to her feet, she whirled on me. "So, you knew all along, didn't you?"

I tried to sound surprised. "Is it up there? I guess that was the only place left."

"It totally stinks that you didn't say anything." She grabbed the back of a leather chair and pushed it toward the fireplace, the wood feet scraping across the flagstones.

I jogged over and blocked her path. "Get your camping

gear. I'll retrieve the gun and give it to you when I drop you at your home."

"No, I'll take the Jag." She pushed the chair, and the seat cushion pressed against my knees.

"You've taken all you're going to get from me." I leaned forward and grabbed the overstuffed leather arms to brace it. "You've got a great job and a place to stay until your first paycheck. That's a helluva lot."

She bumped my knees again with the cushion, despite my effort to keep the chair in place. "So, how do I, like, get to work on January 2nd?"

"Bum a ride off someone." I felt my feet sliding backward on the stones as she continued to force the chair against me. Damn, she was strong—I couldn't stop her.

"I'm not a bum."

Despite bearing down, teeth gritted, I still moved in reverse. Panic sweat pricked my face, and I snarled, "You sure smell like one."

"You suck." She gave the chair such a shove it knocked me onto my butt, and she kept pushing until the wood frame clipped my chin.

I sprawled, and my head bounced once on the smooth stone. Thick wood legs imprisoned me on both sides. I blinked up at the gray fabric stapled under the chair.

Instead of following through with more violence, Tara dashed past me. Tilting my head back, I watched her move, seemingly upside down, to the mantel. She did another pull-up but this time got her elbows onto the ledge and levered herself even higher as she reached to her left.

Afraid of being an easy target once Tara had her gun, I started to push the chair toward my feet so I could wriggle free. I heard a click and then, with a sound of stone scraping against stone, the floor square beneath me began to descend. The surprise temporarily paralyzed me as I continued to sink, still surrounded by the chair. My father's trapdoor-elevator that had scared the shit out of David was doing the same to me.

Tara was no longer visible as I lowered into a basement. Fluorescent lights in the drop ceiling flickered on as I passed them. Over an electric whine and the metal-sliding-on-metal noise of whatever mechanism allowed this platform to go down—and hopefully back up—I heard her say, "So, I noticed a hairline crack between the blocks of stone when I was crawling around. Then I found this, like, switch, up here. I guess your daddy was a tall dude, to be able to reach it easy."

The platform beneath me stopped with a bump. Ten feet above, Tara peered down through the large square hole. She held her father's revolver but fortunately wasn't aiming at me. Yet, anyway.

"Okay, that was fun," I called up to her. "Please push the switch again so I can go back up." Getting claustrophobic under the chair, I squirmed out with zero grace and tumbled off the platform, landing on my hands and knees atop thickly padded carpet. At least my dad had created a well-appointed man-cave. I climbed to my feet and staggered away from the contraption.

"Yeah, no. I tried that, but it's not working now. Maybe it's made that way to keep someone from getting trapped down there—you probably have to find a button at your end."

I looked at the wood columns set around the platform,

searching for an obvious switch, but got distracted by a row of architectural images along one paneled wall. Clearly they had been shot by the same skilled photographer who'd done the ones in the great room. I turned, expecting to see more pictures, but the remaining three walls were bare. Well, not exactly.

When I walked closer, I could make out a row of evenly spaced putty marks that dappled the paneling, slightly lighter than the wood but apparently meant to conceal nail holes on those three walls. Maybe for picture hangers. Dozens of them.

With another click, the flagstone square and chair rose toward the ceiling. Damn that girl, she'd tricked me. It turned out I wasn't a match for this punk after all.

I ran back and grabbed the edge of the stone as it ascended above my head. However, I had several problems: I wasn't strong enough to pull myself onto it, and, if I just hung on, the seam into which the stone would fit up above would squash or cut off anything overhanging the lip. Such as my fingers. Then the basement lights went out.

16

I LET GO AND FELL ABOUT SIX FEET, LANDING HARD ON MY HEELS AND THEN TOPPLING BACKward onto my butt. The square of bleak daylight from the great room above vanished as the stone rose and filled in the gap.

Complete darkness. Disoriented and panicked, it took me a few minutes of patting the carpet around me to find my cell phone, which had popped out of my back pocket. In the soft blue glow of the screen, I swiped through the icons until I found the flashlight.

Previously useful in reading menus at romantically dim restaurants and finding my apartment door lock when the super failed to replace burned-out hallway bulbs, the app hopefully would allow me to discover a way out. My phone showed no signal, so I couldn't call Cade even if I wanted to. Not that I did. No way would I let someone half my age get the better of me.

Still, when things started to go wrong earlier, maybe I should've shouted for Deputy B.J. Tindale or run outside to him. Monday morning quarterbacking was so not helpful.

The flashlight provided a dazzling cone of brightness. I searched around the columns that surrounded the platform mechanism, which rose above me in a series of diamond-shaped metal joints that would fold upon themselves and flatten when the square of flagstone came down again. Much cooler than David's secret pocket door, for what that was worth.

I couldn't hear anything overhead, but I figured Tara had made her escape by now. Then I remembered my purse was up there, with my keys in it, ripe for the picking. She could only steal one car at a time — and clearly she'd fallen for the Jag — but with Christmas only two days away, it would take forever to get someone out to change the house locks. Plus the locks at all of my dad's properties. And only God and Google knew where the nearest German car dealerships were, so I could get the remaining cars towed and rekeyed.

Cussing, I resumed my search and finally found a switch mounted on one column. I half-expected Tara to have disabled the mechanism at her end. However, the platform descended with the electrical whine and scissoring scrape of metal that I'd heard earlier. The massive leather chair remained atop it.

When the overhead fluorescent lights automatically came on again, I returned the phone to my back pocket. I hopped onto the stone square before it had completed its descent, sat in the chair because it took up most of the space, and used the toe of my boot to flick the switch again. Heading back up, I realized my gun was in my coat. Near the front door. Maybe with Tara still there. It was possible I was rising into a trap unarmed.

I considered crawling under the chair again so her first shots would miss me, but then what? Wiggle my way to safety? No, better to dive one way or the other if she turned out to be as murderous as her fiancé. Still, I tried to make myself a smaller target on the chair by hunching over and cringing as I emerged through the floor and back into the great room.

Again before the platform stopped, I was in motion, this time rolling across the floor in the direction of the fireplace. I thought I could grab a poker or something, but my focus on that plan vanished as I bounced across flagstone slabs, accumulating deep bruises.

I peeked over the back of the couch. No sign of Tara. Also, I noticed the lack of three things: my purse, my coat, and the camping gear. Other than my suitcases, the girl had cleaned me out as she was clearing out.

Rubbing my sore knees, I winced and hobbled to the front door. Only twenty years before, I would regularly slide face-first across home plate and hop up to high-five my softball teammates without noticing my sprained fingers and abraded arms. God, I hated forty.

I stepped onto the porch just in time to see Deputy Tindale remove his Smokey hat and lean into his car. "Wait," I shouted.

B.J. popped out so fast, he bumped his bare head on the door sill. It looked like he wanted to spit on the courtyard again. Instead, he lifted his gunk-filled Styrofoam cup and treated me to another display of chewing tobacco extrusion. After sucking wet brown strands from his lower lip, he said, "I ain't going nowhere, Ms. Wright. Gotta get your prints."

He left his hat inside the patrol car and picked up the kit at his feet. "Missed getting them from the little lady with the painted hair, but she said she had to run a errand right quick and would come on back."

"Did you have that conversation while she was driving a green Jaguar?"

"Yes, ma'am. Right pretty thing with a lot of power. Threw stones every which way when she got it revved up good." He indicated huge gouges in the pea gravel.

I said, "I'm glad you got a good look, because I need you to put out an APB or whatever you call it— Tara Glenmont stole that car, my purse, and my coat, which has a pistol in one pocket."

"Is that right? She sure don't seem the type. Well, 'cept for the hair and face studs anyway."

"Tell me about it—if I knew she was a psycho I would've turned her over to you when we pulled up." I led him inside the house.

The deputy set the fingerprint kit and spit cup at his feet, tucked his gloves into his coat pockets, and took a notebook identical to Cade's from his pants. "No call for putting a 'psycho' label on her, ma'am. Chief don't like it when we label folks. Even the dirt bags." He clicked a pen. "You know the tag for that car? Never seen anyone but your daddy driving such a thing around town, so we can spot her easy, but chances are she's on the highway by now."

My shoulders slumped. "I guess the license plate number is on the vehicle registration card Mr. Pearson gave me. Which I'd put in my wallet, in my purse, which she stole."

"I can make a call to Driver Services, see what they got on record. I reckon it's still in your daddy's name?"

"Yes, until I get a local driver's license." Item number twenty-seven on my ever-growing To-Do list. Tearing each painted hair out of Tara's head had become priority number one.

"I'll alert the chief and then track down that-there tag."

As the deputy withdrew his cell phone and lifted his spit cup, I remembered the legal pad on the dining room table. I said, "Maybe I wrote down the car info—be back in a minute." The bruises in my knees still ached as I jogged past the fireplace and into the dining room. Served me right for pretending to be an action hero.

The legal pad was gone—with security codes for the house and garage, all of my notes about the businesses, financial details about the estate, everything Mr. Pearson had told me. It shouldn't have surprised me. How else could she have gotten the Jag out of the garage? I would've been able to recreate most of the details from the mound of paperwork he'd given me, but I'd left the stack on the table, and Tara had snatched that up, too. On a hunch, I went into the kitchen and checked the fridge. Yes, the little bitch had even swiped the lunch leftovers.

She'd taken her revenge for Landry's death, with me as the stand-in for everyone she held responsible. I had an image of her striding to the garage with both arms full and camping gear slung over her back. It might've been the only thing that had kept her from stealing my luggage.

Tim was off filing duplicates of my paperwork with the county courthouse, so I still could retrieve it but not without a lot of hassle—seeing as how Tara had all of my identification. I did remember the security and garage codes, but I had no idea how to change them and no user manuals. And with Tara having the keys to the house, I couldn't stay here anyway.

Suddenly I didn't care how much she was hurting inside; my empathy reserves had run dry. All of this havoc, created so quickly by just one obnoxious, tie-dyed brat. I kicked a cabinet over and over, so hard the pots rattled inside it, and shrieked enough curses to overflow Tara's grandmother's goddamn swear jar and bring Deputy Tindale running, spit cup in one hand and pistol in the other.

From the kitchen entrance, he looked me over and re-holstered. "You okay, ma'am? I thought she'd come back and was giving you what for."

I gulped air to stop panting and tried to recover whatever shreds of dignity I could by standing taller and straightening my black pantsuit. He kept staring at me as if I were crazy, so I fluffed my hair and tried patting down Mom's cowlick as well. Finally, I said, "No luck on the tag number. You?"

"Uh, I just got off my call with the chief." He watched me a moment longer, made another contribution to his Styrofoam, and added, "He says hey."

"That all?"

"No, ma'am, he started out the door as I made my report and is driving through town, in case the girl stuck around. Said he'd call J.D. in early—he's third shift—and get him on patrol, too. Counting me, you got the whole of the Graylee police force working this-here case."

Cade, B.J., and J.D. Hot damn, Tara was toast. There was no point in acting snarky, so I said, "I really appreciate that. Thank you."

He tipped his cap with his free hand and asked, "Okay if I call Driver Services now?"

"Sure. Do you need info about my father?"

"Naw, I helped the chief with all that paperwork back in July. Know your daddy's particulars better'n my own."

"That's good, because Tara also took that from me when she stole all the stuff from my dining room table."

B.J. shook his head. "Snatched that, too? Mm-mm-mm, we got us a regular Bonnie Parker on our hands." Misinterpreting my expression as confusion rather than aggravation, he supplied, "She ran with Clyde Barrow, ma'am. Back in the thirties. Gangsters, they was."

"I got the reference."

He spat, sucked his brown-speckled lip, and said, "I'll just make that call. Then would you mind if I get your fingerprinting out the way?"

I'd temporarily forgotten the incidents that had started the whole avalanche called "What Happened When I Decided to Move to Graylee, Georgia." Putting a brighter tone in my voice, I said, "Oh, here's some good news, finally. It was Tara who vandalized the rental car and statue."

Deputy Tindale scowled at me, maybe thinking about how much work he'd just done in the wintry outdoors with frostbite imminent and snow-maggedon almost upon us. "You know that for a fact, Ms. Wright?"

"Absolutely—she told me."

He removed his notebook again, looked at his two occupied hands, and paused. Then he set his stinking cup full of brown slime on the granite counter between us and clicked open his ballpoint pen so hard the plastic cracked. "Exactly when did this happen?" he demanded.

In this case, the truth would not set me free. The truth, at best, would earn me a stern lecture and make the deputy conclude I was getting what I deserved. At worst, he'd charge me with a crime for withholding evidence. Maybe I had reaped what I'd sown, but I was not taking the fall for giving Tara a second chance. I told him, "Right before she stole the Jag, she trapped me in the basement and taunted me by saying she'd done all that damage herself."

"How'd you get out?"

"I'll take you through the whole thing after you call the DMV and put out the APB. Or whatever," I added, ears burning because of how foolish I sounded.

B.J. eyed me once more, put away the pen and pad, took out his cell phone, retrieved his spit cup, and trudged toward the front of the house. As he scuffed in figure-eights around my wheeled luggage near the front door, I thought about what I needed to do.

It was the same thought I'd had before Tara rang the doorbell only a few hours ago. Way back then I needed to get a weapon for self-defense and pick out which car to drive to Cindy's. Tara had eliminated my ability to choose a vehicle, having stolen the keys for all of them, and she'd taken my coat with the pistol in it. But Dad had owned two firearms, and I was feeling more vulnerable than ever.

I went up the east-wing staircase to the second floor and returned to the master suite. Gripped by an irrational fear that she had snatched the second weapon, too, I rushed into my father's bedroom, dropped to my bruised knees, and winced as splinters of the shattered porcelain lampshade jabbed through the black slacks. Ducking to peer under the bed, I banged my forehead on the wood frame hard enough to blur my vision. I groped blindly, but the gun vault wasn't there.

How was that even possible? Tara wasn't just a resourceful thief and vandal—she was some kind of supernatural monster. With a groan, I fell onto my left side, ignoring the crunch of ceramic that pin-cushioned me with a hundred shards and powdered my hair, face, and clothes with flecks of china.

Gazing into the darkness under the bed, I finally focused my eyes and noticed something blacker still. The gun vault. I'd light-ened it earlier by taking the chrome pistol and ammunition, and, when I slid it back under the bed, it went farther than I'd thought. Tara was just a person, nothing more. I could deal with her.

With mounting relief, I pulled the laptop-size black case to-ward me. Hopefully another confrontation wouldn't come down to violence, but if she attacked me again, she'd get a nasty surprise.

I sat upright in the ceramic dust, pulled the case onto my lap, and tried to open the lid. It didn't budge. The nasty surprise was mine: in my paranoid New Yorker, always-lock-the-door idiocy, I'd closed the case earlier, turned the key in the top without a thought, and blocked myself from accessing some serious self-defense.

Too tired to pitch another fit, I just struggled to my feet and lugged the twenty-pound case back down the stairs by its molded plastic handle. Hopefully Deputy Tindale would pick the lock for me.

B.J. was still on the phone when I walked into the great room. He stopped talking and looked me up and down. It wasn't a sa-lacious leer, and it wasn't the "Jeez, this woman's crazy" onceover he'd given me in the kitchen. His look said, "What the hell hap-pened to you now, lady?"

After glancing down at what had started the day as my fa-vorite black wool Dolce & Gabanna pantsuit, I dropped the gun vault and said, "Back in a minute."

I retreated to the bathroom, where I could gape in privacy at my reflection from different angles in the mirror. The entire left side of my outfit, both knees and butt cheeks, and my hand, hair, and that side of my face bore the glittering, powdery outcome of my latest debacle.

With my right side facing the mirror—Mom's cowlick bobbing jauntily—I still resembled Janet Wright, intrepid heiress and would-be philanthropist and writer who was destined to find true love in tiny Graylee, Georgia. Turned the other way, I appeared to be a hapless office worker who'd been mugged by someone wielding a sock full of ground glass and flour.

Right side: "Before meeting Tara Glenmont." Left side: "After." Right side…left side….

Glaring past my reflection, I noticed the walk-in shower behind me, the glass door still dappled with water from Tara's cleanup. I definitely needed a wash and change of clothes as well. Then what? Hitch a ride with Deputy Tindale to Cindy Dwyer's and either hunker down until a Statie caught up to Tara or I found the energy to see about new ID, credit cards, and everything else.

Hell, I hadn't even thought about money. When the estate cleared probate I didn't think I'd ever need to again, but now I didn't have a single dollar on me. I imagined my next call to Jeff Conway: "Remember that welder I asked you to hire? Scratch that—she robbed me blind. Instead I need an advance on my salary, and, by the way, could you please deliver that to me as a sack full of actual money, seeing as how I have no means of cashing a check?"

Good news: at least I could eat for free at Denny's until the first of the year. Bad news: I'd have to take all of my meals there for the foreseeable future. Good news…bad news….

17

STANDING NEAR THE FIREPLACE, THE DEPUTY CLICKED OFF HIS LATEST CALL AS I TRAIPSED back into the great room. "Word's gone out on the Jag, ma'am," he said. "Statewide."

"Thanks."

"You okay? Looks like you took some kind of fall."

"I was looking for this and got a little dirty." I tapped the gun vault with my boot. "Unfortunately, the key to it was on the ring in my purse that Tara stole. Can you pick locks?"

"No, ma'am."

Damn. In the movies, all the cops knew how to do that. "Can you shoot it open?"

B.J. glanced at the case and appeared to give it some thought. "Not a good idea, what with the ammo that's probably in there." He just looked back at me, apparently not willing or able to offer a solution. His gaze flicked again and again to the powdery ruin of my left side.

I sighed and said, "I need to go to Cindy Dwyer's, but would you mind waiting while I freshen up? There's coffee in the kitchen and leftover pasta in the fridge—help yourself."

"Chief told me to see to you, make sure you got settled in." He spat into his Styrofoam.

It probably was an indication of what he thought about that

duty, but Cade's consideration touched me. I assured B.J., "It'll just take me an hour to get ready."

He blinked at me. "A whole hour?" His examination of my left side resumed, now accompanied by an expression that seemed to say it was a lot of time to spend for such an unpromising outcome. Or maybe I was projecting.

I said, "If you want to go and come back, that would be fine, too. I wouldn't impose, but I don't have money for a cab."

"Naw, it's okay, I reckon." He examined the great room, perhaps trying to decide where he wanted to wait.

After looking at what twice had been my battleground with Tara, I walked over to the fireplace mantel. "Here's something cool you can play with. Sit in that big leather chair."

೮೨

There was just enough lag time between pushing the button atop the mantel and the start of descent to get in position on the square of flagstone. B.J. had taken to it like a kid at Six Flags.

Still damp from the shower—somehow Tara had managed to soak all of the towels, and I'd been forced to wring them out and reuse them—I donned comfort clothes: a fuzzy, roll-neck, mohair sweater in mocha over a plain tee, flannel-lined jeans, and my favorite ankle boots. I assumed the deputy was still taking himself down to the basement and back up again, over and over, as I finished with my make-up and did the right side-left side comparison a final time. It seemed to be me from all angles again, which would have to be good enough.

I called Cindy Dwyer back about returning to the original

plan of me staying with her and scratching Tara's reservation. Then I rolled the two suitcases out of the bathroom in time to hear the click, electric whine, and scissoring metal that indicated a happy lawman, oblivious that an hour had passed so quickly.

Peering down through the square gap at the lit basement below, I said, "Deputy? I'm ready when you are."

His voice echoed a bit as he called from the recesses, "You see all the photo lab stuff and cameras and all? There's a whole 'nother room set up for a shoot."

"No, I must've missed that when I was fearing for my life."

"Come on down and take a look—you came into some right fancy gear."

"Uh, sorry, no spelunking tools up here." Actually, that wasn't true. I'd packed so many belts, I could've linked them all together, secured one end to a couch leg, and shimmied down. The deputy didn't respond, so I pointed out another fallacy. "If I press the switch, the platform will come up and the basement lights will go out."

"Well that ain't good. Never did like the dark much." Soon, the platform started its ascent, and I backed away so I wouldn't crowd him. B.J. rose through the floor, seated in the leather chair like the King of the Rednecks, his .45-caliber sword in its holster, his scepter a radiantly white spit cup. At some point in the last hour he'd exchanged the half-filled one for new Styrofoam, making me wonder if I'd find the used one in my trashcan. Note to self: Don't reach into the garbage blindly.

"Thanks for waiting," I said.

"Sure thing—that was a hoot. I knew your daddy liked to take pictures, but don't that beat all what kind of setup he had."

"Did he just shoot landscapes and architecture?"

"Naw, he'd take picture of just about anything or anyone. Never saw him without a camera around his neck when he was tooling around town." The deputy took in the large shots mounted on the walls. "He loved to shoot high school sports, too. Had a reserved seat at all the games."

He walked with me to the foyer to collect the luggage but then stopped and stared out the windows in horror and fascination. "Uh oh," he said. "It's started."

I spun around to look in the same direction. Outside, fat flakes drifted down. "You've seen snow before, right?"

"Sure. Every five years or so we get a tich of it. Sometimes it sticks around, turns to ice. Trucks spinning out, bumper cars on all the streets, broken bones from falls. We best get moving."

Doing a final walkthrough, I spotted something outside the kitchen windows: Tara had left the garage door open. Why I expected her to show any sort of consideration I didn't know, but it pissed me off all over again. I marched through the back door and out into a fantasy snow globe. Silence except for the gentle tick of flakes settling on everything. Immediately I felt my temper calm and a smile warm my face.

What I still liked best about Graylee was that hush, as if I were a million miles from the chaotic clatter of any city. Deep into the night, I knew my Horsewomen would return with a vengeance to tell me I was, in fact, that far from anyone who possibly could love me. For now, though, I didn't hear those hoof beats — there was only the delicate landing of a thousand tender spots of snow.

"Careful, ma'am," B.J. called behind my back.

I checked the path around my feet. The snow was sticking, sure, but it would need to come down like this for hours just to blot out the ground. "I lived in New York most of my life," I reminded him, as he sheltered under the porch overhang. "Walked on a 'tich' more than this."

At the garage door, I entered the code to lower it and noted there now were three empty bays. Tara has stolen the Jag, the BMW was stranded in the courtyard, and there was the space with only faint oil drips to show some mystery vehicle once had been there.

Back up on the porch with the deputy, he looked at me head-to-toe and back again, perhaps wondering how anyone could've survived such an onslaught by nature. I grinned and did a full rotation for him, to display the fat, glistening flakes stuck to me. "Covered in white again, but at least this will melt."

"Hurry now." He glanced again at the weather and muttered, "This keeps up, it'll be a danged white Christmas for sure."

We each took a suitcase. B.J. refused to let my luggage roll behind him — maybe he thought it was more macho to carry the pink and purple bag. At the front door, I stopped to punch in the security number, in case someone other than Tara decided to drop by, seeing as how I couldn't lock up. And who knows, maybe she would lose the yellow pad with the code and get caught revisiting the scene of her crimes.

Before we headed out, I also hefted the twenty-pound kettlebell I'd created from what had been a perfectly good gun vault. I told myself it balanced the suitcase I hauled in my other hand, down the steps and out to the deputy's cruiser. Cade would've taken these items from me and I would've reluctantly — but gratefully—let him be chivalrous. B.J., however, didn't seem to notice my arms stretching longer with every step, and anyway he did have to carry his spit cup in his free hand.

The snowfall had thickened a bit, making me narrow my eyes as we walked to the cruiser. My cute mohair sweater wasn't exactly wicking away the moisture and promised to be a wet mess for a while. I really missed that coat Tara stole.

With everything stowed in the trunk except the Styrofoam, which went into a cup-holder near his hat on the console between us, we settled into our seats. B.J. cranked up the heat and put the wipers on a slow, groaning sweep across the damp windshield. When the glass cleared, I glanced at my father's house—I was leaving it yet again, with no certainty about when I'd be back.

The deputy sawed the wheel one way and then the other and rocked the car with abrupt starts, stops, and reverses. I saw his dilemma. He'd parked close behind the rental car with the flattened tires, and then I parked the Beamer behind him. Not tight on his bumper like on a New York street, but close enough to make him work hard.

"Think we'll escape?" I asked him.

He only grunted and continued to extricate us an inch at a time. To distract him from wanting to kill me for putting him in this predicament, I said, "Did my father once have a fourth car? There are four spaces in the garage."

"Naw, that last one was for the girls."

I turned to him. "He had other daughters?"

"What?" His tobacco-packed lower lip pushed out farther in ridicule. "No, the girl that would stay there each year."

I imagined a parade of live-in girlfriends, my father replacing one with another annually. Maybe that's why Mom had left him—he got bored easily and just couldn't keep his hands off other women. It also would explain the weird mix of decorating styles—the Hemingway and Laura Ashley mashup. I guess he had so much space he let them have their choice of suites to decorate. Of course, maybe it was just a live-in maid that Dad swapped out each year while he led a monkish existence. Add another mystery to the pile.

The deputy pounded the steering wheel. "Look, I'm gonna have to nudge one of your cars or the other. You pick."

"The rental. We'll just include the dent in the vandalism report Cade wrote up."

B.J. said, "Buckle up." He bared tobacco-flecked teeth, stomped the gas, and banged into the beleaguered sedan probably a little harder than he needed to. Even with the tires flattened, the rental rolled forward a few feet. He moved us clear at last and made a big half-circle across the snow-speckled courtyard to point the cruiser toward town.

My phone rang. The scooped-out seat behind me made it easy to reach into my back pocket. I checked the screen and saw Cade Wilson's name and cell number. Plugging one ear with my index finger so I could hear him over the rubber-on-damp-glass squeal and stutter of the wipers, I drawled, "Darrell's Demolition Derby, what can we do fer ya?"

"Uh…everything all right?"

We coasted onto Brady Stapleton Boulevard, which showed white patches where the snow hadn't melted. I switched to my regular voice. "Sure, Deputy Tindale is moving heaven and earth to get me to Cindy's. Any luck finding Tara?"

"No. I got J.D. checking the neighborhoods, and I've been doing the side streets, but I think she's long gone. We need to quit the hunt anyway, because the snow's starting to stick and we'll be responding to calls soon."

"I heard. Hey, the one bright spot about Tara is that she solved 'the why' for us: Wallace Landry was her fiancé and wanted to get enough cash to buy her an engagement ring. It's like the cop shows always say: follow the money."

"Darn, I knew I should've paid more attention to those shows. Talk to you after I binge-watch some *Law & Order*, so I can do my job better." He ended the call.

Playful friskiness underlay his derision, a good sign. The snow would be a major plus if it kept up: it could strand Bebe way out in the woods at David's, while I would be close by in case Cade had time for dinner. If he didn't, I could help him set out roadside flares at accident scenes and assist with fallen pedestrians. Afterward, we'd warm up with some brandy at his place.

On Main Street, B.J. jounced me out of my fantasy by jabbing my arm and pointing repeatedly at the road, which had begun to show faint tire tracks through un-melted snow. Only a few cars remained parked in the slanted spaces, their windshields, hoods, and roofs slowly turning white. Graylee had rolled up its sidewalks early. Not a single person was outside, and the lights of the diner and other businesses had been turned off. I looked behind me and saw the Denny's was dark as well. So much for my free meals.

"Cade hung up," I said, "so feel free to give voice to your panic."

He frowned at me and replied, "I'm telling you, this is the real deal. We're gonna spend tonight and all of Christmas Eve on accidents, stuck cars, and folks slipping on the ice."

"It'll be a nice change of pace from the weekend drunks, meth dealers, and brawlers Cade told me about."

"That'll be Christmas and the days after. Domestic violence goes way up. DUIs and overdoses through the roof. Snow and the holidays make everything that much worser."

"Bah humbug." He didn't appear to be in the mood, so I dropped the banter and thought back to his earlier comment. "Did my dad have a lot of girlfriends?"

"One a year, like I said." We headed into a neighborhood behind Main Street, nearly all of the houses bright with Christmas lights as the sky darkened further and the snow kept on coming. In one yard, some kids methodically slid all of the so-called accumulation together in an attempt to build the smallest snowman ever. In another yard, a boy used a plastic tarp as a makeshift sled to pull a girl across green grass dappled with white.

We stopped in the driveway of a lovely lavender Victorian with white gingerbread moldings and old-fashioned, big-bulb colored lights draped over fir trees in the front yard and strung across the porch railing. A sign hanging from a wrought-iron pole identified the house as the "Graylee Bed & Breakfast" and promised a "stay in gracious luxury."

"Any of them still live here?"

"Not the younger ones, like Cindy's daughter, but I heard Cindy once dated your daddy for a bit. Long time ago."

18

THE DEPUTY DIDN'T ELABORATE AS HE ASSISTED ME WITH THE LUGGAGE. HE MERELY WISHED me luck and left me on the porch. I waved as he backed down the drive. A blur of white continued to settle in the grass and even balance on the pine needles and narrowest tree limbs.

Behind me, the front door opened, followed by the screen door. "I know it's a cliché," the voice of a middle-aged woman drawled, "but we Southerners do love our snow." I turned to her—trim build, face sagging a bit at the edges, hair dyed raven-black, stylish glasses. Eyes as dark as her hair and not nearly as welcoming as her smile. "Can't drive on it a lick," she added, "but we sure do think it's pretty to look at."

"Janet Wright," I said automatically, putting out my hand.

"I know," she replied, shaking it. "Cindy Dwyer. I'm looking forward to getting to know you better."

I gestured at the snowfall, the accumulation of which might've reached a whole sixteenth of an inch in spots. "I hope so, since we might be cooped up for days."

She nodded in earnest and hugged herself, shivering in her sweater, slacks, and boots. "I went to the store and bought milk and eggs and bread. Good thing I went early—a friend on Facebook said they've sold out of all that now."

"I guess everyone here sees snow and wants to make French toast?"

Cindy laughed. "I never thought of that, but maybe it's what I'll fix for breakfast tomorrow instead of the usual menu."

"You have other guests coming for the holidays?"

"Always a few. They ought to be here soon unless the weather keeps up. It can be fractious at some family get-togethers, everybody cooped up in one house, so my place is a kind of refuge. A sanctuary where folks can recharge before going back into battle."

She helped me get my bags indoors. I carried the gun vault and kept the name facing away from her, worried that she might react badly to me bringing a weapon, even if it was trapped inside a dense plastic shell.

The interior of her home reminded me of any number of bed-and-breakfasts I'd stayed in: woods polished with fragrant lemon oil, sedate blue-yellow flames in the gas fireplace, bookcases, antiques, doilies, and scented candles galore. What always drew me in, though, were the personal items of the host. A family photo on one wall of her opulent parlor showed a much younger Cindy—with authentically black hair—arm-in-arm with a tall, mustached man, an adolescent girl and a younger boy standing in front of them.

We bypassed a large staircase, and Cindy led me to a guestroom in the back of the house. "This one is my favorite," she said, unlocking the door and handing me the brass key, which was labeled "Dan. Mod." The door opened onto a medium-sized sitting room decorated in Danish Modern earth tones, with low-slung chairs, long, narrow tables, and boxy lamps. Either teak was her favorite thing, or she longed for a return to the 1960s.

In the next room, I wasn't surprised to find a platform bed, a dresser with lots of slim drawers, and more horizontal lines everywhere I looked. Even the bathroom had teak cabinets and a sandalwood frame bordering the bathtub. No shower attachments: anything with a vertical orientation apparently would've been in violation of the Scandinavian aesthetic.

The preponderance of horizontals made me want to follow suit and lie down, but B.J.'s comments about my dad, Cindy, and her daughter wouldn't let me rest. "It's lovely," I told her. "Would you mind if I made some coffee? We could talk and watch the snow."

"Hot tea would be even better. Kitchen's this way."

Though I wasn't a fan of hot tea, I decided not to insist. She'd no doubt heard about my "benevolent dictator" crack—and word probably had gotten around about my Denny's meltdown already—so I needed to counteract all of that with a charm offensive.

She led me to the foyer, turned right into a dining room with a maple table that could seat a dozen, and walked toward the back again. We ended up in a large, warm kitchen with a granite island, a six-burner range, a sink large enough to bathe a German shepherd, and a corner fireplace. Blue gas-jet flames there made the ceramic logs glow in oranges and reds.

Cindy filled a kettle and put it on the stove. From a sideboard, she lifted a leatherette case and, in full hostess mode, opened it toward me to display rows of tea bags in different flavors. At random I selected "wild persimmon honeysuckle" or something like that and then helped her set out teacups, saucers, and a full complement of sweeteners in the dining room. I would've been fine sitting at the vintage Formica table on one side of the kitchen, but she wanted to "put on the dog" as Mom would've said.

"Milk or lemon?" she asked.

"Neither, thank you. Please sit—this is too much."

"Nonsense. I haven't had any guests since Thanksgiving, and I don't want to get out of practice." She disappeared into the kitchen again, where the tea kettle had begun to whistle. While I settled in to watch the snow through lace curtains, I heard a microwave purring. Cindy soon returned with a china teapot and a basket of miniature muffins with a sidecar of butter, jam, and honey packets.

She poured hot water into my cup and sat across from me. As our teabags steeped, we each selected a muffin—blueberry for me, cornbread for her—and prepared them with the spreads. She touched up her snack with a little more honey and asked, "What's wrong at your father's house?"

"Just some security issues. I need to get the locks changed and alarm code reset." I chewed a bit of the warm, buttery muffin. "Moving into a place where other people have had access, you want to make sure you're safe."

Cindy looked at me over the top of her teacup. "I guess living up North in that big ol' scary city would do that to a body."

Playing along, I said, "Yeah, typical New York paranoia."

Instead of dropping it, she replied, "Even if the only people with access have been Phil Pearson and the police?"

"I wish that were the case, but I lost my keys."

"Oh, that's too bad. Otherwise, you liking the house all right?"

"If you want to switch with me, it wouldn't break my heart." I gestured with my butter knife at the Blue Willow plates hanging on the walls and faux-British bric-a-brac. "This is much more my style—with the Danish Modern suite for sleeping, of course," I added.

"I haven't seen it in years, naturally," she started, and then paused, perhaps wondering if she'd opened a topic she didn't want me to pursue. "Anyway, what's it like?"

"Imagine Ernest Hemingway and Laura Ashley each decorated half of it."

She sipped her tea. "You mean, randomly? Like an Ernest kitchen and a Laura dining room?"

"No, very specifically. Ernest's hunting lodge exterior carries inside to the great room, dining room, kitchen, and master. Then there are these wings upstairs and down with a suite in each. All four of those are by Laura."

I drank a little of the fruit-and-flower-scented tea and considered the point of no return I was about to cross. "Am I right to think a lot of women stayed there over the years?" I paused and then added, "Or was he mostly into girls?"

She stiffened, making me think B.J.'s comment about "girls" had been more literal than I'd hoped. But they couldn't have been girl-girls. They were girls who drove and whose cars had a space reserved in the garage. She still didn't answer, now feigning interest in the snowfall, her face serious. The friendly mask she'd struggled to wear since my arrival had melted entirely.

Girls who drove. Dad's passion for photography and missing pictures on the basement walls. The hairy eyeball Gloria had given Tara. Cindy and her daughter both dating my father at some point in their lives. It all swirled in my mind and created an ugly picture. In a confiding voice, I said, "I know we're taught not to speak ill of the dead, but I need to understand what happened here, what my father was like. Did he do...pornography with teenage girls?"

"Oh my God, no, of course not!" She scowled at me. "Maybe that sort of thing goes on in New York City, but what kind of people do you think we are? We certainly wouldn't let that happen under our noses." The indignation was pitch-perfect. Either she was as good an actor as Bebe or I'd been way off-base. That was a huge relief—but still didn't give me the real story.

"Sorry," I said, "I put two and two together and came up with seven. No one will talk about things directly, so I'm left to guess."

"Mary Grace would've been so disappointed—having a daughter who could conjure such a filthy idea."

"I think every daughter feels like she's a disappointment to her mother. And sometimes vice versa." I let that sink in. "I heard you dated my dad. Was that before my mom came along or after she left town with me and my brother?"

Cindy blotted her lips, folded her napkin precisely, and said, "It's a good thing you haven't unpacked, because I'm demanding that you leave right now."

So much for my charm offensive. I stood and threw my napkin over my plate and teacup. Time to play the only card I had left. "How much do you want?"

She leaned back in her chair, as if I'd slapped her. "What?"

"How much to talk?" I gestured at the well-appointed room, the plaster ceiling that showed more than a few cracks and water stains. "Place like this must cost a small fortune to keep up. I happen to have come into a large fortune. Ten thousand to talk to me? Twenty?"

She stood, fists clenched. "You certainly are Brady's daughter. He thought he could buy anything with money. Loyalty, silence. You're—"

"So, he paid for your silence? I'll double it so you'll talk to me."
Her voice broke as she screeched, "Get out of my house."

Hopefully just one more push was all she needed, because my
interrogation was starting to feel sadistic. I asked, "Did it involve
your daughter? Do you want me to believe the worst rather than
know the truth?"

Cindy dropped into her chair and closed her eyes. "No, the
truth is the worst. Just a different kind of bad."

"Tell me." I leaned across the table. "Why do so many people
in town look at me like I'm the daughter of the devil or they're
deciding how hard they want to punch me in the face? Do they
think me and my dad are the same person?"

"Not literally." Eyes open again, staring at her folded napkin,
she sounded about a hundred years old. "But maybe we can't believe he's really, truly, finally gone. You show up and it's like what
we feared all along—he's come back to haunt us. Risen from the
grave, like something from one of David's books."

"But I'm not my father, dammit." I found myself still leaning
into her space, so I sat and waited.

She turned and faced the window. A couple of pads of snow
slid down it in long, icy rivulets. "We're all damned," she whispered. "Damned by our silence. Our complicity."

"Tell me why."

She misunderstood, answering the question maybe she and
many others in Graylee had asked themselves countless times.
Not why they were damned but why they'd chosen to be silent,
complicit: "Money, of course. Big-city salaries, huge bonuses, with a small-town cost of living. Well, getting pricier all the
time what with the upscale shops and all, but still—having nice

things, good places to eat out, all in a tight-knit hometown. He would've shut it down, taken it all away, if we went against him."

Cindy finally looked over at me and continued in a rush. "'Pick up my marbles and go,' was how he'd put it. None of us could've had the lifestyles—the luxuries—without his willingness to pay much better than we could make otherwise. Better than Atlanta even. And everyplace else is so much more expensive."

"Golden handcuffs," I said.

"Leg irons, too."

"But why did he need to buy your loyalty and silence? What was he doing?"

She chose to answer another earlier question. "I dated your father after your mother skipped town. He never looked at anyone else when Mary Grace was around, thought she'd hung the moon." Her gaze returned to the window. "I just knew she was crazy for leaving this brilliant man who was due to inherit the biggest estate in the county. Then I understood why she'd escaped."

"Did he hurt you?"

"Not in the ways you'd think. You know he was a genius, right?"

"I remember the newspaper obit calling him 'gifted.' My mom never talked about him."

"Well, he was a genius, let me tell you. Remembered every word he ever read, everything he ever saw. Earned his mechanical engineering degree from Georgia Tech in just three years—and probably could've done it in two." She shook her head in wonder. "You couldn't help but feel dumb when you were with him, that mind going a thousand miles a minute all the time. It was impossible to keep up, and the more you fell behind, the more he let you know it."

"So, he made you feel small, ignorant?"

"It was more complicated than that." Her expression blanked, as if she were lost in memories. Finally, she murmured, "He slept like a cat—twenty minutes here, ten there. Two in the morning, he'd wake you up, want to talk about philosophy or finances or to dance or...other things. He became an expert at whatever he set his mind to."

A blush spread over her face and neck, but she persevered. "So, yes, being around Brady you felt overwhelmed, unworthy. But at the same time, you felt like you were smarter than everybody but him, because you didn't—couldn't—have the same conversations with any of your friends. You were more worldly, sophisticated, because every other guy was a fumbling, bumbling mess next to him, and none of your girlfriends could ever experience what you did on a daily basis. You seemed more alive than you ever had before. And were totally dead with exhaustion of every kind."

"Did he end it, or did you break it off?"

She shrugged. "His attention span could be like a cat's, too. Even while you were feeling those highs, you knew it wouldn't last—because you *were* unworthy. Every girl was, except Mary Grace. You knew he'd start in with somebody else soon enough."

Thinking about her family portrait in the sitting room, I tried again but used a sideways strategy. In a gentle voice, I asked, "How long after that did you meet the guy you would marry?"

"A few years. There was no one in between." She looked away from me, embarrassed again. "It took a long time to get over Brady."

Noting the huge wedding ring on her finger, I asked, "Is your husband home?"

"Died a few years back. Stroke. He was good to me and the kids, had a great job at the plant." She gazed at the ring.

"Either of your children still in town?"

"No, long gone. Joe's in Arizona, Ellie's up in Virginia."

"And Ellie and Brady...?"

I knew my relentlessness could be a bad thing—at least past boyfriends had told me so—but in this case it had worn down her resistance. Her shoulders slumped, breath hissing out. Clearly she wanted to confess to someone; I'd merely managed to push the right buttons.

Cindy struggled to her feet and shuffled past me. I followed in silence as she led me upstairs to the room above mine, the only one up here with a deadbolt. The others all had knob locks, probably guest rooms. Maybe she'd put me downstairs in hopes I wouldn't discover this outlier and get nosy.

She unlocked the door and opened it, flicked on the ceiling-fan lights, and stepped aside. The room was unfurnished, but the hardwood floor was polished and dust-free. On all four walls were framed newspaper clippings, hung at eye level, each one showing a skillfully rendered portrait photo in black and white—maybe my dad's work again. Girls in their late teens, dozens of them. Every picture had been glued to a backing that included the Lord's Prayer in flowing script beside it. Above each teenager's image, the newspaper had printed "Stapleton Scholar" and the year. Below each photo was the girl's name.

The annual award had begun in 1985. Starting on the wall to my left, these handmade plaques went in chronological order around the room, the newsprint going from yellowed to fresh gray-white as the dates drew closer to the present. To my right, the fourth wall was only half-covered, the line of framed clips ending with the previous year.

If Cindy considered the Stapleton Scholarship an achievement, this room wouldn't have been locked up and undecorated. This was not a place for celebration—it was a memorial.

What the hell had happened in Graylee for more than thirty years?

Based on the timeline Cindy had described, I figured Ellie would've been born in the mid-1980s. I went to the wall showing the Stapleton Scholars in the early 2000s. Sure enough, Elisabeth Dwyer was there: a lovely brunette with dark, wide-set eyes and a mouth quirked in a playful smile. It was impossible not to notice beside her beautiful face the middle portion of the Lord's Prayer, which, in this room, seemed more like a plea to the Almighty:

And forgive us our trespasses,
as we forgive those who trespass against us.
Lead us not into temptation, but deliver us from evil.

Cindy sniffed behind me. She wiped her eyes as I turned to her, but instead of looking miserable, she glared at me.

Did she see my father standing before her? For a frightening instant, I thought she was going to shut me in there, with the newsprint faces staring at me for eternity. "I'm not him," I reminded her.

She took a step back and let me exit. As I waited for her to kill the lights and lock the door, I wondered whether the photos confiscated from the basement walls of my father's house were the full-size version of these. If that were the case, who had removed them? Mr. Pearson, Cade, and the deputies were the only ones who were supposed to have access to the house following the murder. The lawyer had tidied up in other ways, so he could've cleared out those photos, too—which meant he knew about them. Knew about all of this.

Of course he knew. Cade, too. As did Tim and David and everyone else who lived here. They all knew, but they didn't do anything to stop whatever had happened for over three decades. I considered the lawyer I respected, the cop I was falling for, my best friend in Graylee, and the author I admired—-and found it hard in that moment not to despise them all.

Standing so close to Cindy in the hallway, with hate still burning in her own eyes and a steep hardwood staircase at my back, I chose my words carefully. "Will you tell me about those scholarships?"

In a chipper voice barbed with irony, she recited, "Full-ride scholarship to any university the awardee could get into—Ivy League, the big tech schools, *any* of them—living expenses, a new car, tutors to help them graduate with a bachelor's degree, whatever they needed. Plus, a huge bonus for the family."

I hurried down the stairs to get away from that room, with Cindy close behind me. Back in the foyer, feeling safer, I said, "But if these girls could go anywhere to college, why was there a spot in my father's garage for their new car?"

She kept up her eerily bright tone of voice, sounding like some of the insane people I used to encounter on the subway. "Your dear daddy made just one tiny little stipulation: to ensure the Scholar was ready for the university of her choice, during her last year of high school she had to live with him."

19

I STAGGERED BACKWARD INTO THE NEWEL POST AS I GROANED. MY REASSURANCE TO TARA Glenmont from earlier that day now taunted me: *There's no conspiracy. No cover up. No deep, dark secret people are hiding from you.* I asked Cindy, "How could you? I don't care how much money he offered, how could you sell your daughter to him?"

"For God's sake, we didn't sell her. Anyway, you don't understand it, the pressure he brought to bear. And the opportunity he offered." She retreated to the luxurious parlor and collapsed into a chair beside the family photo, a moment captured before Ellie had matured enough to catch my father's eye.

I pursued Cindy and planted my feet in front of her, feeling the momentum shift back in my favor. "You could've just moved."

"Some did. Others took a stand, at least for a while."

"And what happened to them?"

She sneered at me. "Things didn't happen just to them. Your father gave everybody sixty days' notice per the law that he was shutting down his businesses and laying everybody off. He also raised the rents on all of those storefronts a thousand percent. The family holding out either knuckled under fast or they fled, because the calls and messages would start coming."

"From my dad?"

"No, he'd sent his message by picking up his marbles. The calls and all would be from more and more folks in town. They'd start out pleading and soon turn to threats. People wanted to save their jobs, wanted to be able to afford the leases on their businesses again, wanted everything back to normal. At any cost."

"So the people of Graylee became his partners in this."

She looked away. "That's how it worked—the reason for the gold in our handcuffs and leg irons. It only happened once a decade or so. Usually if a family didn't like his offer, they moved away quickly, but most people gave in—did it for the good of the town." She stared at the family photo. "At least, that's what we tell ourselves at night."

Not wanting to rub salt in, I made my voice gentle. "But you knew personally what he was like, what Ellie would go through."

"It actually helped in a way. I knew she would learn so much, grow in so many ways. Most of the Scholars have done very well for themselves over the years—we track their successes." She looked around the room. "Their families have done well, too."

Maybe confession had purged her guilt for the moment. Cindy filled that vacuum with righteous anger and went on the offensive again. Rising from the chair, she got in my face. "Don't you judge me. It wasn't like we sold her into slavery. Ellie had her own suite of rooms. He even let her decorate it. She could lock her door and never have anything to do with him."

The horror of it, her rationales, everything about that terrible secret everyone in Graylee shared made me shudder. I sat down hard on a sofa. "But that wouldn't last for long," I railed. "My dad was a genius, you said, an expert at whatever he set his mind to. He'd figure out ways to coax her, to manipulate." I shook my head, grieving for all of those victims. "A seventeen-year-old wouldn't stand a chance against him."

"Ellie swears nothing ever happened between them, that he was a gentleman."

The lies we tell our mothers. I had told plenty to my mom after I started in with boys—and grown men. I knew exactly what happened to a teenager who gained the attention of a charismatic, older guy determined to get what he wanted. After collecting myself, I stared up at her. She'd fully regained her defiance, armed herself with justifications again. I asked, "Why didn't anyone tell the world? Call TV stations and newspapers? Put it on the Internet?"

"It was part of his threat—if word got out, he'd never reopen the plants. Your daddy was a rich man and didn't need Graylee. He'd kill the town out of spite. Most of us grew up here—and thanks to him we grew softer the longer we stayed. We couldn't imagine starting over again someplace else. Even the pastors wouldn't speak out against him, not with the donations he gave every year."

I leaned back to get her out of my space a little. "Your memorial ended with last year's scholarship. Didn't he pick someone for this school year?"

"You can ask your friend Tim Bladensburg about that. I heard you've been hanging out together—maybe you can even shack up with him tonight. Because you're not staying here."

I didn't want to see Tim at that moment, or even Cade or David. The people I'd started to care about had disappointed me greatly, and I knew my next encounter with any of them would be an ugly confrontation. Taking a page from Tara, I decided to pull her stunt of refusing to go. I crossed my arms and stared at Cindy's family portrait.

"Goddammit, I said you're leaving. Get out."

"No."

She stomped over to an oversized purse and started to rummage through it. "I'll call the cops. Surely you can't be sleeping with all of them already."

"What?"

A cell phone came out, not a gun, thank God. Still, she pointed it at me as if it were loaded. "We've all seen you riding shotgun with Cade Wilson. But B.J. spent hours at your place today before he dropped you off, so maybe you're trying out every guy you can."

The gossip network keeping tabs, ratting each other out. It was how my father's commandments had been enforced, and the old habits didn't die with him. Virtually overnight, I'd become the town slut in their eyes. The people of Graylee were primed to hate me, of course, and apparently I wouldn't have the chance to change anyone's opinions.

I said, "You people have dirty minds."

"Your father made us that way." She dialed a number and turned her back on me.

All of my stuff was boxed up in a moving truck, heading down from New York. Probably impossible to intercept it, to get the driver to turn around and head…home? Is that what this came down to—tucking my tail and becoming the absentee owner whose only connection to Graylee would be income statements and tax forms? It's what my New York friends had been begging me to do since I'd gotten the idea of reinventing myself down South.

However, I still thought I could make a difference here, help people heal from at least some of my father's sins, undo the fear and anger that still gripped everyone. It's what my mother would've done, if she'd known what had happened. The only way I'd leave Graylee, I decided, was in a box of my own. Though I didn't want to stay around Cindy for one more second, this was my town and no way would I let her kick me out into the cold.

"Hey, Chief," she said, "it's Cindy Dwyer. Look, I appreciate you referring Ms. Wright to me and all, but it's not working out between us.... Sorry, it's just not. Unfortunately, she's as stubborn as her old man and refuses to leave. Can you or one of your deputies—what's that? No, I haven't looked in a while." She went to a front window and pushed back the lace on a world of white.

I stood and chose a window at the opposite end of the room. A half-inch had fallen, with more coming. It looked like the heavy kind, more ice than snow, which would linger in shadows even after the weather warmed. B.J.'s worst fears realized: we'd have a white Christmas for sure.

Cindy went on, "My stars, look at—yes, I can imagine all the calls you're getting already. Well, okay, but…fine, here she is." She looked in my direction and then at her phone and maybe considered throwing it at me, but then she straightened her back and marched over.

"You can stop right there," I said. "I'm not talking to him."

Into her cell, she said, "Chief, this is how crazy she is: she refuses to talk to you even. I can't have a demented person staying here with guests due to arrive any—" After another pause, she sighed and turned from me again. "Okay, but if I'm found dead, you'll know who did it." She mashed the icon with her index finger to end the call. "Mashed" was a word my mother had used, and it fit Cindy's action perfectly. "Stabbed" would've been too surgical a description; she was crushing a bug.

My host retrieved her purse and stowed her phone, keeping her back to me. She ordered, "Stay away from my other guests and don't expect breakfast in the morning."

"Gosh, I was counting on French toast."

She whirled, lower lip curling under her top teeth to form an F and probably the remainder of a familiar curse often heard on the streets of New York. Then Southern manners and good breeding kicked in. Her mouth clamped shut, and she strode across the hall, disappeared into the dining room, and soon was banging pots around in the kitchen.

Just wait until she discovered I had no money to pay her. My phone buzzed against my butt, and I checked the screen. Cade. I let his call go to voicemail. Earlier, I'd had a fantasy of helping him with road flares and people who'd fallen, and then curling up at his place with a brandy and wicked intentions. Because of what I knew now, I couldn't go through with that, not in a million years. Not with any man in Graylee. Shit.

A startling bump against my shin was followed by a long slide of fur across both legs. I looked down at a fat tabby, which peered back with hazel eyes and meowed a greeting. "Hey," I murmured, "do you like Danish Modern?"

The cat merely reversed course across my legs and batted my knees with a couple of tail flicks. "Good," I said, "because I'm kidnapping you."

B&B cats were used to being handled. This one went limp as I hefted her, all warm, doughy flesh and silken hair, the purrs already relaxing me. I hugged the tabby to my chest and carried her to the suite Cindy had assigned me, with the memorial room bearing down overhead.

Inside, I set the cat on a rug and locked the door. Cindy would have a spare key, and she wasn't the only one worried about an attack. After considering all of the horizontal furniture in the room, I slid a squat chest of drawers across the threshold.

Feeling a little more secure in my bunker, I visited the bathroom, washed my hands, and then opened the bedroom drapes. Bleak light from the cloud-choked sky reflected my mood. Only the drift of more snow over the backyard—flowerbeds, shrubs, grass, and pines all shrouded in white—broke the stillness. Nothing else moved outside, not a single bird flitted and no squirrels scampered. If I pushed up the window sash, I knew I'd only hear the soft hiss of a million snowflakes landing.

The tabby had just settled on my bed when phones pealed from other rooms, startling her upright. She puddled again into a furry orange blob, considered me through slit eyes, and then closed them once more.

Cindy answered in the kitchen, her muted voice coming through the wall. From her comments, I gathered some guests would arrive late due to the driving conditions. Her tone displayed understanding and patience, the gracious innkeeper extending her offer of a sanctuary, a kind of refuge, while she harbored the same terrible secret as did everyone else in town.

Somehow, I'd landed in the middle of a gothic novel. No, darker than that—something David Stark could've written if there were sinister supernatural elements at work. I checked the cat to make sure she hadn't become an undead monster. Nope, just a napping tabby. Something about David niggled at me, though. He knew all about my dad, of course, *"everything,"* he'd said, but that wasn't it. Whatever the insight was, I couldn't grasp the threads before they submerged and were lost under the surface of my thoughts.

The intermittent buzzing of incoming texts had ceased, making me wonder if my New York friends had given up on me, at least for the day, because I hadn't responded to anyone in a number of hours. Actually, my right butt cheek still tingled periodically, the nerves there continuing to fire as if more messages were coming in, but those were phantom signals. Time to get caught up with my peeps.

I slipped the cell out and clicked the power button, but the screen remained dark. Two more tries, same null result. Perfect—a dead battery and an explanation for the cessation of texts. And where were the charger *and* my emergency battery boost? In my purse, with Tara. Cade's voicemail must've been the last thing to get through.

Barricaded in hostile territory, cut off from the world, I joined the cat on the bed and tried to nap. Immediately, though, my recollection of Tara brought updated To-Do lists to mind, each item punctuated by a flare of anger. The rage found new kindling as I considered David and Cade, the tender shoots of romantic feelings ripped out as I imagined the horror they'd allowed to perpetuate for so long. My friendship with Tim, which already had begun to flower, also was destroyed by the secret he'd kept from me. Eliminate them and also consider my track record with at least some of the women in town—Cindy, Paulina, Luz—and I was socially adrift.

My old fears kicked in, the nightmares that had crept up in childhood with the faint echo of hooves that became louder as I progressed from adolescent to teenager: lonely, abandoned, unattractive, unloved. The Four Horsewomen, my constant companions. I slid under the covers, curled my body around the cat, and willed myself to sleep.

℘

When I awoke, the cat had moved. I couldn't see her because the room was dark, but through the covers I felt her against my feet. Night had come on — the uncovered windows merely darkened rectangles against dark walls. Without thinking, I patted my back pocket for my cell, and then felt around the low table beside the platform bed until I touched the cool, glassy front of the phone. Then I remembered the battery had died. I padded into the bathroom, shut the door so as not to disturb Ms. Kitty, and turned on the light. Half-past eleven on my watch.

I used a paper cup to drink from the tap until the dryness in my throat went away. The cat probably was thirsty, too, so I found a small plastic container in one of the drawers, rinsed it clean, and filled it with water. She meowed an inquiry as I approached but ignored my offering when I set the container beside her.

During my return to the bathroom, I heard the cat lapping the water. Although I was starving Cindy's pet along with myself, at least we were staying hydrated. However, only I had an obvious place to pee, so I pulled the chest of drawers away from the exit and opened the door enough for the tabby to depart. She did so without a backward glance, disappearing down the black hallway.

Cindy had turned off every light in the house. Other than the pendulum clicks of a grandfather clock, the inn was silent. Either her guests had arrived and settled in, or it was just me and her, with a long night ahead. I decided to close the door, lock up, and set the barricade in place again. If the tabby returned, she'd let me know.

I went into the bedroom and peered out one of the windows I'd uncovered. Lights from some neighboring houses cast enough of a glow to notice the snowfall had stopped. From the icy glaze of white atop nearby shrubs, I guessed about an inch had fallen. Nothing by New York standards, of course, but it might've set a record for Graylee, and only further emphasized my isolation—I hadn't brought the proper footwear to walk on snow and ice. Even if I gave in to my habitual need for company, no way would I be able to get to Cade, let alone David out in the country. Not that I wanted either of them. But still....

I imagined the stirring of hooves and saddle creaks from my four tormentors. Sleep wouldn't come for a while again, and I needed a distraction to keep them at bay. The tablet computer Mr. Pearson had given to me was in one of my suitcases, and its battery still had a few hours of life, so I switched on the overhead lights and checked e-mail and Facebook to get caught up and share my news.

When I considered telling my friends about what I'd learned, though, I paused. It was too horrible to post in a forum normally devoted to flippant or snarky observations, pet videos, family photos, and tributes to recently passed loved ones and celebrities. I realized I didn't want any of my friends to know, or at the very least I didn't want them spreading it around like juicy gossip.

So here I was, another Graylee guardian of the secret: protecting it with my silence, doing my father's bidding in a way. Without any pressure, I'd chosen to become one of them. The thought made me tremble. However, it also rearranged my feelings about the people here, gave me a dose of empathy. Things were more complex than I'd believed. If I exposed the terrible price my father had exacted from the Stapleton Scholars and their families, I could force the victims into the light as well. They wouldn't want that scrutiny, wouldn't want to tear off the scabs of shame, to dredge up deep pains and dark memories.

Yes, the people here conspired with my father to perpetuate his sins, but they also were trapped by the affluence he'd provided them. For a Graylee resident who didn't have a daughter chosen by my dad, and whose livelihood and lifestyle depended on him, it would've been easy to look the other way and then find someone to blame when those comforts were in danger. People did it all the time throughout history. Much easier to live with the guilt—and rationalize like crazy—than to do something about it.

I tossed the tablet aside. Even with a better appreciation of what the townspeople were faced with, I still couldn't understand why they'd let it go on for decades without real opposition. Could anyone have resisted the lure of the good life and stood up to my father?

Tim and Abby sprang to mind. What if, in actuality, he wasn't renovating their home but repairing—because something had happened to it? For those who stood up to my father and brought about layoffs and skyrocketing rents, people in town could escalate their calls to death threats. Cindy had told me to ask Tim about the current year's Scholar. What if the Bladensburgs refused to knuckle under and someone acted on their threats? The new porch he'd installed—needed because of a firebomb? Maybe those roof shingles had looked dark from smoke and flames rather than decay. But why target his family? My father had never picked minority girls.

I certainly didn't have perfect recall like Dad, but I did inherit a little of his ability—it just took me longer to process and organize my thoughts. I pictured the memorial room again and how the row of frames on my right halted halfway across the wall, missing the current year. Now that I focused on it, the previous year's winner looked different from the earlier Scholars. The newsprint hadn't yellowed, but the teenager's face still looked tan rather than pale. And the name—Isabela…Garcia? Yes, I could see it now.

My father's prejudice certainly wouldn't have stopped him from desiring young women of color. Maybe he'd even gotten a sick, illicit thrill targeting a lovely girl from the ghetto. Unfortunately, there were plenty of examples of that throughout history, too. In the family photo I'd seen in Abby's home, Tim's sister was beautiful and certainly could've caught my father's eye. And she was a senior this year.

Tim had called himself a pariah. Possibly, the status applied to the whole family and only Abby and Tim stayed, to rise above Graylee's scorn. In fact, maybe Tim had struck back. I remembered his refusal to enter the house when we first met—perhaps he'd been inside once before, back in July. Could my best friend in town have participated in my father's murder?

20

I DISMISSED THE THOUGHT AT FIRST, RECALLING ABBY'S SCORNFUL FACE WHEN SHE'D NAILED me for conjuring other slanderous ideas about Tim. However, helping Landry kill the goose that laid the golden eggs definitely would've cemented his pariah status with anyone who suspected him. They'd probably assume Graylee now teetered on the edge of collapse because of my dad's death.

Tim, of course, would remain a sphinx if I asked him. My only chance of piecing together what really had happened was by gathering more clues. Stuck in Danish Modern purgatory, how would I do that? My gaze fell upon the suitcases I'd rolled against the wall and hadn't bothered to unpack. In one of them I'd stowed the case file Cade had given me.

I found the thick folder shoved beneath a pile of bras and panties that would've given credence to Cindy's "town slut" accusations. Settling back on the bed, I started to read. The mound of paper didn't intimidate me. When I'd dated the NYPD detective a few years back, I would pore over his case documents while he snored in the bedroom. Often I ended up more prepared for his upcoming trial testimony than he was.

Not one of my longer or wiser relationships, but at least I'd become familiar with typical criminal file organization. Cade's entire incident report was in caps, which made it hard to read, but

I guess it saved him the bother of using the shift key and allowed him to type even faster.

In the early morning hours of July 8, he was working the first half of a double-shift. He'd offered a week of vacation to the third-shift deputy after an especially raucous Fourth of July weekend that had J.D. racing all over town, making arrests for domestic violence and settling drunken brawls nonstop. Rather than saddle B.J. with two shifts, Cade had volunteered to do the late one and then his usual daylight eight hours. The police chief had been more succinct about it in his report, but I could read between the lines: he was the good leader, taking one for the team.

At 3:27 a.m., the security alarm sounded at my father's house and sent an automated call to Cade's cell. He responded immediately. As he drove across the courtyard and pulled up to the front of the house, he heard the alarm blaring. He discovered the front door jimmied open but found no one downstairs.

As the chief headed up to the second floor, the first of a succession of gunshots cut through the clamor. He determined they were coming from the master suite. Once inside the study, with service weapon drawn, he saw movement through the open bedroom door. That space was lit by a strobing security alarm. Entering with firearm ready, he identified himself as a police officer to the man standing at the foot of my father's bed, and told him to drop what appeared to be a pistol in his hand.

The man raised his gun and Cade shot him twice in the upper chest. With the assailant down and unmoving, the chief found the switch for the overhead lights and illuminated what must've been an unholy massacre, but, in the report, he blandly stated

AFTERMATH

his discovery of Brady Stapleton in bed, with multiple gunshot wounds to the head, torso, and legs.

He identified the assailant as Wallace Landry. After kicking away the man's pistol—which, it turned out, no longer had any bullets—Cade rolled him onto his stomach and handcuffed him to ensure he no longer was a threat. He then checked Landry for vital signs. A weak pulse and gurgling breath soon ceased and didn't recur.

Cade confirmed my dad was dead as well. He removed the cuffs from Landry, rolled him onto his back again, and used the bathroom sink to wash Landry and Brady's blood from his hands. Then, with the alarm still blaring, he hurried outside to phone the county sheriff's office, which in turn contacted the county coroner. He also called B.J. with orders to report to the bottom end of Brady Stapleton Boulevard and block anyone from entering except county officials.

While Cade waited for the sheriff, he rechecked the house and grounds to make sure he hadn't overlooked anyone. He eventually liaised with the county lawmen and coroner and submitted to extensive interviews while officers processed the crime scene, which included collecting his firearm and swabbing his hands for gunshot residue. The sheriff determined that Cade could continue his duties while the investigation proceeded.

An attached supplemental report from Cade, also entirely in caps, provided some background: Cade knew Brady had hired Wallace Landry in late June to do handyman chores around the property—my dad had told the chief and his deputies not to be concerned if anyone saw Landry on the grounds.

The week before, Cade had spoken to Landry after hearing stories from others who'd paid the out-of-towner for yard work. Apparently, Landry had been insolent and aggressive toward them, but Cade's discussion with him had not revealed any threatening behaviors. Nonetheless, he'd cautioned my father, who merely said, "He's just a spirited young buck. I can still handle myself."

Further into the stack of paperwork, I found a ballistics report connecting all of the gunshot wounds in my father to Landry's emptied gun, which had been tampered with sometime before the murder to make the serial number unreadable. Also, a follow-up report from the county sheriff declared Cade's killing of Landry a righteous shoot and determined that Georgia Bureau of Investigation involvement was not warranted. Case closed.

So, the police chief was exonerated, the evil tyrant was dead, and even the murderer got his comeuppance. But was Cade really the hero in this story? He'd lived in Graylee long enough to know what happened annually: a seventeen-year-old girl handpicked in March or April, the arrangement finalized with her family during the summer, the installation of the Scholar in my father's home for her senior year. Driving through town in her new car, taking her meals with my dad at Denny's and elsewhere, she would've been a constant reminder to everyone that yet another young woman had been cursed with the terrible honor.

Yet Cade had done nothing. Less than nothing—he'd gunned down the real hero of Graylee, the man who'd finally ended Dad's hold over the town. The age of consent in Georgia was sixteen, but surely my father had broken other laws to get what he wanted. Extortion, racketeering, something. Why hadn't the chief stopped him long before Landry did?

A memory of Cade surfaced, the casual sliding back of his sleeve to check the time on a chic and expensive-looking watch. Even the lawman had been bound with golden handcuffs. Plus, he was employed solely at the pleasure of the mayor, who had been in office forever thanks to my father. Going after Brady Stapleton would've meant forfeiting his relatively cushy job and maybe returning to the mean streets of Atlanta to battle gang-bangers and drug pushers.

I recalled Cade's haunted face as he drove us up to my dad's house, his look of dread even before I pointed out "MURDER" etched into the frosted car window. Maybe Landry was in fact evil, as Paulina had insisted, or maybe he was just an opportunist who murdered a genuinely evil man in order to make a life for himself and Tara. In either case, he'd miscounted the number of shots he fired, not realizing he used up all of his bullets, and Cade was forced to end him. Now the chief lived with the knowledge that, essentially, he'd killed an unarmed man. In the police car with me, perhaps he'd read Tara's message as she'd intended it: a condemnation, but aimed squarely at himself.

Still so much I didn't know, and the questions kept mounting. My gaze drifted around the bedroom and settled on the luggage where I'd stored the case file. Something continued to bother me about the incident report. I wondered what it was until I noticed the gun vault beside the suitcases.

Why hadn't my father retrieved one or both pistols to handle his own protection after Landry triggered the security alarm? Digging deeper through the paperwork, I finally found the reason in a toxicology report. My dad had gone to bed with a blood alcohol concentration of nearly one percent. A quick Google search on the tablet showed that he could've been arrested for a BAC of just .08%—his was more than ten times higher. Soon after he'd hit his pillow, he would've been figuratively dead to the world before Landry had made it a literal fact.

When I'd explored my father's house, I didn't see a formal bar setup, and my rummaging through the kitchen cabinets in search of dinner hadn't uncovered a huge stash of liquor. It was possible those bottles had been cleared out when the basement photos were taken away, but I didn't think anyone would bother. If my father routinely drank himself into a stupor, he would've had cases of booze around, but I'd only found a few new bottles of scotch, brandy, and the like in a kitchen cabinet. I had to assume he'd gone out drinking that night, a real bender.

While I'd never been so intoxicated, I sometimes imbibed too much when I was younger. From my roommates' jibes, I knew that—besides being a foul-mouthed, hair-pulling kind of drunk—I always forgot to lock the apartment door when I finally staggered home. Sometimes I wouldn't even bother to shut it. My only focus had been crash-landing on a soft surface.

It didn't matter whether my dad had been a big man who probably held his liquor pretty well. The thought of him driving home without incident and then studiously setting the alarm before he struggled into pajamas and collapsed in bed wasn't believable. Especially the alarm part. Not in a town where most people didn't even lock their doors.

Someone must've been with him that night—a person who would know, or could get access to, the security code. A friend who'd set it for their best bud before heading home, presumably less drunk than Dad. My father's lawyer, Mr. Pearson, might've kept that code on file, and Tim had said he'd gone to work in that office in July. But no way was Tim going to be Brady Stapleton's drinking partner. It was much more likely to have been Mr. Pearson himself.

If that were the case, he and I shared a bond: we'd both seen someone on the day they would be killed. As a young girl, I had reflexively told my brother, Brady Jr., to be careful before he headed to his high school classes; that night he died, apparently drunk and trying to beat a train at a crossing. In July, Mr. Pearson would've watched Brady Sr. clump up fifteen stairs before he set the alarm that would fail to save his friend and client, but would summon an avenging—albeit corrupted—lawman.

As I ruminated on that, a gunshot sounded outside my window. I dove off the bed and used it for protective cover. Another shot and then one more, followed by a crash and a thump.

The sounds were farther away than I first thought. When I mustered the courage to peek through the glass, I saw a pile of twisted pine limbs at the end of the yard. With a series of bangs, more snow-covered branches toppled to the ground. Ice, I realized, was putting too much weight on the weak ones. Their splintering sure as hell sounded like gunfire, but all was not as it seemed—maybe like the puzzle I was trying to solve.

❧

Still in my clothes, I gave in to sleep again around two in the morning and awoke before seven. Though I'd managed to dream through more tree limbs breaking, no one could've snoozed through the racket Cindy made in the kitchen. She probably did it on purpose, since my room was on the other side of the wall.

The sun hadn't risen yet. However, houselights from neighbors revealed a litter of icy branches at the base of the pines. An inch of glittering snow covered everything. With Cindy occupied, it would've been the perfect time to sneak out of the house without another confrontation—since I had no way to pay for my "stay in gracious luxury"—but I had no coat, the footing would be treacherous, and I had two suitcases and a gun safe to haul around.

Creaking and clumping on the staircase signaled a pair of guests coming down for breakfast. A further distraction for Cindy. She had landlines in the house, so I could contact someone to ask for help. My inability to pay for anything eliminated both the motel and the cab to get me there or anywhere else. Having entered cell numbers for Tim, Cade, and David into my now-dead phone, I thought I could remember them—thanks, Dad—but who would be the best one to call and beg for a ride?

Tim's sedan wouldn't fare well on the slick streets, so he'd be trapped at home. Cade probably had endured a long night and, assuming he wasn't still working, would be trying to catch a few hours of sleep before going back on snow patrol. That left David. From the Azteca parking lot, I knew one car he owned, but surely the richest man in town also had something more rugged at his disposal, a macho toy for off-road adventures.

After packing away the case file, tablet, and toiletries, I pulled the low chest of drawers aside and unlocked and opened the door. Voices echoed down the hall as Cindy made small talk with a woman and man in the dining room. For the first time, I noticed the closed door across from me. It had the same kind of deadbolt as the memorial room upstairs. Fortunately, this one was unlocked and, as I hoped, gave me access to Cindy's bedroom suite. Apparently she'd put me in Dutch Modern hell to keep me within sight and earshot as well as to distance me from the secret on the second floor.

The woman must've loved teak, low profiles, and horizontal lines, because she'd decorated her rooms in a nearly identical fashion to mine. Everything was neat and orderly, as if her living space were just another guest bedroom. However, she had quite a few more accessories, including a cordless phone on her nightstand. Just to be spiteful, I sat on her perfectly made platform bed as I dialed David's number.

After a few rings, his deep voice said, "Tell me a story, and make it a good one." A beep followed.

"Hi, it's Janet. I'm at Cindy Dwyer's. We're, uh, not exactly hitting it off, so I want to take you up on your offer of a place to stay. I know you're writing now, but if you could pick me up here, I'll make it worth your effort." Another ploy that had worked wonders since I was a teenager, when I discovered what that pledge immediately conjured in most guys' imagination. "I'm going to be barricaded in my room —"

Behind me, Cindy said, "Not anymore."

I cussed and nearly dropped the phone. Turning to look at her, I said into the mouthpiece, "Correction: I'll be wandering the snowy streets like the Little Match Girl. Hopefully you'll find me before I freeze to death." I clicked the Off button and told her, "I really had hopes for a reconciliation between us."

"Coming in here uninvited and sprawling across my bed is not

GEORGE WEINSTEIN

endearing you to me." In her hands she didn't hold a gun exactly—she held my gun vault.

I replaced the handset in its cradle and smoothed the comforter. "Sorry, my cell phone is dead, and I needed to call someone."

"David Stark. I caught the 'writing' reference. It's fitting that
y'all would end up together, the richest ones joining forces against
the rest of us."

"I'm not against anybody. Is David?"

"He never put Graylee's interests ahead of his own. We hardly
even see him anymore—sends that actress bimbo to run all his
errands." She gave me a once-over. "His tastes must be changing."

I started to respond, but Cindy tossed the gun vault onto the
bed. She said, "I rolled your bags onto the porch. This one's too
heavy to lug, but it's a good idea for you to carry a gun—with
the way you behave. You can wait outside with it until David or
Bebe fetches you."

Looking down at the big black case, another detail unex-
plained by the file sprang to mind. "Did you ever see Wallace
Landry's gun?"

"No, but I didn't think it was right to make myself at home in
his bedroom, unlike some people."

"How about—"

"Enough." She gestured at a dressing table that displayed a
row of petite perfume bottles. "Get out right now, or I'll start
throwing these at you."

She looked serious. Despite being in yesterday's clothes, I
probably would smell better as is, rather than doused in Obsession. I hefted the gun vault and tried to sweep past her with as

much panache as I could manage while burdened with a twenty-pound weight in one hand. She marched close behind me, so I let the momentum of the case swing my arm back to force her away.

I walked past the staircase, where the tabby sat on the third step, watching me, tail swishing. Dining room chatter paused as, coatless, I fumbled with the front door knob, shoved the screen open, and then strode onto the porch. Behind me, the door slammed hard enough to rattle its diamond panes. In all likelihood, I'd ruined my chances for a book club invitation.

My breath puffed out as the cold settled into me. True to her word, Cindy had left my roller bags near the front steps, which she'd scraped clean for the safety of her guests. The cloud cover had departed, allowing for a sunrise that made the snow and ice blinding. My sunglasses, of course, were in my purse. Maybe Tara was wearing them on her way down the Florida coast or wherever she'd chosen to escape with my car, my money, and my peace of mind.

From deeper in the neighborhood, I heard kids laughing and hollering and dogs barking. Sledding and snowball fights, no doubt, with hot chocolate and warm, dry clothes awaiting them afterward. The images made me shiver and bounce in place. I couldn't bear standing around, hoping David would show up before hypothermia claimed me. Better to remain in motion.

Squinting in the glare, I carried the gun vault and luggage, one piece at a time, down the steps and hid them in the space between a waist-high row of snowy azaleas and the foundation of the house. So far, the footing wasn't bad despite my city-girl boots, which were intended for pavement, not cross-country treks.

Out on the street, though, I started to slip and slide. Overnight, people with four-wheel-drive vehicles had taken the opportunity to live out their tundra fantasies. They'd turned the inch or so of glittering powder into overlapping ruts of densely packed ice. After falling twice, I hobbled onto the pristine white canvas of the sidewalk, brushed snow off my bottom and knees, and made my slow, careful way toward Main Street. I swore I'd never make fun of winter in the South again.

David would be able to track me down; he could just follow the footprints. In the meantime, maybe I'd encounter Cade or one of his deputies or someone else who would invite me to sit in the heated bliss of their car or truck. The fantasy kept me going as I waddled along on numb feet, my bare hands held out from my sides for balance. I had to keep checking to make sure they were doing their job because I couldn't feel them anymore. My face, too, had lost all sensation. So much for my imperviousness to the cold—I was a Southern girl after all.

Once on Main Street, the going was easier because awnings and porticos over front doors had blocked much of the snowfall. I stomped my boots a few times to knock off the white stuff and wake up my feet. I saw only one truck ahead, parked in front of the Law Office of Philip P. Pearson, Esq. As good a place as any to warm up, and possibly he could help me clear up a mystery or two. If nothing else, we could compare notes about what it felt like to be with someone who was destined for a violent death.

21

I KNOCKED A COUPLE OF TIMES WITH COLD-NUMBED HANDS BEFORE I TRIED THE DOORKNOB. Locked—just my luck. I resorted to kicking the brass plate at the bottom. A drape stirred to my left, and then the door was opened not by Mr. Pearson, but by Tim, dressed for work in a suit that no doubt concealed superhero boxers.

"Hey, stranger," I said, trying to mask my chattering teeth with good cheer. "Long time, no see."

He stepped aside, ushered me in, and closed the door. With a glance at his cell phone, he asked in his soft voice, "What are you doing out in the cold before eight? And with no coat on?"

I sighed as the heat of the hallway enveloped me. "Long story. What are you doing in the office before eight on Christmas Eve? Is your boss practicing to be Scrooge for the town play?"

"We're closed next week, so I'm helping him finish some end-of-the-year stuff. He had to pick me up in his truck, since my car couldn't hack the ice." Tim led me to a break room where a full pot of coffee sat on its hotplate. "A mug, or something taller?" He opened a cabinet.

"I could drink right from the carafe, but I guess I'll take the biggest thing you've got."

As he poured, I thought again about how to discuss the reason for his pariah status and the way it fit into the terrible secret.

When he handed me the insulated tankard, I thanked him and took a long pull of scalding bliss. A flush spread over my skin and started me shivering all over again. "Look," I said, "you know I've long-since lost my Southern manners. Would you mind if I come right out with some Yankee bluntness?"

"No problem." He grinned and leaned against the counter. "Hit me with your best shot."

"I just walked over from Cindy Dwyer's B&B, where she evicted me for verbally beating a confession out of her. I know about the Stapleton Scholarships, what my dad put everyone through for so long."

"Okay, yeah. What he did, that was messed up." He turned, took down a mug, and busied himself with pouring again.

"The people in your neighborhood had little to lose—why didn't you or someone else on your street go public with it?"

"When you only have a little to start with, you can't afford to lose one bit of it, and you don't want anybody you know to catch the blowback either." He shrugged. "Besides, what do those scholarships have to do with me?"

"Your sister—LaDonna—she was his pick for this year, wasn't she? Your grandma said what happened to your family was hardest on her."

His face remained inscrutable while he sipped his coffee. "That your best shot?"

"And you stopped him. I can't prove how, but a bunch of people are still holding something against you. Because you were behind it."

Before he could react, Mr. Pearson said, "That is a powerful accusation, Ms. Wright." I whirled to find him standing in the doorway, decked out as usual in a three-piece suit and silk tie. Contrary to our previous meetings, his expression showed no trace of amusement. "We must talk."

Dammit, if one more person snuck up on me.... Ready to do battle, I took my coffee and strode behind the lawyer into the conference room, while Tim brought up the rear. Mr. Pearson slid aside stacks of files to make room at the table. He sat opposite me, and Tim joined him, making his loyalty clear.

Despite the hurt and disappointment in their eyes, I persevered. "The timeline works. The Scholar was picked in March or April, and I'm betting it was LaDonna. In June and early July, my father's largest business had no revenues—Conway and his boys forgot to conceal that in the presentation materials they gave me. After sixty days' warning, all nice and legal, my dad had made good on his threat to lay off everyone, because the Scholar's family refused to give in. That's how the Bladensburgs were made into the bad guys."

I pointed at Tim. "Your whole family are pariahs, not just you. Someone even tried to burn down your house. Your mom and dad left with LaDonna, but Abby wouldn't abandon the old home place, so you stayed with her and continued to stand tall. Then, you came to work here in July, and uh—" I came up with the rest on the fly, combining my two lines of thought as I shifted my focus to Mr. Pearson. "Somehow, Tim makes a deal with Wallace Landry to murder my father, and brings you into the plan. You get my dad drunk and set the alarm after putting him to bed. This double-crosses Landry because Cade shows up and silences him."

"I see." The lawyer steepled his fingers. Gold and diamond cufflinks glinted below soft, manicured hands. "So we have a conspiracy, in fact, where I work with Timothy to perpetrate the contract killing of my most lucrative client." He shook his head. "Though you have described an interesting theory, there is a discrepancy in your timeline. I did hire Tim in July, but *after* Brady Stapleton's murder, not *before*. The purpose was two-fold: first, I needed a talented paralegal—" he gave Tim's arm a gentle pat "—but I also wanted to derail a second killing brought on by the turmoil that preceded and followed your father's death. By vouching for Timothy, I think I succeeded."

"You should've hired him in June or even sooner, before my father shut down the town, and spared his family the death threats."

"Back then, my most lucrative client was still very much alive and feisty, Ms. Wright. 'Enlightened self-interest' often contains at least as large a portion of the latter as the former."

It was an admission of sorts, so I trotted out another theory kicking around in my mind. "My dad made you draw up the scholarship contracts for the families to sign, didn't he?"

"There you have it wrong again. I refused to play a role in that, claiming a conflict of interest, as I handle many other clients in town. Brady had the contracts done in Atlanta."

"But...but...." I slapped the table. "You did clear out the Scholar photos from the basement so I wouldn't get suspicious."

"Yes, I am indeed guilty as charged on that count," he said. "I wanted to spare you the pain of learning what your father was like. An impossible task, as it turns out, because you refuse to leave the past alone."

"That's because there are so many details that don't fit. I've learned too much to still believe Landry simply shot my father so he could rob him."

Tim glowered at me and said even more softly than usual, "I didn't kill anybody. Or set anybody up to be killed."

"You both know who did, though. I can see it in your faces. You know who's guilty."

"We are all guilty," Mr. Pearson said. "If you know about the scholarships, you know the whole town is culpable, from the mayor down to the lowliest citizen. We all went along because — " he adjusted one of his cufflinks and then tapped it with his finger " — well, because of this, symbolically speaking. And if there is more to the deaths of your father and Mr. Landry than meets the eye, then we are all guilty of conspiracy, because everybody believes as you do: it was not simply a crime of opportunity." He spread his hands. "Yet we continue to do nothing, because now we live without the annual guilt and anguish of 'scholarship season,' and business is even better than before."

I stammered, "But two men died."

"Tragically, yes." Mr. Pearson rose. "The accusations you leveled are understandable, given the shock of learning what Graylee has endured, and kept secret, for more than three decades. We certainly do not hold them against you." He walked to the door. "Clearly, your discoveries have left you overwrought. Please rest in my office while Timothy and I finish our work here."

Once again I followed him as we went deeper into the building, but now I barely managed to shuffle behind, feeling wrung out after my epic failure. I even forgot to bring my coffee.

He gestured toward a lovely office of mahogany furniture, leather chairs, and glass-fronted bookshelves. "Make yourself at home. We will not be long."

I plopped into his swivel chair and spun one way and then

the other, trying to gather my thoughts. While acknowledging so much and correcting my facts, the lawyer still hadn't cleared up any of the deeper mysteries. Instead, he'd basically advised me to stop obsessing about the truth and be happy with my blood money, as he and everyone else in Graylee were happy with theirs. His frankness and lack of remorse were jarring—the man would've put Machiavelli to shame.

What to do? I distracted myself by glancing at a wall of framed photographs, a combination of family mementoes and souvenirs with glad-handing celebrities, a little of Abby's decorating style and a little of David's. Some black and white shots showed boys at play from probably as far back as the 1950s, while many others were in color and more recent, with the Pearson family growing older and prosperous.

The American Dream. I think most of us assumed we could live that dream without others getting hurt. But maybe for one person to get ahead, someone else had to suffer. Perhaps a rising tide swamped some ships instead of lifting them all. At least in Graylee, Georgia.

If I blew the whistle on what had gone on here, despite my desire not to shine a spotlight on the victims, would the feds or some state law enforcement find enough cause to charge anyone? Would they target only Graylee's leaders? Cade and his deputies? Nearly the whole damn town? And the people who were left—how would they behave toward me? Even if I fled back to New York or headed somewhere else, I'd always be looking over my shoulder.

Losing myself in the photos again, I examined the oldest one more closely. Mr. Pearson was in the center of the shot, a bare-chested boy of maybe ten years old, his arms around the shoulders of two other boys who also were shirtless: a scrawny kid in thick glasses who looked a little like David and a taller, athletic boy who must've been my father. They stood in the glade of a forest, the three musketeers posing in a beam of sunshine, ready to take on the world.

David had told me he knew *everything* about my father. Now that I knew what questions to ask, he could put an end to this crazy quest for the truth. Hopefully he also would have some ideas about how I should bring about the healing and reconciliation everyone needed.

As I perused the other pictures, a horn honked twice on Main Street. I peered between two slats in the drawn blinds and saw a black truck even bigger than Mr. Pearson's idling on the road. My ride had tracked me down. What a relief—I wouldn't have to face Tim and Mr. Pearson anymore that day, or see the pain in their faces because of more wild accusations. I was so relieved to escape that I jogged down the corridor.

Tim stepped out and intercepted me. He said, "Hey, I really don't blame you for thinking what you did. I should've been more upfront. I just didn't want to overwhelm you with our drama. You know: welcome to Graylee, here's our big, bad scandal all thanks to your daddy."

"We'll have plenty of time to talk it through," I told him as the truck horn blared twice more, "but right now I've got to collect my luggage and settle in someplace where I might sleep for more than a night."

He grasped my arm with surprising intensity. "You're going to stay—"

I broke free and backpedaled toward the door. "Yeah, with David Stark." Grinning at his expression of disbelief, I called back, "Maybe you've heard of him?"

Before he could reply, I turned and exited. Only the icy street kept me from sprinting to the freedom David's ride represented.

Huge wheels elevated the truck cab so much that I needed to use the built-in steps and handholds to climb up. Cade would've stood there and helped me; David merely raced the engine, but I appreciated his confidence in me as I managed to climb into his testament to torque and testosterone.

I closed the door and said hello. Despite the heat blasting from the vents, he'd outfitted himself in black leather: jacket, cap, and gloves, as well as the ear stems of his sunglasses. The ensemble looked good on him. He dropped the transmission into drive and started chewing up ice and snow with each revolution of his tires.

"Making friends all over the place, I hear," he rumbled, his voice pitched even deeper than the truck engine.

"No point in being rich unless you're also willing to be a troublemaker," I said.

He laughed. "Now you're getting it. Actually, you don't get points for pissing off Cindy. Even as a kid she had a stick up her ass."

I described where I'd stowed my bags. "Think she'll pull out that stick and chase us with it?"

"Naw, she was never the energetic sort. Be more likely to spin Blue Willow plates at us like Frisbees from her porch."

"Or launch Chanel grenades."

In short order, David parked in front of her house and actually helped me, hauling one of my suitcases across the snowy yard and setting it in the spacious passenger compartment behind his seat. On the other hand, he did let me retrieve two myself, including the useless gun vault, which seemed to grow heavier each time I lifted it. He was right—Cindy didn't even make an appearance, much less give chase.

Warm and dry again in the cab, I entertained him by telling about my encounter with Tara. The highway was as iced over as the streets of Graylee. Dozens of cars had spun out and were abandoned off the shoulders and big rigs had jackknifed across the road. Despite going extra slow, it took most of the trip to tell because he kept asking for more details. Writers!

I concluded with, "And so that's how Wallace Landry's fiancée got her revenge. Unfortunately for me, I was the stand-in for my father and everyone responsible for Landry's death."

"You mean Cade?"

"I mean the whole town. You and Bebe, too—you said you knew *everything* about Dad. You could've told me about the scholarships and the pressure he put on those poor families, whose only crime was to raise the most beautiful girl in her graduating class."

"No, they had to be whip-smart, too. The girls he picked weren't always the prettiest—he wanted the complete package." He glanced over at me. "I think he was constantly trying to replace your mom. Looking back on my marriages, I wonder if I was doing the same thing."

"You and my mother were an item?" Subconsciously, I knew it must've been possible, but the fact of it took him off the dating board for sure.

"It was the late 1960s — free love had made it all the way to South Georgia. Mary Grace didn't like to be tied down to just one man."

"Then how'd my father get her to commit to him?"

"You'll love this: Brady appealed to her altruistic side, pointed out how much good they could do together." He touched my arm in what I chose to interpret as a fatherly way. "Your looks aren't the only thing you got from her. Maybe I reacted so strongly to your philanthropy pitch because it was like being with her all over again, and I couldn't face that."

David turned off the highway. His road showed only a single set of monster-truck tracks across the otherwise undisturbed strip of white that led to his home. Demonstrating a bit of OCD, he tried to stay in the same ruts as he guided us toward his amalgamation of architectural styles.

"See?" I said. "You could've helped me understand it all. I probably would've handled myself differently with Tara and not lost so much to her." He only tapped out a rhythm on the steering wheel in response, so I thought some more about the case file and started in a new direction. "Here's another thing I can't figure out: why did Landry shoot my dad seventeen times?"

"From what I heard, the guy had an angry streak." He made a sweeping left around the corner of the stone manor wing and rolled up to a garage modeled after a Victorian carriage house. With the tap of a button on the visor, he raised the solid white door, and then we coasted inside. He'd needed a wide, high-clearance building to accommodate the height of his truck and leave room for his Hyundai sedan on one side and, on the other, a white Mini Cooper with thick green and orange racing stripes, suggestive of the Irish flag, which surely belonged to Bebe.

I shook my head. "No, seventeen times is sending a message or acting out some kind of hatred. If he'd gone to the house to steal, he knew he would have to deal with my dad, but surely only one or two shots would've been enough."

"Could be the first few bullets were meant to loosen his tongue, but then Landry went nuts when it didn't work, and he emptied his gun into Brady out of frustration. Lord knows I wanted to do that to your daddy about a hundred times over the years." He replaced his sunglasses with his narrow, iconic specs and climbed down.

I dropped to the ground and pulled out the gun vault and a rolling suitcase from behind my seat. "Did my father do his drinking at home, or did he have a favorite bar?"

David yanked the remaining bag from behind his seat. "What are you getting at?"

"He had a blood-alcohol level of point-eight-four percent. Where'd he get so drunk and, if he did it anywhere but home, how could he manage to drive or fiddle with the alarm before dragging himself to bed?"

"Hmm, you've got a good head for details. If you ever start writing, think about doing mysteries."

"Afraid of some competition in the horror market?"

"No, it's just that mysteries sell well. I'm offering helpful advice—why do you always turn everything into a goddamned argument or some kind of challenge?" He didn't wait for my response, which was a good thing because I was speechless. Once again, he'd nailed my personality squarely.

Instead of guiding us out and across the icy patio, he motioned me toward a dark, open passage built into the side of the garage. He touched a button there, lowering the garage door. I propped the gun vault on top of my suitcase, turning it into a makeshift dolly. Before we started to walk, David tilted his head, as if listening for something. I didn't hear any sounds but the tick of the engine as it cooled and the drip of melted snow from the truck undercarriage to the garage floor.

He shrugged and turned toward the opening. "Here's another spooky effect," he said with a boyish grin. As we crossed the threshold, a series of gaslight carriage lamps flickered to life on both stone walls, continuing the Victorian motif and illuminating a short tunnel that evoked secret hallways and haunted sewers. In the barrel ceiling, heaters with glowing orange coils began to blow warmth on us, drowning out conversation and the clatter of rolling luggage wheels. It ruined the *Phantom of the Opera* effect, but balmy spookiness was fine with me.

The opposite end of the tunnel brought us to French doors and the tiled kitchen at the rear of the house. As we wiped our boots on a thick coconut-fiber mat, the heaters and gaslights cut off behind us. David indicated a hall to the right, leading to the Cape Cod wing. "Your suite is down yonder. I assume Cindy didn't offer a meal before kicking you out?"

"No, it wasn't exactly the gracious sanctuary she'd advertised."

"Unpack first and then get some breakfast."

The click of heels from that hallway announced Bebe before she made her appearance. Instead of red again, to match her hair and nails, she'd opted for a royal blue long-sleeved blouse, a matching, knee-length skirt, and pumps dyed to complement the outfit. "Great to have you back with us," she said, turning on the brogue with a roll to her R and a beguiling lilt at the end. "I've got your room all set, and I laid in enough food to keep us stuffed for weeks."

I said, "I hope I don't impose for that long."

"Nonsense," David drawled and gave my hand a squeeze that felt decidedly un-fatherly. "You haven't even settled in, and you're already talking about leaving?"

22

MY SUITE BOASTED PLENTY OF RUFFLES, LACE, AND PILLOWS, BUT THE OVERALL FEEL WAS maturely feminine, not girly-girl like the rooms decorated by one Stapleton Scholar after another during their senior year with my father. Not a bad place to hole up while putting my affairs back in order. As long as I could keep David at bay. He definitely was looking forward to my stay more than I was. Friends often accused me of having no dating standards, but I did draw the line at sleeping with men my mother had tagged.

As I hung my clothes, put things away in drawers, and placed toiletries on the wide double-sink of the bathroom, I wondered if he saw my mom whenever he looked at me, just as he'd speculated that my dad was forever trying to find her in the Scholars he tutored and no doubt seduced in his gross, Svengali-like way. If that were the case, I needed to make it very clear we could only be friends. Besides, I still couldn't believe he and Bebe had gone from being lovers to mere associates. Not with her acting as jealous as she was.

To keep David from getting any more ideas about me, I had to put him on the defensive and keep him there. Thinking back to our conversation in the truck and garage, he'd dodged or deftly steered me away from some of my questions, as if he were protecting someone. Bebe immediately sprang to mind, but maybe because I was feeling jealous about Cade's relationship with her and way over-thinking everything.

I took the case file into the bathroom, to flip through it again as I cleaned up. It felt good to get out of the clothes I'd lived in overnight and to scrub off the odors I'd accumulated. On the downside, as I lathered my hair, I did have a *Psycho* premonition and wondered if David and Bebe could see me through a peephole or, more likely, with a hidden camera. Another note to self: Never again bathe in a horror writer's house with my imagination set on overdrive.

However, better to be modest unnecessarily than to amble around naked as I usually did after a shower and end up on their highlight reel. Not that seeing me naked would be a highlight for either of them.

Body towel tucked into place, seated before the mirror, I worked on my hair first as I started from Cade's incident report and read through the file, page by page. By being more methodical this time, I hoped it would pay off.

Once again, I read the supplemental report, where Cade detailed learning that my father hired Wallace Landry in late June to do handyman chores around the property, and how Dad dismissed Cade's caution after the police chief related stories from others who'd paid the out-of-towner for yard work. Behind that was a page I'd overlooked the night before: the police chief had included the names and addresses for three people who had mentioned Landry's insolence and aggressiveness: a couple of men whose names I didn't recognize and Bebe McLaren.

Finally, a connection between Landry and someone else I knew. Significant? I had no idea, but I dog-eared that page and started in on my make-up. The coroner's report was such a disturbing mix of clinical detachment and lurid description that I nearly flipped past that section to pick up reading elsewhere. However, the associated forensic reports were a reminder that more had gone on than mere gunshot carnage.

The laboratory doing the toxicology had identified the percentage of alcohol—which they referred to as "ethanol"—in his system but didn't specify what kind of liquor my father had consumed in such quantities. That forced me to go back to the coroner's meticulous account, where I flipped to the page that detailed the gastrointestinal system. Stomach contents had consisted of partially digested, semisolid food consistent with Mexican cuisine and a quantity of liquid that retained the odor of tequila.

I remembered how, a few nights before, Tim had sort of freaked when I suggested a pork chimichanga and strawberry margarita. He blamed it on his concern that I'd get him drunk and grill him about his pariah comment, but maybe he felt some guilt about eating at Azteca, as if I were forcing him to return to the scene of the crime. Then again, there was no chance he would've been slugging down shots of Jose Cuervo with my father, and he didn't yet have access to the alarm code: motive but no means. Mr. Pearson did have that means, but, as he pointed out, no motive. Coming in a distant third, David ate at Azteca all the time, but he had neither a reason to kill my father nor access to the alarm code.

Bebe, on the other hand, clearly despised my dad. Maybe she'd seduced him to give herself the chance to get the code. Then she did Landry as well, filled his head with hate, and sent him to kill my father, who she could've gotten drunk for the occasion.

Tying up loose ends, she tripped the alarm once Wallace was in the house so her other lover, Cade—primed to be wary of the young man because of her warning—could end him. So, that would've been three men she had to sleep with, two of whom she knew would be killed. Would she really be capable of that? It was hard to imagine a sitcom actor becoming a real-life femme fatale. Still….

Plotting my breakfast conversation, I finished touching up my eyes, gave my cowlick a bit more mousse, and went to get dressed. Somehow I had to get some answers without being evicted again. Just in case, though, I chose my warmest jeans, a crème turtleneck topped with a jade jacket, and low heels.

Following the smell of frying bacon, I felt my stomach rumble, a reminder I hadn't eaten since my lunch with Tara the day before. I found Bebe in the kitchen whisking eggs. An apron covered her outfit, and she'd pushed up the royal blue sleeves to her freckled elbows. The domestic scene and the sweat-damp bangs she kept blowing out of her eyes made her seem less intimidating and even harder to envision as a bloodthirsty siren.

"Put me to work," I said. "Can I flip the bacon?"

"Oh my goodness no, you'll ruin that cute outfit." She tonged over the four slices before pushing chopped green onions, tomatoes, and cubed ham from a cutting board into the eggs. With a practiced hand, she poured the mixture onto the griddle and set to work scrambling it.

I asked, "Will David be joining us?"

"He eats early—has to feed his muse, don't you know." She glanced at me. "If you're here long, you'll get accustomed to his ways. Do you prefer soft or hard?"

"What are we talking about?"

"How do you like your eggs, Janet?"

"Oh." I felt my cheeks flush. "Soft is fine."

She plated up an equal portion for each of us and put the dishes on a table she'd already set with napkins, flatware, sliced toast, and spreads. Trying to contribute, I poured the coffee. Bebe removed her apron, dropped it over a chair back, and we sat across from each other in a nook that overlooked the ice-glazed snow of the backyard.

I quieted the urgent growls of my stomach with a forkful of eggs. "Do you have to do everything around here?"

"You mean all the chores?" When I nodded, she said, "We have a housekeeper, comes twice a week to clean. I've always liked to cook, so that part's a snap."

"How about yard work, leaf blowing, that kind of thing?"

She shrugged, but tension in her shoulders made the gesture look spastic rather than casual. "There're folks in town I call for that." She picked up a crispy slice of bacon and bit it in half.

"I heard Wallace Landry did handyman work for some people before my dad hired him."

Bebe gazed out the window. "Cindy Dwyer felt sorry for him. She's been so lonely since her husband died, she'll take in any vagabond off the street—not that we get many of those in the back of beyond. Anyway, she put out the word he was looking for work." After a morsel of eggs and a slug of coffee, she said, "I'm surprised you didn't get on with her. You strike me as being a lot alike, the kind whose heart goes out to strays. Ever been married?"

I frowned at the sharp conversational pivot. "Um, no. You?"

"Engaged though, right? You have that shell-shocked look of someone left at the altar."

I dropped my fork on the table. "How did you hear about that?"

"Just a gift I have for reading people. It was a tremendous help in my acting career." She looked innocent, but the truth was that I'd filled Facebook that summer with an hour-by-hour account of my shock, hurt, and bone-deep sorrow caused by Andy. Easy enough for her to find with a little digging.

"Well, I wasn't left at the altar—thank God it didn't get that far." The words were out before I realized I was offering information instead of obtaining it. "Ancient history."

"Oh, you don't look that old," she said with a wink, although she was at least five years my senior.

I drank some coffee and forced myself to eat as my temper rose. "Did you know your name was in the police reports about my dad's death? You knew the killer."

"It's a small town, as I'm sure you're realizing. Lots of people knew, or knew of, Wally."

I seized on that. "You're the only one who calls him that, except his fiancée." My smart mouth—my father's legacy—once again was primed and ready to let fly. After a pause for effect, I added, "You didn't just hire that young man, you slept with him."

Bebe didn't even blink. "Why are you behaving like someone who doesn't care about burning bridges? When I said Graylee is small, I mean it's *small*. Not like Dublin is small compared to New York City. I mean, you won't be able to avoid running into me and Cindy and everyone else you've offended in your short time with us." She crunched up more bacon, teeth snapping. "You're indeed Brady Stapleton's daughter. What's next, shutting down the town until we answer all your questions? Or, like your father, will that be your last resort when no one will sleep with *you*?"

She resumed eating, as if waiting for me to deliver my next line in a script she'd already memorized. I realized much too late I couldn't scare or influence her. With Cindy, I'd tapped into her guilt and shame as a Scholar's mother. All I had with Bebe was speculation—I couldn't prove anything. Still, my obsession with piecing together the answer wouldn't go away, so I tried a new approach.

"What does it do to a woman," I asked gently, "as she watches families give up their teenaged girls to a tyrant, one after another, for years? It doesn't matter if most of the Scholars go on to great things. This woman—blessed with beauty and smarts just like them—knows the kind of damage a man can cause, the scars that don't show but also never fade."

I continued, "What happens when she sees a family make a stand despite the pressures brought to bear, and instead of the whole town turning on the tyrant at last, she sees them target the family? Threats become actions, and the family nearly burns along with their home. Meanwhile an angry young man, down on his luck, has come to town. Does she see a way out for everyone? Stoke that man's rage and point him at the tyrant, promise that at last he can be the hero instead of the goat? After so many innocent girls' lives have been affected, is the sacrifice of one unlikable stranger really so wrong, when it's in service of the greater good?"

While I spoke, Bebe had worked her way through the eggs and bacon and polished off a slice of toast. She drained her mug and said, "Ah, but you do tell a fine story. A stirring tale, like something from the old country. You don't understand one thing, though."

"What's that?"

"The only reason I'm in South Georgia is because of my dream job with David. I don't give a flying fuck about Graylee or the people here." She glanced at my coffee cup. "Refill?"

I didn't believe her cynical act. "Are you sure anyone had to die?"

"Still a dog with her bone? Won't you give over?" She stood and started to clear the table. "You shouldn't live in a town that will take generations to recover from what your father did. Where the mere sight of you brings back the bad old days. Take your riches and go."

"Except that maybe I can help speed their recovery. It'll only take generations if no one talks about it openly." I snatched away my plate and cup as she reached for them. There was something especially awful about being waited on by the same person I was fencing with. As I deposited my dish, flatware, and mug in the sink, I said, "Maybe I can help undo some of his damage. Set up, I don't know, a sort of truth and reconciliation commission."

She placed the other items in the adjacent stainless steel basin and laughed in my face. "Well aren't you the grand lady, the savior come to rescue us all from our terrible troubles?"

"No, I think that's the role you want to play. I'm just dealing with the aftermath of what you did."

I stalked out of the kitchen and halfway down the hall filled with David's celeb photos before I forced myself to stop and breathe. To my left was the doorway into the study, with the secret pocket door that would take me into his writing space. Was he involved at all in the scheme Bebe had enacted? Assuming he wasn't, did he have any idea about what she'd done? If I brought my theory to him, would he mostly be pissed off that I'd interrupted his muse?

Behind me, water ran in the sink as Bebe scrubbed away the residue of our breakfast. She'd been right in one respect: I was burning bridges all over the place, acting like an inquisitor passing through instead of someone planning to live in Graylee. If I kept alienating people, I'd turn my worst fears, those Four Horsewomen, into self-fulfilling prophecies.

Once again seeking distraction in photographs—maybe another trait I'd picked up from my dad—I marveled at how many A-list politicians, actors, and entrepreneurs David knew. I recognized someone in every shot. At least until I reached the end of the wall, with what probably had been the first framed photo he'd hung there.

As I stared at it, two other pictures popped into my head in succession. First, the photo on Mr. Pearson's wall of three shirtless boys hamming it up in a forest glade, a clearing that could've been the very one where this house now stood. The second was a Stapleton Scholar image from Cindy's memorial wall, notable because, in subsequent years, the newspaper editor had settled on a recurring presentation style, with "Stapleton Scholar" and the year printed above the teenager's image and, underneath, the girl's name. For the first Scholar, in 1985, a larger portrait photograph showed a blond beauty with the headline "Stapleton Scholarship Winner Named" but the text below her picture had been sacrificed to fit the clipping within the uniform frame size Cindy had chosen.

I now saw that teenager again, on David's celeb wall. Slightly older, with a more mature hairstyle and an obviously forced smile, she displayed his first hardback, *Witch's Requiem*, the book that launched him into the publishing stratosphere. David had slung his arm around her in the casually affectionate way countless fathers posed with their children. The way I'd fantasized as a kid that my father would one day appear and hug me for the camera. That unhappy girl was his daughter.

What if my dad had tapped some connections through his wealthy family's network of contacts and made an offer to his childhood buddy? By David's own account in interviews, he'd obsessed over getting his manuscripts published but had been luckless early on. I imagined my father asking him how he would like the chance to see his work in print, for sale in every bookstore in America. Just one condition.

There had been no fabled summer intern who'd brought his work to the world's notice, as he'd told countless journalists. The girl he owed everything to was, in actuality, the one he'd raised and then traded to my father for a shot at fame. If I recalled correctly, David's first wife had left him before *Witch's Requiem* came out—maybe soon after he'd agreed to that deal with the devil.

Had he told Dad to fuck off, would my father have abandoned the Stapleton Scholarship notion, and settled on a far less horrible means of finding a girl who could remind him of my mother?

It was impossible to say, but as the one who carried perhaps the most compelling backstory of guilt and shame—the man who'd enabled the launch of those scholarships—David also had the perfect motive: to finally save the town from what he'd unleashed more than three decades earlier. Maybe he just needed the final push that came after my father shut down Graylee for longer than ever before and threats against an innocent family turned to actual violence. Wallace Landry's arrival had provided him with the perfect way to do it without bloodying his own hands.

I'd been gunning for the wrong person. No doubt Bebe had welcomed my accusations, because they kept my focus off her idol. At most, she probably had played a supporting role: finding the ideal fall guy and seducing Cade so that her warning about the drifter stuck in his mind. Then, David had gone to work on Landry. I knew first-hand how persuasive the author could be—it was easy to imagine the righteous fury he could kindle in the man, along with promising a reward commensurate with the deed. He even could've coached Landry about how to ingratiate himself with my father, to get a job and learn the alarm code.

All David had to do after that was give the recently hired handyman an untraceable gun and reassure him that the burglar alarm was a necessary part of the scenario—to make it look like a random break-in, not perpetrated by someone with access. Then David delivered my father home tanked on tequila, entered the code Landry had given him, and let Tara's fiancé show up at a designated time to finish the job and be finished as well.

Maybe David and Bebe saw themselves as heroes. They had achieved what even the cops and politicians had been unwilling to do, and everyone was the better for it. Except the drifter who'd been trying to earn enough to start a life with his fiancée and except Tara herself. As badly as she'd treated me, she didn't deserve to have her love stolen from her forever.

My attempts to compel Bebe to confess had failed, and I was

sure I'd fare no better with David. So here I was, in a trap of my own making: stuck in a house in the middle of nowhere, surrounded by ice and snow, with a couple of murderers. No means of transportation, no cell, no accessible weapon.

Tim's expression when I left him now made more sense. It wasn't disbelief—he suspected David, too, and, given my recent habit of making wild accusations, he'd been afraid for me.

I did the only thing I could think of. In a room near the front door, I found a cordless phone and called the chief of police.

23

I ROCKED FROM ONE FOOT TO THE OTHER, LISTENING TO CADE'S PHONE RING WHILE I TOOK IN my surroundings. The front room was a large space with an impressive collection of art and artifacts David probably had bought while on book tours all over the world. Statuary, paintings, ceramics, and much more totally overwhelmed the groupings of couches and armchairs.

Cade answered his cell, voice slow and hollow, the sound of a man who hadn't slept in a long time. "Graylee Police. This is Chief Wilson. How can I help you?"

"It's Janet."

"I was hoping it was you." He sounded relieved instead of happy. "Tim called me about Stark taking you to his place."

"Tim did?"

"He's worried. I've been trying your cell for over an hour. What do you need?"

His innocent question hurt like a kick to my ribs. Clearly he saw me as always asking for something. And, dammit, I always seemed to be. "Needy" had been one of the words Andy bludgeoned me with while booting me out of his life. Maybe he hadn't been wrong.

To salvage my pride, I contemplated ending the call after a little small talk. But then I reminded myself I'd gotten in way over my head. "I know you're overwhelmed," I stammered, "but I ne — uh — have to see you." Glancing at the two doorways in the room, I didn't spot anyone. Still, I lowered my voice. "It's about my father's murder."

"I figured. Not sure it's a good idea to be calling me from Stark's phone."

"My cell battery is dead," I said automatically, and then I replayed his comment. Did he suspect David, too? If so, why hadn't he done anything about it? Or at least warned me?

Paranoia set in, making the *absence* of sound from anywhere in the house seem ominous. Noticing a pair of samurai swords in curved scabbards on one wall, I transferred the phone to my left hand and selected the shorter of the two. I gripped the leather-wrapped hilt and drew out a two-foot arc of shiny steel. The blade rang as it came free. While no lighter than the gun vault, I could actually use this as something more dangerous than a shot put. I'd been pretty good with sparring weapons at the Y. A real sword was something else entirely, but I had no alternative.

Cade asked, "What was that noise?"

"Just arming myself. A girl can't be too careful."

"Tell me what's happening there. Right now."

How could I explain that nothing happening was even scarier than dealing with something? I replied, "I'm leaving. Can you meet me on the highway?"

"Just hunker down inside and wait for me. It's too easy to slip on this ice and break something. I'll come out there as quick as I can."

"Cade —" I clicked the Off button to hang up on him. A little suspense, I figured, might bring him sooner rather than later, as well as save me some hiking in the wrong footwear.

As I replaced the phone in its charger, I noticed a message on the screen: "Line in Use." Except I'd already ended the call, which was odd. Then the message vanished, and I realized what it meant.

Someone had been using another handset and clicked Off after I did. Here I'd been worried about an eavesdropper lurking nearby, but I hadn't considered that as soon as I'd pressed the Talk button, every other phone in the house would show I was making a call. Either Bebe or David, or both, had listened in. I'd so screwed myself.

No way was I waiting around to be rescued. I hurried to the front closet where Bebe had hung my coat the day before. There, I found a heavy, wool number, which came down to my ankles and would keep me warm during my trek to the highway. At the front door, though, I was thwarted by a locked deadbolt that required a key.

Hopefully I could still get out the way David and I had come in. I considered my route to freedom: straight shot back up the hall, through the kitchen and French doors, into the passageway, and then outside via the garage.

With my sword point leading the way, I crept along hardwood, passing the wall of photos, and paused before crossing the entrance to the study, in case Bebe or David was waiting to ambush me. No one there. I made it to the opposite end of the hall and stood still again, listening. The refrigerator compressor hummed, but I didn't hear anything else.

Scary scenes from David's books flashed through my mind,

which made me even more paranoid. I kept checking behind me to make sure someone hadn't snuck up.

Halfway across the tiled kitchen, I remembered how the gaslights and overhead heaters switched on when we had entered the tunnel. An electric eye must've triggered them, so after I turned the knob of one of the French doors—mercifully unlocked—I stepped high across the threshold. My exaggerated stride left me off-balance and feeling ridiculous, but the passageway stayed dark and quiet.

The pale light from the kitchen faded, and the garage at the other end had no windows, so I was soon navigating nearly blind. My boots seemed to crunch every bit of gravel and grit on the concrete floor. Worse, the air tickled my nose with the smell of damp stone, making me want to sneeze.

My right arm started to ache from holding the weapon up and ready. I knew I'd have to be careful not to trigger the lights and heater at the opposite end, too. With my left hand, I touched the nearest stone wall and proceeded that way, walking in darkness with both arms out and a curved short sword waving ahead of me. I soon felt the edge of the wall and stopped. The electric eye would be at ankle-level. Again I held my breath and took an arching step. So far, so good.

Once inside the large space, I saw only one, faint light source: a greenish bulb glowed on the wall button that would raise the garage door. I imagined the chain-ratcheted clatter as the panels curved overhead. Not a good choice, but I hadn't noticed earlier whether there was a regular door through which I could exit in silence.

My eyes had adjusted a bit, allowing me to make out the

vague shapes of vehicles before I blundered into any of them. As I eased between David's Hyundai and truck, however, my sword point clunked off the passenger side mirror of the sedan. I sucked in a breath and held still.

"So, you're, like, the lamest samurai in the world." Tara's voice, soft but unmistakable, somewhere in the dark. "I'm just saying."

It took a moment to calm myself—I'd nearly shrieked and leapt straight up to the rafters like a cartoon cat. Once I remembered how to breathe again, so many questions crowded my mind I whispered the first one that occurred to me, "Tar, where are you?"

"Other side of the truck. Don't come over here because I'm, like, scared you'll poke out my eye by accident, or whatever."

It wouldn't be accidental, but I needed to remain civil. She could make a racket louder than the garage door and bring Bebe and David running. I crept around the side mirror and made it to the tailgate of the truck without further incident. "You can see me?" I asked.

"Daddy's night vision goggles. They're great for hunting."

She had her father's pistol and one of mine, but hopefully she wasn't hunting for me this time. I eased around to the opposite back corner of the truck and lowered the sword so she wouldn't view me as a threat. "How'd you get in here?"

"Well, duh. You had a hand-drawn map to this place in your purse, which is a total mess by the way. I almost threw out the napkin thinking it was just more crap. So, when you and the writer dude rolled up in his truck, I made a break from my cover in the woods and got inside right before the door closed—dived under it total commando style, way cool—and hid on the other side of the Mini, which looks cute, but I really like the Jag better.

Sorry, I got it, like, stuck out at the tree nursery—not exactly an off-roader, but I didn't want to be on the streets in case you went loco on me and got the Graylee Gestapo to put out a BOLO or whatever. Once the snow clears and the dirt trails firm up I'm sure it'll be totally drivable again. Might need a new suspension, and I think I sort of bent, like, one axle. Well, both."

At last she inhaled, so I had a chance to murmur what probably should've been my first question: "But *why* are you here in David Stark's garage?"

"I took the Jag and all back to my campsite, and the snow started to fall, so I cranked up the heater and got snug on those great leather seats and went on Facebook to see if I could get more, like, intel on why this place is such a hot mess. With the way that Denny's waitress kept going on about your daddy and looking at me sort of like I was jailbait but definitely not the first hottie to sit in that booth, I wondered if he had a thing for, you know, young chicks or whatever, so I started searching for girls that listed Graylee as their hometown."

She kept her voice low, but the patter was machine-gun fast and nonstop. I just leaned against the tailgate in the dark, set the sword at my feet, and let her continue to spew. "So, this one chick who lived in town friended me back and was, like, 'Whoa, you need to write to this other girl to get the 411 on what's been happening here forever.' And then that girl friended me back and was, like, 'Your fiancé's a hero for shooting that dirty old man,' and she introduced me to a whole bunch of other girls—some older than you even—and they've got this secret society, or whatever, because their parents all made them spend their senior year of high school with your daddy, who was a major creepster it turns out.

"So, some of them have gotten over it, but lots are still bummed their folks sold them into, like, slavery. This one chick was the very first but didn't want to talk about it and unfriended me real fast after I told her what my connection to Graylee was. I recognized her last name because it was the same one on your napkin map, and I remembered my daddy keeps a ratty David Stark paperback in his gear for when it gets boring in the tree stand, or whatever. Anyway, by then it was, like, midnight and the windows were all covered in snow, so I hunkered down in my sleeping bag in the tiny back seat. When I woke up today, I decided to track down this Stark dude and get him to tell me more."

As much as I would've liked to observe a conversation between those two, I wanted to make a run for it even more. Part of me was in awe of her ability to get to the heart of the scandal so much more quickly and effectively than I did. If I hadn't grilled Cindy, I still would've been figuratively in the dark. Of course, what had led me to interrogate Cindy was Tara forcing me to flee my home without ID, money, or keys, so most of me remained seriously pissed. And all of me was literally in the dark thanks to her.

I hefted the blade but kept it against my leg as I went around to the other side of the truck. Still unable to make her out in the gloom, I whispered, "I'm pretty sure 'this Stark dude' set up Wally to kill my father and then get killed by the police. Now he knows I know. That's why I'm carrying around this sword."

"Not, like, the best choice of weapons. I'm just saying."

Through gritted teeth, I snarled, "Well, you stole one gun from me, and I'm not able to get at my pistol with the laser sight because you also took my keys, so I can't open the gun vault I've been hauling all over goddamn Graylee."

"Uh oh, Miss Pottymouth is back. Dollar for the swear jar."

My voice had risen along with my temper. Stifling a further rant, I said more quietly, "I figure a sword is better than nothing. And now here I am: in the dark, in danger, and with no idea what to do except get out of here."

"In those boots? The snow's all crusted over with ice. You'll, like, slip and break something."

"Well, I need to try. The police chief is on the way, but I can't wait."

"I'm staying. From here I can see what's going on in part of the kitchen—I watched you wheel your bags toward your bedroom and come back to eat breakfast with that curvy chick. When I spot the writer again, I'll, like, make my move. Get him to tell me if he framed Wally."

"And then what?"

"Maybe I can rig it so the police chief shoots him, too. That would be sweet. Total poetic justice."

In spite of what I thought David had done, I didn't want Cade to have to shoot him. Too many people had died already. Now, instead of saving my own ass, I wondered if I should stay to broker some sort of deal, so no one else got hurt. Maybe the best way to produce a stalemate in the violence department was to make sure I had a decent weapon myself. I said, "Since we're on the same side and friends again, can I have my keys back?"

I heard a hand patting synthetics, as if checking half-a-dozen pockets. Then Tara said, "So, I guess I left them in the Jag with your purse and coat. I ran the heater some this morning, and I didn't think I'd need keys out here."

Another of her lies? No way to know. "That's okay, just give me my other gun."

"How can I be sure you won't try to, like, shoot me for making your life a little less boring?"

"What if I promise?"

"What if I hold onto it for safe keeping, in case the Stark dude sort of catches and searches you?"

"What if I sic the police chief on you when he gets here?"

"What if I, like, shoot you now? I'm point blank."

That made me thrash around with my sword. The blade banged off the rear quarter panel of the pickup and a side window of the Mini Cooper.

Tara giggled. "Even in night-vision green that was great. I wish I was videoing this."

Totally stymied, I said much too loudly, "Don't you want to stop waiting around and just do something?"

"So, I guess you've never gone hunting. That's, like, the question every little kid asks their first time."

"I'm out of here, but we're not done with each other—I still want all my stuff back." I turned and edged around the low shape of the Mini and then held out my sword until its tip poked the garage wall. Once again I felt with my free hand, this time searching for a door.

"A little to the right," Tara said. "Getting warmer. Warmer still."

I kept moving that way until I touched one of the metal tracks for the overhead door. "Thanks a lot," I spat and reversed course.

"No problem. Want to play Marco Polo?"

What I wanted was a normal Christmas Eve: last-minute

shopping, too much drink, indecent portions of food, and a favorite holiday movie or two with a man I loved before a vigorous roll in the sack that made visions of sugarplums dance in both of our heads. I was about as far from that as possible.

At last, my left hand touched wood molding and slid across a regular door. Then I found the deadbolt that required a key. I rattled the knob anyway, but no joy. After all of that, I could only put my back to the cold, smooth surface and slowly slide down until my legs stretched invisibly in front of me and the sword clattered to the concrete.

"So," Tara said, "I was going to tell you but you were all, like, woman-on-a-mission, and I didn't think you'd listen."

She was right—I wouldn't have. God, I was tired. I wanted to sleep forever.

The deadbolt clicked, and the door bumped my head and back. I tried to dig in, but my heels couldn't gain traction, and my fingernails were even more useless. As the door continued to push me in a slow but inexorable slide across the concrete, a whimper escaped my throat. I reached for the sword hilt, but it had moved as well. My fingers closed around a blade so sharp I didn't realize I'd cut all four fingers to the bone until the outpouring of blood made my hand warmer than the rest of me. I wanted to cry for Tara to open fire, but my throat wouldn't work.

Cade's voice, not David's, drawled above me. "Sorry, I didn't know you were on the other side. It felt like I was pushing sandbags out of the way."

Blinding sunlight streamed in through the partial opening. All I could make out was the silhouette of his Smokey Bear hat and head above me. I'd never seen anything so beautiful in my life. Instead of challenging him on the sandbag remark, all I could manage to say was, "How?"

"It was Bebe. Came out to the cruiser as I pulled up and said you'd freaked—started running around with a sword and were holed up here in the dark."

"Hidden cameras," I murmured to myself. I'd ended up on their highlight reel after all.

"Hunh? Anyhow, she gave me a key and said to get you out of here before you got hurt."

Now shaky with chills, I put my trembling right hand into the brilliant sunbeam and gasped at the thick scarlet that coated it. "Too late," I whispered.

Cade took out a handkerchief, which was still warm from his pocket as he tied a makeshift tourniquet around my fingers. He told me to make a fist and squeeze hard. Red quickly soaked through the white cloth, but the pressure felt good.

"Let me help you up." He edged inside and crouched, knees appearing on either side of me. I slumped against his inner thighs and let my head fall back until it struck his flat stomach. If I didn't feel totally wrung out, I would've paid more attention to all that body contact.

He slid his hands beneath my armpits and stood, hauling me upright with him. Getting to second base would've been as easy as shifting his fingers, but he remained a perfect gentleman. Cade turned me to face him, took a pair of sunglasses from his coat pocket and shook them open with one hand while the other supported my back, as if I were his dance partner. "Sun's awful bright," he said, "and you've been hiding in here with the mushrooms." He eased the ear stems into place and leveled the lenses against my cheekbones. "Need help walking?"

I nodded, mostly because I wanted to feel his arm around me. It was a good call on my part, because we didn't get very far after we shuffled out of the garage and into the glare. Without Cade's support, I would've pitched forward in lock-kneed terror.

David Stark blocked our path. He leveled a pump shotgun at us.

24

"STEADY," CADE MURMURED. HE HELD ME UP ALONG HIS RIGHT SIDE, WHICH WAS ALSO WHERE he kept his holstered gun. Because of me, he couldn't get at it. Also, we were standing between David and the door set into the garage, so Tara wouldn't have a clear shot.

David's deep voice seemed to boom in the frosty air as he said, "Thought you'd be in there forever." He shrugged inside his heavy plaid jacket and wriggled his leather-gloved fingers beneath the pump shotgun. "I was starting to get cold. Bebe, fetch his holster and utility belt and anything else he's carrying."

Bebe emerged from the shadows alongside the house and tottered toward us on the ice-slick pavement, her royal blue dress covered by a full-length sable coat I'd rejected while inspecting the hall closet. Her high heels were an even worse choice of winter footwear than my city boots. She refused to make eye contact as she approached. Face pinched, lips tight, she looked as if she were willing herself not to cry.

I was doing the same, and my shaking had returned, forcing Cade to grip me even tighter. David looked at ease, aiming from about twenty feet away, as if he threatened people every day. In his books, some of his characters did—it made me wonder if he'd always wanted to try this for real. Because I wouldn't let things lie, he was getting his chance.

Scuffing behind us, Bebe whispered, "I'm so sorry. I never

wanted it to end this way." Her hands shook worse than mine as they edged between my ribs and Cade's hip. She fumbled with the front of his equipment belt before finally managing to pull the leather free of the buckle and slipping it through the loops in his trousers. The holstered pistol, Taser, handcuffs, and the rest clattered behind us on the snow-glazed driveway.

Next, she came around front, hands still jittery as she unzipped his leather jacket and felt its inside and outside pockets, only tossing a pair of gloves aside. She removed his hat, checked the inside, and, still not meeting his eyes, flipped that onto the pavement as well. I tensed, ready to grab her as a hostage and a shield, but Cade's arm held me in place. Maybe he figured David wouldn't hesitate to mow down all three of us, seeing as how Bebe had given Cade the key so he could rescue me. She'd probably told David a story about how Cade had grabbed it from her, but he'd be pissed off and suspicious for sure. Bebe backed away, head down, but David called, "Pants pockets and ankles. Come on, hon, don't get shy on me now."

She added Cade's phone, wallet, and keys to the pile behind us and gave me a pat-down for good measure. After easing onto her knees, using the fur as an expensive cushion, she pulled up his trouser cuffs to reveal calf-high boots and ran her fingers along the tops of them. She pivoted to face David and raised her voice: "There's nothing more."

"Okay, let's get them inside."

Bebe stood, brushed futilely at the icy ovals her knees had crushed into the fur, and then stepped gingerly behind us again. She gathered up the armload of Cade's gear, making a keening sound that reminded me of a trapped animal.

The chief called to David, "This doesn't have to get ugly. Janet thinks she knows something, but she can't prove it. Just like I couldn't back in July. That's why my report is so cut-and-dried. Drifter breaks in, kills Brady, I kill him—simple. We know it's not, but I'm willing to live with the ambiguity. Always have been."

If only I had been as well, neither of us would be about to die, probably only minutes from now. Cade hadn't shared his suspicions because he'd wanted me to avoid this very scenario. I whispered an apology to him, but he kept his focus locked on David.

The author replied, "I don't think that's true anymore. She won't turn loose of it. Gonna back you into a corner, force you to reopen the investigation." He gestured with the shotgun barrel at an open door in the back of the house. "Now walk."

"I'm not interested in what happened anymore," I said, hating the mewling terror in my voice. "I'll even leave Graylee."

"No, darling, I think it's a family trait, from your daddy to your brother and you. Some people just can't let shit go."

The inclusion of my brother was a sucker punch. "What's this have to do with Brady Jr.?"

He took more careful aim at us. "Walk or die. Your choice."

The door David motioned us toward was on a line that kept us between him and Tara. I had to give her a chance. Hopefully she was only waiting for us to get out of the way so she could start shooting. Just one viable option occurred to me. With Bebe bringing up the rear, though, I couldn't risk telling Cade.

The police chief's grip on my shoulder loosened as we took careful steps on the slick pavement. Looking down to my right, where my kerchief-wrapped hand remained clenched, I watched a steady drip of blood mark our reluctant progress toward the door.

From behind us came the sound of a gun clearing its leather

holster. Bebe had drawn Cade's service pistol. Now two weapons were pointed at us. Did she know what I had in mind?

I still had to risk it. Letting my right boot slide in front my left, I yelled with feigned surprise and pitched onto my side, knocking the sunglasses off my face. Stupidly, I trapped my injured hand under me, and an intense, fiery pain in my forearm finally brought the tears I'd been holding back. My momentum pulled Cade onto his knees, out of Tara's line of fire. I heard Bebe slip and then hit the deck, too, cursing.

Near the door, David shouted, "What the—" before gunfire drowned out the rest. Beside his head, stone chips exploded from the wall. He whirled toward the garage and fired, then pumped and fired again.

Tara shrieked. Her scream died down to a whimper. Then silence. At least, that's how it sounded to me, with ears ringing from the gunfire. I had just gotten her killed. Now I had two reasons to cry.

Cade touched my back and asked, "You know who the girl is?" After I nodded, he studied my tear-streaked face for a moment before asking whether I'd hurt myself. I tried to push upright, but as soon as I put weight on my forearm, a fresh wave of pain made me howl.

David pumped the shotgun once more and aimed at us again. "Who was that?"

Ignoring him, the police chief helped me sit up and cradle my right arm with my left. The thick coat sleeve spared me from seeing the fracture. He checked the pulse on my right wrist with two gentle fingers, nodded, and said, "You're getting good blood flow to your hand. Run your thumbnail over your fingertips and tell me if you can feel that." I did and could, and he told me it was another good sign: the lack of nerve damage meant I probably had nothing worse than a clean break.

Cade hollered to David, "I think she broke her forearm."

"I don't give a fuck. Who was shooting at me?"

I wailed, "Her name's Tara. She was Wallace Landry's fiancée."

"Shit," he barked, "that damn night just won't go away. Bebe, make sure I finished her."

Bebe picked herself up and took her time walking to the garage in her heels. Dime-sized holes from David's two sprays of buckshot pocked the building. As I watched her unsteady steps, I glanced at Cade's gear on the ground behind us. I hadn't seen her take his pistol, but I knew I'd heard her draw it. Then I noticed the bulge in the back of his leather jacket, at his belt line. She'd tucked the gun in his pants.

Her heroics made me tremble again. There was no need to do what I had done—she'd already given us a fighting chance. Tara's death had gone from tragic to pointless. Cade must've felt my shuddering, and maybe he knew why, because he stroked my back in comforting circles.

Bebe disappeared through the doorway and came back out a minute later. Her complexion had gone from pale to chalky. "She's dead, shot in the chest." Her voice cracked. "She was just a girl."

David muttered, "They were all just girls. That's why we did what we did."

I said, "But what does it have to do with my brother?"

"Chief, get her up and inside. C'mon, hon, grab his shit and let's get this over with." He looked at the garage one more time. "Have to tell the cops I shot at a deer and missed or something." He then felt the three white craters Tara's bullets had gouged from the gray stone near his head and groused, "And somehow explain how the deer shot back. Fuck me." He trained his shotgun on us again.

Cade lifted me by the armpits once more, careful to make sure he didn't aggravate my fracture. Shock must've set in, because the pain had gone from hellishly intense to merely excruciating. Sounds had muted, and I felt as if I moved underwater.

I looked back, pretending to check on Bebe's progress toward us but really seeing how noticeable the pistol was beneath his jacket. The leather seam rode higher than his beltline — the gun definitely showed. As we approached the threshold, I let Cade get ahead of me so I could block David's view of the chief's back. Even in this situation, Cade hesitated over entering a room ahead of a woman, but his good sense prevailed over his idea of good manners.

When to act? David had a clear view through the entrance and stood just ten feet away. If I moved aside so Cade could draw, David would cut both of us down with a single shot.

I stayed close behind the chief as we walked farther into what appeared to be a business office. It featured the same kind of large standing desk as in his writing space, but paper stacks of varying heights were mounded like white anthills around the laptop and on every other horizontal surface. Marked-up calendars and bulletin boards with clippings dangling from a hundred pushpins cluttered three walls. The fourth wall sported the exterior door through which we'd entered, along with flanking windows that allowed dusty light to stream in. To our right, a short hall led to his writing room, with its clean airiness and blaze of sunshine.

"That's far enough," David said to us, closing the door. "Bebe, drop the pile on the desk. Afterward, we'll put everything back in his pockets and all."

We still faced away from David. Cade tapped my thigh with three fingers, then two. At the touch of his index finger alone, I turned to face David, still cradling my right arm in my left, and partially shielded Cade, who pivoted in sync. What a damn shame—we would've made excellent dance partners.

Bebe dumped everything on the table in front of David, who looked at us for a moment, then at his shotgun. He aimed it one-handed while he opened a drawer in his standing desk with the other and came out with a chunky, matte-black pistol that looked like a hand cannon. He thumbed off the safety and said, "Shotgun's too fucking noisy and messy for inside the house. Besides, I think I've just finished writing this scene in my head, and it's a helluva lot better than y'all getting blown in half. It's always satisfying to create the perfect ending to a story."

Holding my gaze, he added, "Sorry you're never going to experience that bit of writing bliss." He kept his eyes on us as he leaned the shotgun against the exterior door. The fact that he still wore his thin leather gloves—no fingerprints or gunshot residue on his hands—gave me some idea of what he had in mind. No amount of martial arts heroics on my part could save us.

Bebe had ditched her sable over a chair in the corner and edged toward the hall. She wrung her hands, eyes flicking between David and Cade. The royal blue fabric under her arms had turned black with sweat.

"Janet," David rumbled, "you're a fan of my work, so you know I like my books to wrap up plausibly. Keep that disbelief suspended all the way through. Tell me how you think this sounds:

I'm picturing a love triangle—a classic story everybody understands—involving you, me, and Cade. I'll flatter myself by imagining you'd been with Cade but have now fallen for me. Cade's furious and comes here to—"

"Tell me about Brady Jr.," I said. "What does any of this have to do with him?"

"After I finish my story—don't be rude now, I'm the one with the gun."

"No, not until you tell me about my brother." When he started up again about the love triangle, I shouted over him, "Lalalalalala."

"Goddammit," he yelled and shook the pistol at me. After a breath, he said, "Okay, fine," and then grinned. "It's another good story, actually. I'm assuming you now know about my daughter, Lisa, and my agreement with your father that started this town's nightmare. Not to mention costing me my first marriage and Lisa's love." After I nodded, he continued. "What you probably don't know is that Lisa and Brady Jr. were childhood sweethearts and stayed in touch even after Mary Grace took the two of you and hightailed it north of Atlanta."

He glanced over at Cade. "Chief, I don't like that calculating look in your eyes, as if you're deciding when to try something. Don't know what you have in mind and don't care. You can be dead right now or dead after she finally lets me spin out the story I have in mind. If I shoot you now, I'll just have to do a minor rewrite, but I'm used to that." He aimed the gun at Cade's head.

The chief put his hands in his jacket pockets and said, "I'm not planning anything. It's your show. You're in control."

"Damn straight." He lowered his arm and pointed the gun steadily at Cade's chest, looking as though he could keep it trained there all day. To me, he said, "Your dad makes his offer. I know you want to ask how could I and all, but I'm not going into that ever again. You'll reach the afterlife soon—ask my first wife. I had to pay hush money to her for more than three decades. The bitch finally died of cancer last year, hallelujah. Anyway, Lisa tells Brady Jr. what's going on and brags to me that they're going to elope and live in Atlanta.

"I call the boy and tell him I've seen the light and support their decision to get married, but I'm worried my daughter will be starting out in a hole, so I want to give him what amounts to a dowry. I meet him up in Acworth, outside his high school after class, and talk him into following me to a dive bar I spotted on the way up, the kind of place where they won't card a minor as long as you keep the cash coming. I treat him to some burgers and drinks, get him liquored up good, dump him in his passenger seat, and drive his car onto a busy rail line."

As David recited the synopsis of what I realized was going to be my brother's murder, Cade put his left arm around my waist to comfort me. The worst part was the lack of inflection in David's voice—just talking through another plot summary. Who cared if the victim's sister stood before him?

He finished with, "I move him into the driver seat, pour more whiskey down his throat for good measure, leave the bottle at his feet, and hike back to the bar to get my wheels. Came up with the ideas for my next two bestsellers, so I didn't mind the walk. What's more, your father only learned about the 'accident' long after and never connected it with me. Broke the poor guy's heart for a while, so I guess I've gotten my revenge twice now."

The certainty of being shot to death in the next few minutes and the shock of my broken arm overwhelmed me so much I couldn't fit in many other feelings. Between rage and sorrow, the heartache won out. Cursing David wasn't going to save me, but my doomed brother and grief-stricken mother both deserved more tears while I could shed them. Cade held me up as I fell apart.

My hiccupping sobs might've provided a good distraction for him to draw his pistol, but I knew he was afraid David would shoot me in the melee. Maybe I should've collapsed again to get out of the way, but the thought of landing on my fractured arm was scarier than a bullet blasting through me.

David's only reaction to my breakdown was a look of pride: his story had achieved the desired effect. Another notch for the master of terror. As I bawled, he repeated, "Lalalalala," until I'd settled into quivering silence. "Now then," he thundered, "back to our originally scheduled program. The love triangle: you, me, and Cade. Chief finds out about your duplicity and flies over here in a fury. Bebe and I are in the other wing of the house. Cade goes through the unlocked front door and discovers you lounging in the kitchen. Temper out of control, he snaps your arm. That doesn't satisfy his jealous rage, though, so he shoots you to death and, finally realizing what he's done, takes his own life."

"No booze?" Cade asked, still keeping me upright. "I thought that was your MO—you used it twice and then let someone else, or something, do the killing for you."

"I'm branching out, and hoping like hell it's the last time. I'm getting too old for this shit. Let's go to the kitchen." He reached for Cade's equipment belt and paused for a moment over the empty holster. With a look of resignation, he said, "Aw, hell, Bebe."

She turned and started to run down the hall as Cade shoved me aside and reached around for his pistol. David didn't flinch—he shot Cade and then pivoted and fired into Bebe's back, pitching her into a face-first slide that ended in his writing space.

Ears buzzing again, I somehow kept my balance. Cade sprawled on the hardwood nearby, left hand pressing against the blood-spattered leather covering his right shoulder. As I dropped to my knees, David swung his pistol in my direction but held his fire. I laid my broken forearm in my lap, hissing at the pain, and put my left hand on top of his to push down harder.

David hurried over and snatched up Cade's weapon. "Okay," he said to me, "I think I can use this. You were anticipating his outrage and waiting here with my gun. He comes at you, and you wing him before he disarms you, breaking bones in the process. Still, you reach for my fallen pistol, but he draws his first and kills you and then Bebe, who heard all the gunfire and came running. Now he's murdered not just one of his lovers but both of them, so he kills himself." He gave me a self-satisfied smile and asked, "What do you—"

The sound of wood sliding on wood interrupted him. Someone had found the switch for the pocket door. The author aimed both pistols toward the hall. "Christ, now what?"

"It's my deputies," Cade said through clenched teeth.

"Bullshit."

An electronic hum sounded from the writing room, which gradually darkened as blinds slid into place over the huge panels of glass. Still applying pressure to Cade's wound, I thought about poor, conflicted Bebe. She'd tried a couple of things to help us, and I was betting there had been a third and final gambit. If it failed as well, we'd soon be dead. I swiveled my gaze to focus on the sunlight streaming through the office windows and then caught David's eye.

David said, "Yeah, two can play at that game." He looked toward the hall, and I knew what he was thinking: to make our room dark as well and even the odds, he'd have to cross the line of fire. "Janet, pull the shades."

"But Cade needs—"

He aimed at Cade's head. "Do it or he won't be needing anything but a eulogy."

I struggled to get to my feet without jostling my broken arm. Cradling it again with my left, I mentally said a "Please don't shoot me" prayer as I crossed in front of the open doorway. It was impossible to ignore Bebe's body, face down, at the threshold to the writing space. One blue shoe lay in the hall, and the sight of her pale, bare foot broke my heart all over again.

At the windows, I drew one shade, dimming the room somewhat. The shotgun was propped upright against the exterior door. Certain David was watching me, I made a big show of studying it.

He drawled, "Don't even try, darling. Remember, it's the chief here who'll catch the first bullet, square in the face, and then I'll gut-shoot you so I still have a bargaining chip. With you wailing like a banshee from the pain, it'll be a fast negotiation."

I made a wide arc around the shotgun. For the second shade, I pulled it down slowly, allowing the office to get darker by degrees. Trying for maximum drama, I kept glancing between David and the nearby weapon.

As the room was cast into gloom, he shouted, "Okay, get away from there." I didn't, and he took a couple of steps toward me, pistol aimed. "Do it, goddammit."

Then I saw something even better than I'd hoped for, what Bebe had made possible with her last bit of deceit. A shimmering laser dot of red appeared on David's plaid jacket at stomach-level and moved rapidly toward his chest.

At that moment, he seemed to remember the threat in the other room and turned that way as a pistol crack resounded from the writing space. A bloody, quarter-sized hole appeared in his coat, below his heart. He toppled backward into a filing cabinet and crumpled to the floor.

"You got him, Tara," I shouted. "Hold your fire."

"No problem," came the reply from the next room. I imagined her watching me through her father's night vision goggles, still clutching the laser-sighted pistol she must've taken from my gun vault. Which meant she'd lied about not having my keys. Tough to hold it against her. Bebe had done an even better job of lying—though she would've called it acting—to convince all of us that Tara was dead. Her final gambit had paid off.

David peered at me. His narrow, iconic glasses were askew, and blood bubbled on his lips. He looked like he wanted to make a final pronouncement, some famous last words, while he clawed the hardwood. His gloved fingers closed around one of the dropped pistols.

I snatched up the shotgun with my left hand, which was sticky with Cade's blood. Stock pressed between my elbow and ribs, I swung it around as he aimed at me. Mad, sad, glad, scared. Somehow, I felt all of them at the same time when I pulled the trigger.

25

"AREN'T WE A PAIR?" I ASKED CADE IN THE PATIENT LOUNGE OF THE COUNTY HOSPITAL LATE that night. Along with Tim and Tara, we slouched in a ring of upholstered chairs, which surrounded a low table where vending-machine coffee steamed in paper cups. Cade and I both wore our right arms in slings. My fingers had been stitched and taped, and a splint held my forearm in place. Fortunately, I'd just broken the ulna, not the radius as well. Cade had undergone surgery to patch the wound to his shoulder.

"We could be," he replied. He looked like he meant it.

"Whoa, Chief," Tim said in a louder, more confident voice than usual. "I thought this was a place for holding a vigil, not a pick-up spot."

"Yeah, no, totally," Tara said, twining a raspberry-dyed lock of hair around her finger as she gazed at Tim. "So, they've been operating, like, forever on Bebe. You think they're doing other things to her, you know, sort of getting it all out of the way at once? A boob reduction maybe? What? The girl's really top-heavy. I'm just saying."

The problem with Tara was she did enough brave, brilliant things to force me to forgive the antics that were just plain wrong. Tim grinned and shook his head. He seemed to find everything about her to be guileless and charming—the guy was falling hard. They both were.

After Tara had called 911 at David's house, I'd recited Tim's number to her from memory so he and Mr. Pearson would know what had happened. They arrived at the hospital ahead of us, Tim stayed on, and he and Tara had bonded during the long hours while Cade and I were getting fixed up. She'd even talked him into taking a cab with her back to Graylee, hiking to the slushy pine grove, and retrieving my things from the stranded Jaguar. He ruined his dress shoes, but came back to the hospital a new man, chattering away as they held hands.

They'd found me resting in the lounge and deposited an armload of items beside me. There were no electrical outlets nearby, so I'd plugged my phone into the emergency charger, more out of habit than a desire to reconnect with the outside world. My interior world had been in turmoil since I pulled the shotgun trigger.

I'd killed a man, literally blew him apart. While I'd been careful to avoid looking directly at David's body, I could still feel the bone-rattling recoil through my left arm and ribcage and conjure the explosive boom. His dried blood flecked my slacks and boots. At the time, I thought I was defending myself and even avenging my brother, but afterward I felt as if he'd forced me to do it, so I would corrupt a piece of my soul.

Cade's soft drawl drew me back to the present. "It gets easier to live with. Time heals."

Somehow he knew. I wondered if my face reflected the same haunted look I'd seen in his when he'd driven me to my father's house that first time. There should've been something glorious when you not only confronted evil but destroyed it. However, I now realized what Cade had told me was true: no matter how complete your victory, some of the darkness will touch you. And leave scars. Maybe the three people seated there would always remind me of that darkness; maybe all of Graylee would affect me that way until I followed my mother's course of action and fled.

In answer to the police chief, I said only, "I hope so."

Tim and Tara had been staring at their phones during the slightest conversational lull for hours now. It seemed like a good distraction, but I couldn't lose myself in my New York friends' Christmas Eve postings and texts. While I cared about their lives, I was too far removed from them emotionally now, as well as physically.

I wondered how many of those old friends I would bother to trade pleasantries with in a year's time. My life already had taken such a radically different trajectory. Despite their sophistication and witty banter, their knowledge of wines and fashion, the countless times we had laughed together and shared in each other's triumphs and disasters, I realized I felt a much deeper bond with my brand new Graylee friends. We were survivors of the same war.

When I looked at Tim, Tara, and Cade, I saw three courageous people who had my back. Rather than merely remind me of the darkness, they could help me keep it at bay. Together, we could make Graylee a special place to live.

Squeaky wheels in the hallway announced the arrival of an orderly. He stuck his head through the doorway. "Y'all ain't supposed to be in here. Visiting hours —"

In unison, Tara, Tim, and I pointed at Cade, who raised his badge high in his left hand.

Immediately the guy put up his arms, as if surrendering. "Hey, it's cool. Second shift didn't tell me the five-oh was on a stakeout."

In a solemn voice he said, "Y'all have a blessed day and a merry Christmas." The squeak of wheels diminished as he pushed his cart down the hall.

Tim checked his phone. "The dude's right—it's officially Christmas morning." He asked me, "Got any plans?"

"All my spare clothes are at the crime scene, so I guess I'm going to spend the day in my own bed for a change." I realized how that sounded out of context and blushed. Adding "alone" to clarify things wouldn't help, especially with Cade staring at me and Tara whispering in singsong, "Awkward," so I simply drank some coffee and looked at the police chief. "You?"

"New case file to work on, obviously. If Bebe pulls through, I'll have to charge her as an accessory to the murders of your daddy and Wallace Landry and have the sheriff put a guard on her door here. The county prosecutor might go easy, given her last-minute help, but you never know."

He rubbed his baggy, bloodshot eyes. "Also, I've got to come up with a story to feed the media. The world will want to know what happened to one of their favorite writers. B.J. and J.D. have been giving out the usual 'investigation in progress' line, but that's not going to work much longer. Anytime now, some reporter's going to get word about Bebe and show up here with a camera-man." Making a circle with his left hand to encompass all of us, he said, "We're going to be in the spotlight for a while."

"Not only that," Tim said, "but somebody like Cindy Dwyer will start talking to the press, and then the whole story will get out. I can see the headline in *People*: 'A Small Town's Shame.'"

He was right—the victims and their families soon would be thrust into the glare, no matter what I did now. However, if I didn't try to do anything more but just let the feeding frenzy run its course, I wouldn't be responsible merely for killing David Stark—I would kill all of Graylee. I told Cade, "When I launch a truth and reconciliation commission to help people start to come together, the media will make it especially ugly for you. Lots of finger-pointing and questions to answer."

"I deserve it," he said. He brought his left wrist close to the sling so he could use the fingers of his right hand to remove the sleek, expensive watch. Then he dropped it onto the linoleum and stomped down, crushing it under his boot heel. The sudden violence made me jump, and I anticipated an embarrassed apology from him, but he kept his face lowered and rocked his foot side to side, grinding the pieces into ever-smaller bits. Maybe he finally was coming to grips with how much he'd allowed himself to be corrupted and the pain he'd now have to endure to make amends. Taking a bullet might prove to be the least of it.

My initial impulse was to reassure him, connect with him physically, make myself indispensable in his journey back to honor and righteousness. Here's a guy who wants you, said the scared voice that had been my constant guide on all matters related to the opposite sex. Make sure he doesn't get away. It was that or face the Horsewomen again with their condemnations and prophesies. Lonely. Abandoned. Unattractive. Unloved. Right?

Wrong. I'd gone six months without a man and thought I could go six years or sixteen if I wanted to. In the past few days, I'd finally come into my own. I had embarked on a quest that turned into a purpose, a reason for being. Not only had I made a difference, but now I could do even more that mattered.

Perhaps Cade continued his hospital vigil in part because he still had feelings for Bebe. Or, possibly, he only was interested in me romantically. Until I decided I was genuinely interested in him, though—and not merely giving in to my fears—I didn't care either way. There was real freedom in vowing never to be needy again.

Cade cleaned up his mess as best he could with one arm in a sling, dumped the watch fragments into a trashcan, and slumped again beside me. Since he was on my right, I couldn't pat his knee, so I nudged his boot with the toe of mine. That was as much contact as I wanted to commit to for the moment, and his smile told me he was grateful to get it.

Obviously trying to lighten the mood, Tim said, "Hey, Janet, after you've got everybody in Graylee healed through the power of story and shared tears, and we're all singing 'Kumbaya' together, what are you going to do? Run your businesses? Run for mayor? Wander from town to town fixing their problems like some kind of TV hero?"

His snarky "power of story" comment reminded me of David Stark's quip that I would never know the satisfaction of creating the ideal end to a tale, "that bit of writing bliss." The natural follow-up to my truth and reconciliation commission would be something that connected my mother and brother's tragic journeys with the scandal of the so-called scholarships—and how the knots of a seemingly perfect crime came undone.

"I'm going to write a book about all this," I said, "seeing as how Graylee now has an opening for the job of best-selling author."

Tara asked, "Seriously? What are you going to, like, call it?"

"*Aftermath*."

SPECIAL OFFER TO READERS OF *AFTERMATH*

I find it impossible to adequately express my gratitude to readers of my books. There are so many other ways you can spend your precious time and money, so I am humbled whenever anyone selects my work for entertainment and hopefully—borrowing from David Stark—to feel genuine, deep down, real emotions.

Without readers, writers are superfluous. Without readers' reactions, writers can't know whether they succeeded in their purpose, and other readers won't have guidance about whether a book is likely to suit their tastes. To encourage you to share your reaction to *Aftermath* with me and fellow readers, I propose a two-for-one trade: two more pieces of Janet's story (before and after *Aftermath*) in return for your public feedback about the novel.

If you will post your review of *Aftermath* on Amazon.com or Goodreads.com and e-mail the URL (web link) of your review to me at **AftermathNovel@gmail.com,** I will send you electronic versions of the Prologue—when Janet is five years old and her mother choses to flee Graylee with Janet and Brady Jr.—and the Epilogue, set a year after the conclusion of the novel, with Cade, Tim, Tara, Bebe, and a new mystery for Janet to solve.

Thank you in advance for sharing your comments with other book lovers and with me. I hope you also will enjoy the adventures of Janet Wright at ages five and forty-one!

ACKNOWLEDGEMENTS

Feedback from my critique partners helped me to improve the prose, develop the characters, better define the settings, and (hopefully) correct any errors. It's a privilege and an honor to share my work with such talented writers and insightful readers.

The reason *Aftermath* exists in book form—and not merely as a manuscript on my outdated laptop and a cheap backup drive—is because of the team at Deeds Publishing: Bob, Jan, Mark, and Matt. Y'all remain as professional and topnotch as ever, and I thank you.

ABOUT THE AUTHOR

George Weinstein is also the author of the contemporary novel *The Caretaker*, the Southern historical novel *Hardscrabble Road* and the multi-cultural historical novel *The Five Destinies of Carlos Moreno*.

His work has been published locally in the Atlanta press and in regional and national anthologies, including *A Cup of Comfort for Writers*. His first novel, the children's motivational adventure *Jake and the Tiger Flight*, was written for the nonprofit Tiger Flight Foundation, which is dedicated to the mission of leading the young to become the "Pilot in Command" of their lives. He wishes that there had been such an organization in Laurel, Maryland, where he misspent his youth.

George is the former President of the Atlanta Writers Club (AWC) and former everything else there too. Having run out of term-limited positions for him, in 2012 the AWC Board bestowed on George the lifetime title of Officer Emeritus, which means he can never leave. Not that he would, but it's nice to be wanted. The AWC was established in 1914. George was established only a few years later; he has a self-portrait in his attic that looks like hell.

He lives with his wife and three furry, four-legged children in Roswell, GA.

CPSIA information can be obtained at www.ICGtesting.com
Printed in the USA
LVOW11s1328201016

509586LV00003B/153/P